DEATH AT DUSK

THRICE NINE LEGENDS

Joshua Robertson

Published by Crimson Edge Press, LLC
www.robertsonwrites.com

Printed in the United States of America

First Printing, 2018

ISBN-10: 1-945397-86-1
ISBN-13: 978-1-945397-86-8

Edited by Christie Stratos at Proof Positive Pro
http://www.proofpositivepro.com

Cover Art: Venkatesh Sekar
Mapwork: Josephe Vandel, Michael Baker
Character Concepts: Simon Walpole
Formatting: Susan H. Roddey

In celebration of Death at Dusk, several talented composers have dedicated or created songs for the Thrice Nine Legends Saga. You can find the music at the link below and listen for free while you read. Enjoy the works of Anthony Abdo, Zaalen Tallis, and Stephen A. Jacobi.

https://www.subscribepage.com/deathatdusk

Dedication

To anyone strong enough to find beauty in their tears, and
to those who recognize that the losses in life that cannot be
fixed must be carried. Remember—to know grief is to know a
profound, irreversible love.

There once was a time when the gods were gods without question. When men were men without example. When heroes were only the frivolous dreams of lurid mortality. It was a time when truths and untruths were indistinguishable, hatred and love were equally excusable, and life and death regaled all of humanity in the same breath. Myths of old were realized and legends were born from the very dust man was formed of, to be told and retold until the grace of time altered them beyond knowing or forgot them completely. Still, some tales were preserved deep within the hearts of mankind, for reasons that could not be fathomed. Perhaps bearing the fruit of some profound truth or kept alive merely by the strength of the men who lived them. Some tales would never be forgotten.

Table of Contents

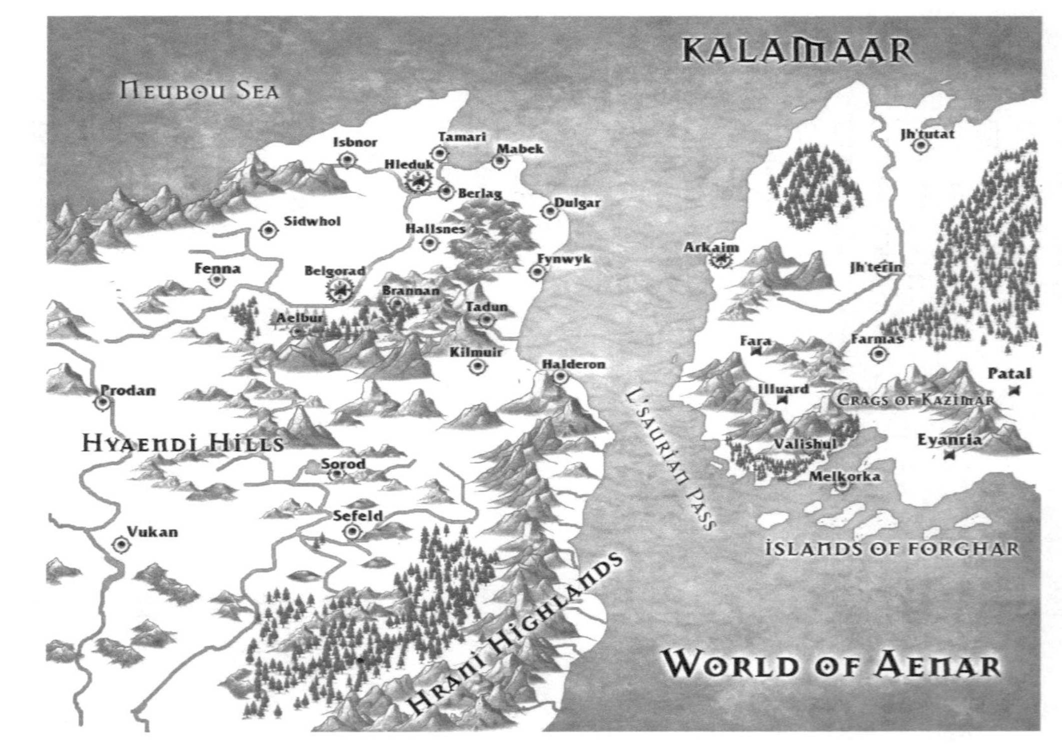

KALAMAAR
Neubou Sea
Isbnor
Tamari
Mabek
Hleduk
Berlag
Dulgar
Sidwhol
Hallsnes
Fynwyk
Fenna
Belgorad
Brannan
Tadun
Aelbur
Kilmuir
Halderon
Prodan
Hyaendi Hills
Sorod
Sefeld
Vukan
Hrani Highlands
L'Saurian Pass
Arkaim
Jh'tutat
Jh'terin
Fara
Farmas
Illuard
Crags of Kazimar
Patal
Valishul
Eyanria
Melkorka
Islands of Forghar
World of Aenar

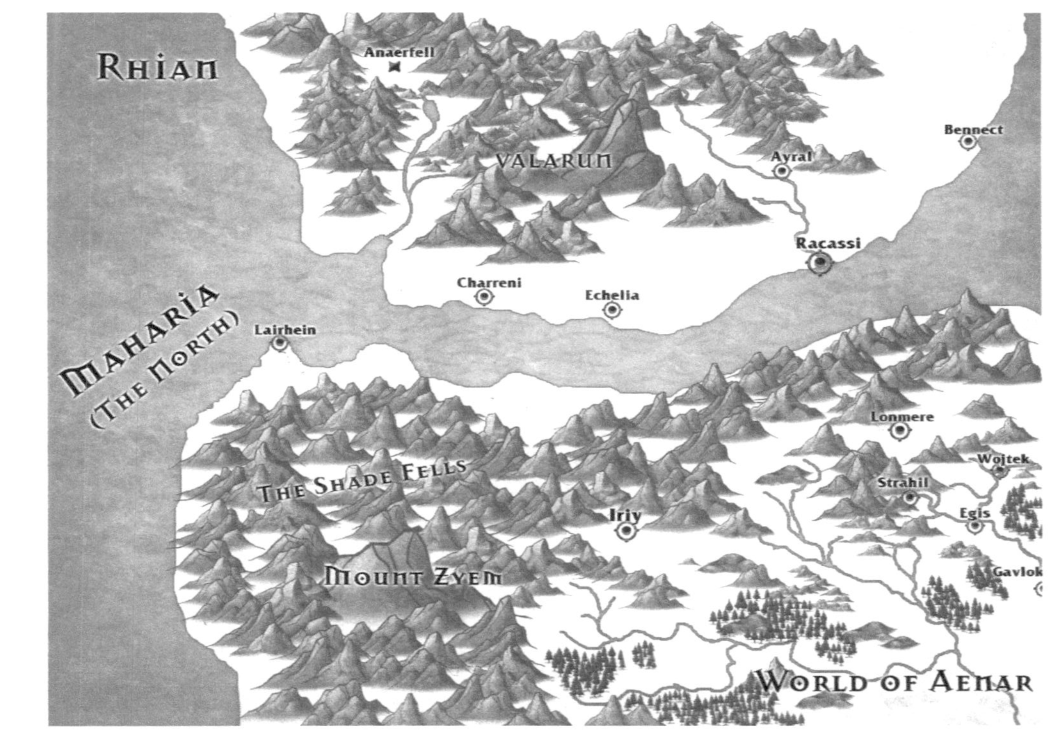

Rhian
Anaerfell
VALARUN
Bennect
Ayral
Racassi
Charreni
Echelia
MAHARIA
(THE NORTH)
Lairhein
Lonmere
THE SHADE FELLS
Wojtek
Strahil
Iriy
Egis
MOUNT ZYEM
Gavlok
WORLD OF AENAR

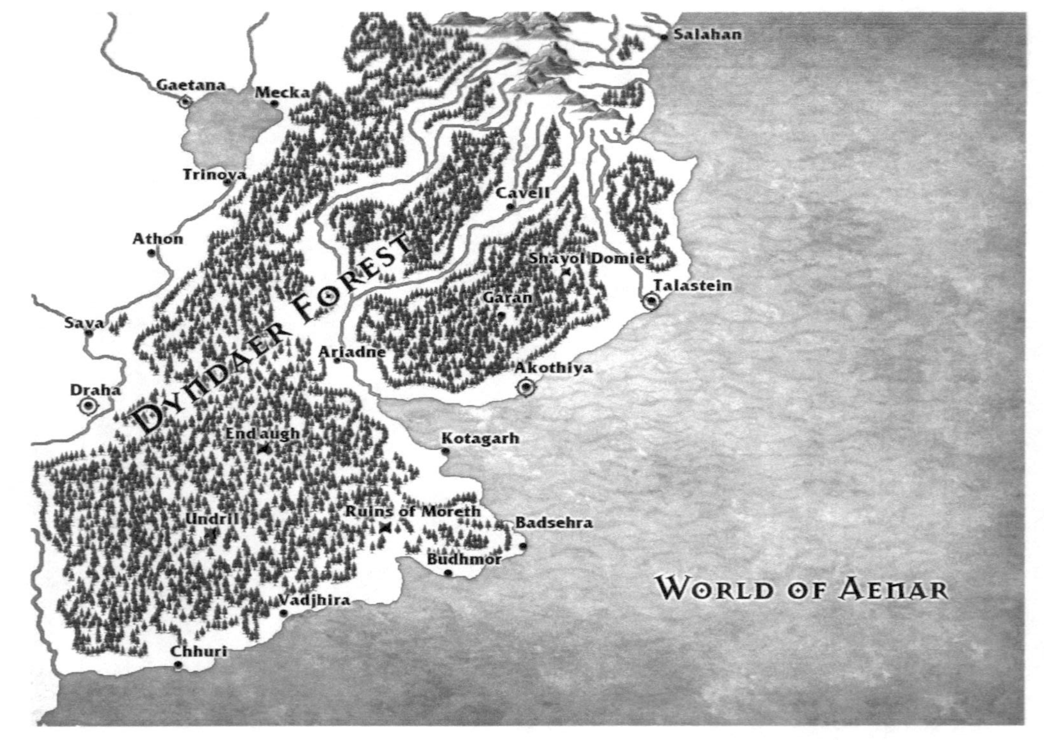

DYNDAER FOREST
WORLD OF AENAR
Salahan
Gaetana
Mecka
Trinova
Cavell
Athon
Shayol Domier
Talastein
Garan
Sava
Ariadne
Akothiya
Draha
Kotagarh
End augh
Undril
Ruins of Moreth
Badsehra
Budhmor
Vadjhira
Chhuri

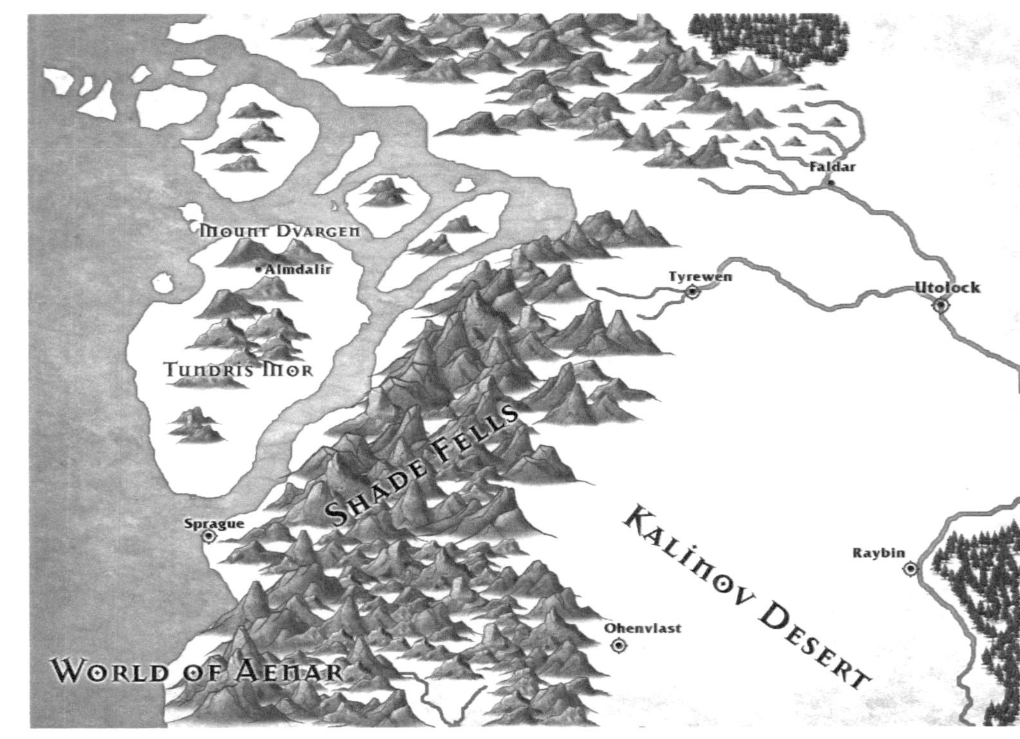

World of Aenar
Mount Dvargen
Almdalir
Tundris Mor
Shade Fells
Sprague
Kalinov Desert
Faldar
Tyrewen
Utolock
Raybin
Ohenvlast

Thrice Nine Legends Saga

The Blood of Dragons by Joshua Robertson & J.C. Boyd
ANAERFELL*
HESHAYOL*

The Kaelandur Series by Joshua Robertson
MELKORKA*
DYNDAER*
MAHARIA*

Other Thrice Nine Legends Saga by Joshua Robertson & J.C. Boyd
WARDEN OF THE ASH TREE*
UNDERSUNG*
A SONG AND SILVER*
STRONG ARMED*
WHEN BLOOD FALLS*
THE NAME OF DEATH*
THE SKINCUTTER'S DAUGHTER*
THE HIGHBORN LONGWALKER*
OF LIFE AND DEATH*
DEATH AT DUSK*

Additional Works

Legacy Series by Joshua Robertson & J.C.Boyd
BLOOD & BILE*
WRACK & RUIN**

THE HAWKHURST SAGA*
GRIMSDALR*
THE PRINCE'S PARISH*
JACK SPRATT*

*Published by Crimson Edge
**Forthcoming by Crimson Edge

DEATH AT DUSK

THRICE NINE LEGENDS

BRENN DARDROGAN

Month of Rutting
Second of Frost
1348 CE

Chapter I

BRENN, *The Dusk Legion*

"Wise men say all great ideas first come from gazing into infinite darkness," Brenn Dardrogan poetically remarked, peering into the damp tunnel ahead. Roots and rocks decorated the inside of the wet hole. His partner, Krel Traelador, stood next to him, cold and unyielding, like one of the stones lodged in the earth. He expected Krel to grunt at him or, at least, tell him to keep his mouth shut. When he said nothing, Brenn went on in a clipped tone, "Please enlighten us, Krel. In what sunlit meadow did you plot this scheme?"

Krel lingered in silence, pushing his brown bangs from his eyes and tightening his lips so that his mustache scratched against his lengthy pointed beard.

Brenn offered a small smile and loudly cracked his knuckles, one by one, looking at the crown of branches above them. He could not see the grey clouds through the thick canopy, but night

1

must have come by now. In the Dyndaer woods, it was hard to tell. Not only were the trees thicker than molasses, but a rolling haze often filled the skies, keeping the sun hidden from sight.

Brenn clicked his tongue, seeing that his partner had not moved. Krel's gaze was fixated on the disgusting hole ahead of them.

With an elongated sigh, Brenn looked over his shoulder at the rest of their company kneeling in the dirt. Rehor Malankov and the two sisters, Quinn and Taryn Caluum, looked back at him with indifference. The three were hired on a month ago when he and Krel passed through the northern town of Egis. To the trio's knowledge, they were here to see the mission completed and receive their payment. He and Krel had done well to hide their true intention to cut their throats once the job was done.

The pieces of Gaetanean silver in Krel's coin purse would be planted on each of the hired hands after killing them, so that any who found them might think they were hired within Gaetana.

Brenn blinked, pushing the thoughts to the back of his mind. He did not want his face to give any hint of their scheme, and he knew he tended to smile when thinking. Though it was hard not to ruminate over completing the job, especially now that they had reached the Dyndaer, a forest fouled with worshippers of Czern the Grey-Clad. He wanted to finish it all and return home.

"Krel—" he started again, shifting his gaze from the hired hands and back to his fellow assassin.

"Shut up, Brenn." Krel's response came at the end of a growl, steady and low-pitched, nearly swallowed by the sound of the gurgling swamp nearby. "The Legion and the senate mutually agreed to this assignment. If we kill the princess, the desert people will be valuable allies in the years to come. Her death will give rise to the Lonmerean Kingdom. If you are dissatisfied with the plan and want to stand on the opposite side of history, go home."

"Dissatisfied? Not in the least. I am happier than a first-timer in a cathouse." He ran a hand over his bristly facial hair, slightly shorter than Krel's, and held back his delight. His partner's blood was easier to boil than salted water. He squinted his eyes, saying, "But like the first-timer, my mind is swirling with confusion."

"Oh, I can help you, Brenn. I have been to a number of cathouses in my time, hmm?" Rehor said, his eyes so naturally wide that the entire white of his eyeballs might as well have been visible. His whistle-pitched voice was coupled with a western accent. He pointed at the tunnel ahead of them. "The hole you are looking for is right there."

Brenn smiled again. He could almost hear the titter on the edge of the ruttish man's tongue, bespeaking the endless lewd jokes they had been subjected to over the past weeks. Brenn kept his attention on Krel, not wanting to get wrapped up in the Stuhian's rhetoric. "We cannot be certain the Uvil will keep their armies from Lonmere's gates. At the end of the day, the Uvil do not see us any less human than the others."

He refrained from listing the three kingdoms besides Lonmere: Gaetana, Tamarri, and Ariadne.

"You cannot know the minds of the Uvil, but you are too smart to think we are on equal standing with the other kingdoms. Anshedar or not, other men treat us like swine." Krel looked over his shoulder long enough to examine the three silent sellswords at their rear. Brenn heard stories of how Krel's father once wanted to be a member of the senate, and although he never gained position, he raised Krel with the prejudiced thinking practiced by their government toward the other Anshedar. Krel outwardly grimaced, his crooked teeth scraping together. "It is not our place to worry about what the Uvil might do in the end. We answer to the Legion and they answer to the senate. I did not hear you complaining when you took the assignment."

Brenn patted Krel between his shoulder blades as though comforting a child. He knew an argument with the Dusk Legion or the Lonmerean politicians would result in him being replaced. Even after a decade of service, he did not have influence to speak against his betters; at least, no more than any other assassin with the Dusk Legion.

"I was saving my concerns for you," he said.

Krel moved the hair from his eyes again, pulling away from Brenn's touch.

Clearing his throat, Brenn changed his voice to a more solemn tone. "But in all seriousness, why not wait until the princess is out and about? You are insisting we go into the castle which, in my opinion, is a surefire way to get killed. I have a family back home—"

"You have a brother."

"And a mother and father," Brenn hurried to add with a half-smile. "All who would be unhappy to find my head on a pike before Lonmere rises to power. And if we are caught, you know that is where we will end up."

"We discussed this. They will have guards protecting her on the road too. We will have a fight no matter where we strike," Krel said. "No one will expect a hit in the castle. If we can keep to the shadows, we might balance the scales in our favor."

"I agree," Rehor said. "Cavell is a dull place, but a fight on the road, even a mile out, will draw attention from someone. Remain inside the castle walls and muffled, the sound of our glorious battle will be."

Quinn, the elder sister, bobbed her head so that the two strands of braided hair hanging behind each ear bounced. The age lines around her cheekbones were a clear indication of how much older she was than the rest of them. She added, "The worst anyone expects here is for the weekly shipment of salt to be delayed from Ariadne. We strolled right through the gates and learned about this *secret* pass from a page boy in under a day's time."

Looking to Taryn, Brenn waited for the nice-looking girl to speak against his reason too. But she did not even look in his direction, fiddling with the ends of her fingernails. His eyes fell to her full lips and small round chin. She would be the hardest for him to kill in the end.

Brenn turned from her. He said, "Salt is hardly the biggest concern in the Dyndaer. I have heard stories that would give grown men nightmares."

"I am not sure the simargl would instill nightmares in anyone," Quinn said, "especially the residents of Cavell. They grow up being aware of the beasts."

"I am speaking of monsters worse than the winged wolves," Brenn replied. They had passed by a few simargl on the way to Cavell but were able to avoid them by staying low and downwind. He was glad the simargl were all they crossed. When no one responded, he shifted his eyes to Rehor. "Come to think of it, what did you do with the page boy anyway?"

Rehor lifted his hand and placed it on his forehead, holding his wavy hair back as though the pressure on his skull might help him remember. "He swallowed some *felpoppies*, and then I drowned him in the swamp."

Brenn tightened his jaw at the heartless answer. The redhead was a dragon-man, a Stuhian, which already marked him as being difficult to trust, primarily due to his strange magic, but the westerner upped the ante with his study of herbalism, collecting plants in his side satchel to craft his toxins. Anytime they stopped to rest during their trek, he was off picking flowers and digging up roots.

Knowing little about the craft, Brenn recognized felpoppies could numb someone for hours. Giving the page boy a few flakes would have certainly eased his disposal. He searched for a fitting response. "You could have said something an hour ago."

"I could have," Rehor agreed.

Brenn rotated back to Krel. "We should probably pick up the pace, Krel. The boy will be missed in a small town like this."

"We wanted to cover our tracks, hmm?" Rehor cooed. Brenn didn't bother to look at him but imagined the man lifting his thick eyebrows with feigned innocence.

"Yes, but drowning kids in swamps was most definitely not what we discussed," Brenn said.

"It was one kid. One swamp," Rehor clarified.

"What's done is done," Quinn said, scooting forward to his side as though they were going to finally advance down the hole. Brenn lifted an eyebrow at the older sister. He somehow expected her to have a more visceral reaction to murdering children, but her face remained like stone.

Quinn ignored his look, straightening the interlaced twine of the bola at her side. Brenn surveyed the strange weapon. Three cords diverged from a single knot with smooth iron stones, a quarter the size of his fist, tied to the end of each one. A second bola hung on her left side, seemingly more lethal, with spiked stones instead of smooth ones.

Her face was dead of emotion, despite the eagerness in her tone. "Now, can we please move forward? I am a hundred feet from a castle full of riches, and I'm getting antsy."

Krel rejoined the conversation. Maybe he finally lost interest in the hole ahead or was drawn back from his own thoughts with Quinn's movement. "Robbing them was not part of the plan."

Quinn narrowed her eyes, gesturing at the hole as though a hoard of treasure awaited them. "I don't see why we would waste the opportunity."

Krel grumbled, scratching the strands of hair hanging off his cheek.

Brenn looked to the youngest sister again. Her tongue massaged her bottom lip as she gathered and twisted her hair back to the crown of her head, exposing her decorated ears. The silver loops in her earlobes were slightly larger than the silver lining Quinn's ears. "Anything you want to add, Taryn, while we are giving in to our indulgences? Should we expect you to seduce the prince amid the killing and plundering?"

"Mm. I had my eyes set on the king," she said, "but I will take what I can get." The younger sister smiled deviously with her perfect white teeth.

"Wait till you see the king," Krel said under his breath.

Brenn shook his head, briefly trying to recall how he and Krel found these three miscreants at the Underhorn Inn. The entire exchange was a blur. No matter what was said, they each had their own goals, and it was becoming apparent that they planned to act on them.

Rehor hummed in Taryn's direction as though he might respond to her quip about sleeping with the king. Instead he decidedly held his lips together and puffed out his cheeks in restraint when Quinn whipped her head around.

"Don't even look at her."

Taryn tittered softly. She winked at Brenn while leaning closer to Rehor and whispered, "You can look."

"Cock and pie," Brenn cussed with a shake of his head. The young girl was more of a trull than the wenches who slept with the sailors at the port north of Lonmere.

"I cannot wait to be done with the lot of you. Let us go already," Krel said, starting into the tunnel toward Castle Frantisek, the heart of Cavell. The excitement in his tone, the hunger for killing was unmistakable to Brenn.

Somewhere beyond the tunnel was their quarry.

The chilled wind of autumn swept under Brenn's long brown cloak. After a month of travel, he was more than curious to see how this would play out. He reached into a pouch at his belt, retrieving his two cestuses, his preferred weapon. He slid on the fitted gloves made with iron plates bound over his knuckles with leather strips.

He traipsed over the decaying clumps of moldering grass with Krel at an arm's length ahead and the hired hands moving softly behind him. The hole was barren and dank, growing darker with every step until they were blinded by blackness.

Before Rehor had led the page boy into the woods, they learned the veiled path would give them access to the castle's cellar. Brenn presumed the tunnel to be an escape route for the royal family if ever the stronghold was overrun. Even with the Uvil armies advancing from the south, the chances of Cavell being the target of a real attack was slim. Count Frantisek, the ruler, may be the younger brother of the king, but the hamlet hardly held a strategic position in the deep wood.

"Rehor, give us some light," Krel directed. A moment later an orb of orange light sprang into existence over Krel's shoulder, illuminating the cramped space. Brenn covered his eyes at the sudden brightness. The glow wavered, outlining the slender frame of the man in front of him. Krel waited a moment for their eyes to adjust. The hand crossbow strapped to his belt swayed against his side. "Take it slow," Krel said, skulking forward.

Brenn shadowed his partner, who he'd met ten years ago when joining the Dusk Legion. They had suffered one another, mission after mission, ever since.

For nearly thirty paces, they walked in silence under Rehor's magical light until they reached a narrow door coated in dust. Krel gently traced the frame as though he expected a trap to spring, possibly dropping the ceiling on top of them. Then, without a word, he pulled a long knife from his belt and slipped the blade between the stilted casing and the door, forcing the blade up. A clash sounded on the other side of the door as he knocked loose a barricading crossbar, causing the beam to topple to the ground.

"Let's hope no one heard that," Quinn mumbled.

"Yeah," Krel grunted, pushing the door open to reveal a musty, unlit room with barrels and crates lining the stone walls. The cellar was no larger than a room at the local inn. The prop of wood Krel knocked loose lay on the floor among the collected dust and scattered hay.

Rehor moved the orb of light into the vacant shadows of the cellar. "Guess we would not be lucky enough to have her already wrapped up and waiting here for us."

Quinn stepped over the crossbar after Brenn, ignoring Rehor. "How did you know the door was barred?"

Krel headed for the staircase leading to the next level of the castle while Brenn answered her. "The door was forced too far back from the frame. We saw the same thing once in Eldhaft."

"So the rumors are true. You do confront the Guardians then," Quinn said.

"Sometimes," Brenn said. Most of the north knew the assassins of the Dusk Legion and the thieves among the Guardians of Gero had their own private war taking place in the shadows, one which the Guardians had been winning for the last several decades.

Krel hummed in agreement. Neither of them had permission to discuss the faction's blood feud with strangers, especially mere hired hands.

Brenn followed Krel, who silently inched up the few stairs and paused at the door.

"What is it?" Brenn asked.

Hovering his hand over the handle, Krel said, "This does not feel right." He pressed his ear to the door, waited, and then leaned back to tug the long bristles on his chin. "I do not hear anything. We should turn back."

"Turn back?" Taryn said with disbelief, poking her nose over Quinn's shoulder. "We cannot spend another night in Cavell."

"They are probably in bed," Quinn muttered.

Brenn hesitated. Krel's gut feelings were rarely wrong.

"Taryn is right," he finally said. "We cannot stay another night, not with Rehor killing the page boy. Once he is found missing, we will be the first accused."

"I am being singled out because of my red hair, hmm? That is what this is!" Rehor feigned an indignant gasp. "We are all here because we support the Dusk Legion, who, if I recall correctly, are assassins. We *all* kill people. That is our thing, hmm?"

Brenn rolled his eyes. "You are not part of the Dusk Legion. You are a sellsword. You do not bear the mark of an assassin."

"And yet," Rehor chirped back, waving his hand in Brenn's face, "I am the only one who killed someone today, so stop picking on the redhead."

"Blood and spit," Taryn laughed. "He has a point."

"Nine lands." Krel tensed his jaw, springing the latch on the door. He slowly creaked it open to reveal an unoccupied foyer. Besides a few torches lit along the walls and a closed iron door at either end of a diverging hall, the area was barren. Hunching over into a crouch, Krel led them down the hallway.

"Not much to steal, Quinn, hmm?" Rehor mused.

Krel glared at Rehor. "Shut up. I need to listen."

Rehor squeezed his lips together and widened his eyes at the command.

From the opposite side of the door ahead, Brenn heard soft voices, clinking metal, and padded boots nearing them at a leisurely pace.

"We need to—" Brenn started.

He did not give his warning quickly enough. The door burst open and two guards emerged. Their full armor was colored pitch, casing all but their heads, looking as though they were prepping for war. They abruptly stopped whatever conversation they were having.

"Shoot!" Brenn hissed at Krel. His partner spun away from Rehor to face the front.

The first guard flailed backwards, wailing like a lost child to alert whomever might be in the room behind him. The second, however, did not make it far before a quarrel from Krel's crossbow tore into his face, penetrating the flesh beneath the nose.

His head snapped back from the impact and he dropped to the stone floor.

Krel waved them forward. "Find the princess!"

Chapter II

KREL, *The Dusk Legion*

K rel unfastened the leather casing, a small quiver, on his belt and retrieved a single crossbow bolt. He scarcely caught Taryn's sweet voice as she skirted by him.

"Oh, this will be fun," she purred, pulling two iron daggers from the back of her belt. She moved swifter than any other, the piece of purple lace wrapped around her neck tucked under her light-brown cloak.

He observed the dark-haired beauty sail into the room ahead and bit the end of his tongue. She either did not see the crossbows the two guards carried with them, or she did not care. His smaller crossbow was deadly enough, having the power to penetrate through armor; what the guards carried would certainly cleft her lithe frame in two. He hated to see the young tart die first, but he supposed if she got herself slaughtered, he and Brenn would have one less body to cut down. The senate would pay handsomely for a mission well executed, and he had no intention of disappointing those who filled his pockets.

The din of voices and footsteps echoed from the chamber and down the hall, giving clue to the number of men on the opposite side of the doors. Krel's throat tightened, realizing the danger ahead. He fumbled with his bolt, trying to grab Brenn as he trailed closely behind Taryn.

He choked. "Bre—"

Quinn raced after them, pulling her bola from her waist. Her voice was shrill. "Taryn, wait!"

Krel looked over his shoulder to find Rehor gazing at the fallen guard. The Stuhian merely strolled forward, having a quarter of the vitality of the others. "I will be of better use back here with you."

"Get in there and do your part," Krel ordered.

Rehor lifted his hands out from under his brown robes and wiggled the small finger on his left hand at Krel. The digit was ornated with a small silver ring. "Do not worry. I will earn my cut."

An imposing voice from inside the chamber bellowed, "Detain them!"

Krel growled, turning from Rehor, and rushed to the doorway. He lifted his crossbow to take aim, immediately sensing the warmth emitting from the two central firepits. One sat between two long tables near the main door and the other lay between the thrones on the dais. By a quick calculation, he counted a dozen armored guards scattered on either side of the tables, awkwardly twisting away from the main doors and lifting their larger crossbows.

They may have been lying in wait, but they had been securing the wrong door. By some strange luck, Krel's band had caught them by surprise.

The battle was already underway, giving Krel no time to consider how Count Vlaskhorn Frantisek knew that they were coming. Ahead of him, Taryn pitched a dagger into the nearest guard's gut, then rolled to the side to dodge a bolt fired by another guard.

Next to her, Brenn roared with enough ferocity to startle another guard. His tenor was hardly subdued by the purple and black tapestries hanging against the castle's walls, a depiction of the long history and lore of the royal family of Cavell. His unlucky target fumbled with the crossbow in his hands, staggered by the violent cry. Brenn smashed his right fist into the guard's lower ribs with a heavy undercut. Krel imagined the power behind the iron plates of his cestuses sinking into the side of the man. The armor surely protected him from serious harm, but the hit forced the guard's body to bend. Brenn leaped straight into the air, giving the guard no chance to react. He brought his weight down, the knuckles of his left hand pummeling into side of the guard's temple. A hollow groan escaped the guard's lips, eyes rolling back.

Krel watched Brenn catch the guard with a single hand before his legs wilted beneath him. He then lifted the body to use as a shield against the rest of their enemies.

Several bolts whipped through the air, two finding their place in the guard's back. The man thrashed for a moment with a startled cry before losing consciousness again.

A heavy-set guard by the farthest firepit dropped his crossbow and reached for his blade. Krel fired his quarrel, hitting him in the leg before his hand touched the plain hilt. He fell to a knee about the time Quinn advanced through the array of bolts. She wielded her bola with clear precision, spinning the weapon in a series of arcs, hitting the same guard in the back of the skull.

He hunched over, unconscious.

She then danced forward and back, twirling the smooth stones over her head. Her braids bounced, a look of determination painted on her face as she raked the room for the best target. With a few twists of her wrist, she launched the bola at another guard who hastily tried to equip his crossbow with another bolt. The twine caught around his face, spinning in motion, before the three weighted ends smashed into his head and dropped him where he stood.

Quinn was pulling her spiked bola from her belt when Count Frantisek, the father of their target, retreated from his throne. His large belly jiggled, and his purplish cloak swirled. He raised a chubby finger at them as he fled behind his guards. "Stop them!"

"Come on!" Krel said through gritted teeth, looking to Rehor. "You could easily kill them on your own."

"Maybe," Rehor mumbled, lifting the hand with the silver ring and scanning the room, "but the princess we sought is not here. Your mission is botched, I think. The count must have been alerted by someone. Do you really want to kill him?"

Krel squinted an eye at the room, knowing Rehor was not wrong in his swift assessment. Killing the count would hurt the Dusk Legion and Lonmere more than aid them. Even if they murdered the king's niece, he could not frame the Gaetaneans if those in Cavell knew the Dusk Legion was truly to blame.

"If we do not complete the job, we lose favor with the desert people. They need these brothers to be squabbling," Krel whispered as he reloaded his crossbow.

Brenn shouted at him to shoot, ducking behind a table. The body he carried was bloodied and full of arrows. Taryn kneeled behind him, smiling wildly with one dagger left in her nimble fingers. Quinn advanced on the count, the spiked bola spinning at her side.

Krel affixed his eyes to Rehor. "We need to know what he knows."

The Stuhian tilted his head, his red bangs falling over his eyes. "Then question him, we will. Stand aside."

Rehor's fingers spidered through the air as he stepped into the doorway. Krel observed in near horror as one of the guards holding a sword went rigid, eyes glossing over, then viciously turned on his allies. He grabbed the nearest guard from behind and sliced his neck, immediately gutting a second guard before the others realized what was happening.

"Tomas!" a guard bawled, lifting his crossbow in defense. "No—"

Swatting the weapon to the side, Tomas struck his blade across the guard's cheek, ripping the man's face open. Red splattered across the chamber floor.

Krel gaped at Rehor, seeing the power of the dragon-man. Casting a ball of light in a darkened tunnel was one thing but causing a man to slaughter his friends was another. As an Anshedar, a human, Krel could never truly understand the scope of the magic called Koldovstvo wielded by the mysterious Stuhia from the west and the Kadari of Kalamaar. He once heard that the magic caused life to drain from the spellcaster's body, aging them with every spell. Yet Rehor showed no signs of being affected.

"How?" Krel's heart pounded with a sudden realization. The Stuhian could slaughter them all with a simple thought.

Rehor's voice was without emotion as he controlled Tomas. "*Faegrim.*" He named the ring on his finger. "An old heirloom of my family. You cannot use it unless you are a Stuhian, though Koldovstvo is not required to harness its power."

Krel deliberately tore his eyes from the simple-looking ring. Trying to calm his nerves, he watched Tomas run through another guard, the edge of his sword dripping with blood as it tore through either end of the armor. If he and Brenn were meant to kill the sellswords, they were going to have to catch Rehor while he was sleeping.

Krel counted four guards remaining including Tomas. Lifting his hand crossbow, he aimed and fired at one. The bolt zipped through the air, striking the wall on the opposite side. He gritted his teeth. He hated missing.

As he reached for another bolt, Taryn charged from her protected spot behind Brenn. She used her free hand to hold the sword arm of another guard at bay and then struck the guard twice in the stomach with her dagger, then the neck. She pulled him to the ground, holding her blade firmly in his jugular.

The last guard, besides Tomas, moved across the chamber to shield the count. He balanced his blade defensively. "Glory to the Grey-Clad," he muttered.

Quinn rushed him, her spiked bola spinning twice before wrapping around the back of his leg, well under his lifted sword. With a quick jerk, she pulled his feet out from under him. By Rehor's command, Tomas then lunged forward and stabbed him through the chest.

The older sister let go of her bola and moved clear from Tomas, blinking rapidly at the guard. Before she could raise a question, Brenn slugged him across in the jaw.

Tomas collapsed.

"Good." Krel slipped the bolt back in its casing. He cleared his throat and dipped his head at Rehor. He wished he would have known of the Stuhian's power before they picked them up in Egis. He did not need the dragon-man thinking he was intimidated by his magic.

He entered the chamber, sensing Rehor close behind him, and approached Vlaskhorn Frantisek. The man was horror-filled, his complexion completely without color as he gawped at the dozen fallen guards. He sank against the far wall, falling to his rear, looking as though he hoped to burrow through the stone and escape into the Dyndaer.

Brenn stepped over Tomas, his wide frame cutting off the count from any hope of escape. Taryn, on the other hand, went in search of her missing dagger and Quinn collected her two bolas from the dead guards.

Count Frantisek fumbled to pull a knife free from his decorated belt. His hand got wrapped up in his fancy cloak before he finally was able to point the dagger at Brenn. "Czern curse you. My brother will hear of your betrayal."

"How can we betray something we have no allegiance to?" Brenn leered. "We did not swear fealty to the Gaetanaen king."

"He is the king of all four kingdoms of Maharia. You cannot change that fact," the count said. "The *Peace of Sekan* granted the Frantiseks the throne. For one hundred and fifty years we have governed."

"Sounds to me like the Frantiseks have had their fill of power. Did your mother never teach you how to share with others?" Brenn smirked.

"Enough." Krel came shoulder to shoulder with Brenn, his hand crossbow latched at his belt with a leather cord. Glancing at the count's iron dagger, he folded his arms across his chest. "What exactly do you think we have come here to do?"

The count answered in a scathing tone, pointing the dagger at Krel while he sat on the floor. "To kill my daughter, Nitalia, but you are too late. The Crimson Sun knows your plot. She already left for Gaetana!"

"The Crimson Sun." Brenn's smile went stiff in a clear effort not to lose it. Krel did not blame him for displaying his frustration. Pegging the murder on the sellswords, or anyone in the Gaetanean Kingdom, would prove difficult if the Crimson Sun was involved. Brenn looked to Krel for an answer. "How in the Nine Lands did those *righteous do-gooders* catch wind of anything?"

Rehor cleared his throat, coming uncomfortably close to Krel. "They have eyes and ears everywhere."

"Not in Lonmere," Brenn said.

Krel scowled in response, causing Brenn to snap his mouth shut. Rehor, on the other hand, only grinned all the wider before puffing his cheeks full of air.

The two talked too much, risking the count learning of their motivations before they discovered what he knew. Krel needed a genuine report. He did his best to hide his disappointment and scrunched his face to look disgruntled instead. "Count, why in the Nine Lands would we want to murder your daughter?"

"Do not be coy with me, assassin. Your senate wants to weaken Cavell, so we will be incapable of providing aid to my brother when you infiltrate the capital. Do you forget he is aligned with the Kadari, the Guardians of Gero, and the Crimson Sun?" The count sneered as he named major factions across Maharia, his voice thick with ire. He pulled his feet underneath himself as though he meant to stand but stopped to lean against the wall. He huffed, his large stomach rising and falling with each breath. "And what about the Ariadneans? Do you think the *hero-warriors* won't come to aid their king? We are too strong for you to undercut our alliances with your undermined ploys. You are fools."

"Clearly so." Krel did his best to flatten his expression, suppressing his relief. The count clearly knew nothing of the desert people attempting to distract from the growing war in the south, meaning the Crimson Sun may be ignorant to their true purpose as well. He could only hope they lacked the insight; though anyone thinking Lonmereans considered themselves strong enough to outright challenge sovereignty in the north was either stupid or completely paranoid.

"So, what are we doing?" Quinn vigilantly skimmed over the guards lying around the chamber. Her face looked to be etched from stone as she neared, hooking her spiked bola on her belt. She held her side as she approached, showing how the toll of battle impacted her differently than the rest of them. She may have been closer to the age of the count than any of them.

Krel did not care enough to ask.

Taryn traced her sister's steps, eyeing the count with a gleam in her brown eyes. "Are we going to kill him?"

"No," Brenn answered, faintly shaking his head in response.

The count frantically shuffled the rest of the way to his feet. Krel searched the room for some answer to their dilemma. "Taking his life does not serve us."

"He knows our faces and our plot," Quinn said. "I am not sure leaving him alive helps us either. He will have the entire north searching for us."

"Krel," Brenn started, "she has a point. This will ruin Lonmere. Every kingdom in Maharia will raise arms against us."

"Your pathetic nation is already ruined. You have invited a war upon you that you cannot win," the count said, still clinging to his knife. "Even now, you stand here and admit to me what I knew to be true all along."

"Shut up," Krel said. "I need to think."

The silence did not last more than a couple breaths.

Taryn crossed her thin arms and leaned against Quinn. "Does that mean we aren't going after the princess either?"

"We may have reason to pursue her yet," Rehor offered, reaching for his satchel of herbs and vials. Krel jutted his jaw at the Stuhian, unsure how a toxin could help them. He gestured for him to spit it out. "I have a bit of *fumeweed* on me. A mixture of *shadbush* and felpoppies, it is."

"Which will do what?" Brenn asked.

"Go on," snapped Krel at the same time.

"Put him to sleep," Rehor said, pulling a clear phial from his pouch, "and muddle his memory for the past half day or so. He will not even remember we were here."

Count Frantisek's eyes widened, lifting his knife in defense. "You will not get me to take anything."

"How will that help us? He will awaken to dead guards filling his throne room, his daughter gone, and will probably remember the Crimson Sun has her under their protection," Quinn said. "He would be able to deduce the truth."

"Suspicion is better than knowing. He might remember the Crimson Sun took her if he remembers anything at all," Brenn said.

"I am standing right here." The count flared his nostrils. "I am hearing your conversation."

A flash of light sparkled in Rehor's eyes as he snubbed the count. He wobbled the phial at Krel. "If you made it look like the Crimson Sun killed her, would it serve your purpose?"

Shifting blame to the mercenaries was not far off the mark from targeting the hired hands. He suspected the desert people would be satisfied with any unrest they could muster between the other nations, especially if they could keep the esteemed Crimson Sun from advancing southward. The king would have to rely on lesser-skilled mercenaries. Krel rubbed his chin. "Brenn, what do you think?"

"Might be hard to pull off," Brenn admitted with a shrug, "but a better situation than where we currently find ourselves."

A smile split Rehor's face from ear to ear. "Does this mean I am a legionnaire now?"

"That is not how this works." Krel squinted at the red-haired man. They would undoubtedly have to kill the sellswords after catching the Crimson Sun, if for no other reason than to leave no witnesses to their deed. He lied to the dragon-man, "Though if this works, I will be certain to put a good word in for you."

Rehor held his smile, turning to the count.

"I am not taking your liquid magic, Stuhian," the count growled. "You will have to kill me first."

Krel sighed, motioning at Brenn. "Hold him."

"Oh, no, no, no." Rehor stepped forward and put his left hand on Brenn's shoulder. Faegrim shimmered on his finger. "That will not be necessary. He will drink it on his own."

Chapter III

TEODOR, *The Crimson Sun*

Despite the bite within the walls of Castle Frantisek, sweat gleamed off Tyr Og's flesh. Teodor Bacheva looked at the droplets for only a moment in the faint flicker of torchlight dancing off the walls before averting his eyes and continuing to follow the bare-chested giant through the corridor. The Ispolini, as Tyr was called, breathed heavily, keeping his head tilted beneath the wooden high beams. At command, he led them back to the great chamber where the count awaited their return. The only other sound, which overpowered the giant's breathing, was the clopping hooves of the Svet, named Farthr, who trailed Teodor.

"Bah! You should have sent me with Eisliev and Seigfeld," Tyr said abruptly, clenching his six-fingered fists at his sides. The giant's shaggy red hair recoiled over his bright eyes with every word. "The Dyndaer is riddled with beasts that will tear a man's head off. How do you expect to keep that lass safe with only two men?"

"They are capable enough," Teodor replied, resting his hand on the hilt of the longsword at his belt. He lifted an eyebrow at the volatile giant, towering a head and a half over him. The Ispolini was a recent addition to the Crimson Sun, along with Eisliev Kluk, the dragon-man from the west. Teodor remained uncertain if he could trust them but would not place blame where none was due. "Seigfeld is a seasoned warrior, and Eisliev's magic will keep any beasts at bay."

"Eisliev will not allow himself to become a pawn to be used and cast aside," Tyr said. "Koldovstvo steals his life. He is not going to destroy himself to save the neck of a random princess leagues away from his own home."

"He will if he wants to remain among the Crimson Sun," Teodor said delicately, attempting to hide the frown that surfaced from the bold assessment. Tyr did not exactly evoke confidence. "Let them do their part while we do ours."

"Bah! You speak in the same tenor of noble bitches and bastards. I would not be surprised if you were raised with a decorated goblet in one hand and a quilled pen in the other, so you might dictate the lives of those you think to be lesser in quality." Tyr scowled.

Teodor spun the signet ring on his left hand, bespeaking his aristocratic heredity. He could not say he allied himself with the sullied beliefs of his Bacheva home, though he could not escape the affiliation, especially while serving the Crimson Sun.

He did not know what Tyr's issue was with noble families or from whence his anger originated, but Teodor knew his onus and allegiances. He spoke with conviction. "Our duty is here."

"How do you figure?" Tyr rattled. "Ivarr sent us to protect the lass, and then you whisked her off to Gaetana with half of our party. Why would we split our numbers? And before you say *to protect the count*, hear this. Our orders were not to keep the count alive."

Teodor considered the argument, pulling at his thick short beard and twisting his neck to admire the few tapestries hanging on the walls. Scenic images were threaded into the fabric, including towering buildings overlooking the crashing waves of Strega's Deep. He wondered if those who lived within the woods their whole life dreamt of the sea. Although he'd spent his childhood in Eldhaft, an inland city, Teodor never longed for the water. In his adult life, however, he found his place with the Crimson Sun in Tamarri, a city built next to the sea. The illustrative embroidery was certainly comparable to the northern city.

"We cannot be sure what the Dusk Legion intends for the Frantiseks. We must be strategic," Teodor finally said, slowing his pace so he would not collide with Tyr's bulky frame. "The Crimson Sun is charged with keeping peace in the north. No matter what task we set out to see done, harmony between the four kingdoms is forever our concern. The count's death would undoubtedly upset that mission."

Farthr blew air from his oversized nostrils, crossing his arms over his chest. His black skin almost camouflaged him in the dark hall. His clopping hooves slowed behind Teodor. "Listen to him."

Tyr growled in his chest.

Farthr mirrored the snarl as though Tyr were directly challenging him.

Pausing to eye Farthr, Teodor's mind peppered with thoughts of the centaur's loyalty. Half-man and half-horse, standing nearly the height of Tyr, Farthr's long black mane flowed from the top of his head and down his back, where it blended with the dark fur of his lower half. With triangular ears twitching beneath his curved horns, nostrils as wide as a horse's in his human face, and sharpened fangs, he was a dangerous creature with which to come face to face.

The Svet, too, only joined the Crimson Sun in the past several months at the request of Seigfeld Brecher, who currently accompanied the princess on the road to Gaetana. Considering most of the centaurs were enslaved to humans, Teodor had not expected Farthr to have any interest in strengthening the kingdoms of men, yet here he stood in service to the shield of the north.

"Listen," Teodor sighed, "if the Dusk Legion does not arrive in Cavell by sunrise, we will follow after Seigfeld and Eisliev. Once we have seen the princess to Gaetana, we can return to Tamarri. In the meantime, let us remain calm and pray this has only been a sick joke."

"Doubtful," Farthr said. "Maybe a distraction. The way the warning was delivered hints at a greater scheme."

Teodor pursed his lips, seeing the chamber doors ahead. Farthr was not wrong. The note tipping off the Crimson Sun to the possible attack had been found on their doorstep, delivered with unmarked sealing wax and without a signature. Tracking the identity of the sender was impossible. "That begs the question—a distraction from what?"

Before Farthr could respond, a pained cry emanated from the closed doors ahead.

Tyr stopped, instinctively reaching for the double-sided axe at his back. His meaty hand clasped the thick branch of a handle and pulled it to his front. Farthr moved to the corner of Teodor's eye, already lifting the heavy crossbow from the leather strip hanging at his side.

Following suit, Teodor yanked his sword from its scabbard and charged through the doors. He did not want to wait around for his mind to conjure images of what he might find on the other side.

With Tyr and Farthr thundering at his back, Teodor crashed into the great chamber, quickly surveying the room. Withholding his shock, the litter of dead guards were ignored at the sight of several shrouded figures looming over Count Frantisek, who lay near the dais. The sovereign did not move, crumpled into a ball. Even at a distance, Teodor could see the fat man's chest rising and falling.

"The Dusk Legion," he snarled. The assembly of assassins, three men and two women, faced him. Teodor elevated his sword, pointing the tip of his iron blade at them. His words boomed through the chamber. "Stand down! Lay down your weapons!"

"They have a Stuhian among them," Tyr indicated in a hushed tone at his right.

Teodor gazed at the redheaded man in the brown robes.

A slim, bearded man at the dragon-man's right with a hand crossbow glowered, shifted his feet, and then offered a whispered directive to the rest.

Tumbling to and fro, the assassins fanned out while the dragon-man stepped forward and pitched a bolt of fire at Teodor. Dropping his axe to the floor, Tyr moved quicker than the magic, stepping around Teodor, grabbing the underside of the short end of the long table, and flinging it upward. Clay mugs and plates soared in every direction as the magical fire blasted against the wood. Tyr was already returning to scoop up his weapon when the wrecked table smashed back down to the ground.

Teodor ducked as a crossbow quarrel zipped over him. He veered left to circle around in the direction of the count. Leaping over a dead guard in black armor, he caught sight of a young woman in his periphery, her arm extending in a flash. He narrowly registered the movement, shifting his weight and arcing his sword upward to deflect a thrown dagger from burying itself in his flesh. The dark-eyed girl smiled widely and winked, then rushed around the rear firepit where the other woman whipped a bola over her head.

A fist suddenly drove into Teodor's breastplate, staggering him back several feet. The clang of iron on iron reverberated through his chest and shoulders. He swung his sword upward to stall the assassin so he could regain his balance, unsure from what shadow the man had materialized.

"Teodor Bacheva," the assassin identified him, pressing one fist into his open palm to crack his knuckles beneath his wrapped hands. He stood more than an arm's length away, smiling softly between his thick mustache and beard.

"Do I know you?" Teodor asked.

The man gently shook his head. He pointed a finger at Teodor's breastplate. "I would recognize the emblem of Gero anywhere, and what other thief dances among the mercenaries of the Crimson Sun?" The assassin scoffed, advancing. "You are almost as well known as your father. It would be an honor to kill you."

Teodor held his chin steady despite the impulse to look at the horse head emblazoned on his armor. A reminder of his faith, his birthright, and his legacy. He could never escape Eldhaft and the Guardians of Gero, even if he was never a member among his father's guild of thieves.

"I am no thief," Teodor said.

"Says he who reveres a god of lies," the assassin remarked, holding his smile.

The series of blows, high and low, were in rapid succession. Teodor stayed on the defensive as the assassin attacked aggressively, his balled-up fists empowered with the weight of the iron plates hidden beneath the leather wrappings. Having little use for his sword in close-quarter combat, Teodor could do no more than twist the blade to offset the pinpointed punches. He took every opportunity to swing with his free hand and kick—ineffectively— at the assassin.

He moved side to side, keeping his head bobbing as though he were young again, boxing with his cousins in the courtyard of his home in Eldhaft. Unlike his childhood days, he knew one solid hit from the trained assassin would leave him in a world of black from which he would never awake.

The assassins did not tire as they maneuvered around their corner of the room. In the backdrop, tables and chairs crashed, crossbows twanged as their deadly bolts fired, and faction members shouted muffled commands. At one point, he saw Tyr get flung across the room by some unseen magic. The giant bawled in pain, tearing through a hanging tapestry and into a wall, but the fight continued.

Teodor finally put distance between the assassin and himself, then angled his sword at the enemy. He moved his blade through the air briskly to keep the assassin at sword's edge and gain his breath.

The assassin smirked with amusement and settled back.

"And what of your god, assassin?" Teodor asked, stalling, doing his best to keep his breath steady.

The stranger lifted his shoulders to his ears, speaking with ease. "No god exists worthy enough to worship me, let alone one worthy enough of my worship."

Farthr roared behind Teodor. Stepping sideways to keep his eye on the assassin, he tilted his head to see the centaur with a bolt sticking from his foreleg. Dark blood dribbled from the wound and into the beast's dark fur. The assassin who fired the shot dropped behind the throne to reload; the Stuhian approached the dais too, turning his back on the fight.

It looked as though he was having a casual conversation with the bearded assassin.

"Kill them!" Teodor heard the crossbowman bellow.

The bola soared through the air toward Farthr, but Tyr— without the threat of the dragon-man—snatched the weapon out of the air and flung it to the side.

Farthr wasted no time, firing his heavy crossbow at the bola-thrower. The bolt struck true, hitting the woman in the chest. Her shriek was silenced by a gurgle as she fell to her knees.

"No!" The scream of the dark-eyed girl was deafening as the dying woman slumped sideways. The enflamed color in the younger girl's face already spread to her exposed neck, resembling the color of the blood spilling over her fingers.

Under the explosive cry came the babbling moaning of the count, who stirred against the wall.

"Nine Lands." A curse spewed from the lips of the assassin standing opposite Teodor. He backed away with little caution, leaping over a cracked table toward the distraught girl. "We have to go! Come on!"

The crossbowman and dragon-man stumbled off the dais and out the side door, while the brawler dragged the truculent girl from the lifeless body.

"Teodor!" Tyr roared, rushing to the side door where the assassins escaped. He whipped his head back, red hair matted with sweat. His wide nose flared with bloodlust. "Teodor!"

After taking a couple steps forward, Tyr waved him off and sheathed his sword. "Our duty is here."

Chapter IV

TEODOR, *The Crimson Sun*

"Teodor!" Tyr shook with fury, his muscles visibly tightening in his shoulders and chest. "The bastards are escaping. We need to make them answer for their crimes."

Spinning the signet ring on his finger, Teodor kneeled beneath a decorated tapestry at Count Frantisek's side. He made no move to follow Tyr's direction, resting his hand on the count's shoulder before responding. "Let them go, Tyr." He gestured to the dead lass. "Farthr has assured that we have evidence of the Legion's betrayal. Even if they run back to Lonmere, we will have the support of the king and the remaining kingdoms to bring them to justice."

Teodor watched the giant from the corner of his eyes, concerned he might lash out or charge down the hallway anyway. Tyr snarled, knuckles whitening around the handle of his double-sided axe. The muscles twitched in his face, seemingly taking all his willpower to holster the weapon back into its binding.

Farthr's dark hand rested on the bolt in his foreleg while crossing the chamber, as though his grip would keep him from feeling the pain. The centaur rumbled in his throat, oblivious to the Ispolini's rage. "Tell me that he is alive."

"Unconscious," Teodor replied, hoping he was masking his concern well. He shook the count in an attempt to rouse him. Another stifled groan escaped the ruler's thick lips. He could see the older man's eyeballs rapidly moving behind his eyelids. "Count Frantisek?"

The sound of thin shoes slapping against the stone floor rang into the chamber from the direction the assassins absconded. He twisted his neck with intent to call to arms but saw the flowing purple-and-white dress of the count's wife, Countess Maja Frantisek. She burst through the side door with her arms held rigid, fingers clasped to her face. Her golden hair was wrapped in a bun on the center of her scalp, fringes of hair wisping over her cheeks.

"Vlaskhorn!" she blubbered, the color draining from her face while her wide eyes raked the room for her husband. She scarcely looked at Farthr or Tyr, whom she would have known from earlier that morning, and gaped at the arrangement of dead guardsmen. She stopped on Teodor, faintly gasping to herself. Her mouth formed a perfect circle, and then she cried out, "Czern's breath! Is...is he dead?"

Her long skirts dragged along the ground, over several bodies, and through pooling blood before reaching her husband's side.

"He is alive," Teodor answered her, watching Farthr lower himself to the ground and lie on his side. Curving his upper body and with a low growl, he tugged on the bolt in his leg. He snapped at the air, thrashing his head back; he quickly stopped pulling at the bolt.

"Did it pierce the bone?" Teodor asked.

"No," Farthr breathed, flashing his sharp teeth. His arm flexed against his side, preparing to jerk at it once more. "But it twisted into the meat."

"Pulling it out might cause more damage than good until we see an herbal healer. I do not need you to catch fever and die, Farthr," Teodor said.

"I will be fine. I just need to get it out," Farthr said.

Teodor pushed air from his nostrils. "Okay. Tyr, help Farthr. Find something to use for bandages. He is going to need to go back to Tamarri."

Farthr rumbled again while Tyr acquiesced. The giant made his way to the fallen assassin. He removed the black cloak and began tearing it into uneven strips.

As if being summoned, the count suddenly coughed, shuddering in Teodor's hands, thick saliva seeping from his lips. Vlaskhorn's eyes fluttered open, shut tightly, then opened again. "Wha—"

"Husband," Maya dropped next to Teodor and grabbed the count's hand, "tell me Nitalia has not been harmed. Please."

"I promise she is safe," Teodor reassured her.

"We don't know that," Tyr mumbled. He kneeled at Farthr's side and wrapped his six fingers around the end of the bolt. He did not see the harsh squint Teodor shot his way; the Ispolini had a lot to learn.

Vlaskhorn's words were jumbled and airy. "My daughter? What of her? Why would she not be safe?"

"You are lucky it didn't bury itself deeper." Tyr spoke to Farthr loud enough for them all to hear, clearly losing interest in the count. "We would have never retrieved it."

With a mighty tug, Tyr ripped the bolt free. Farthr roared, swinging a hand wildly through the air.

"Bah! I have been through the same and worse, and I survived. Stop squirming and allow me to bandage it," Tyr said.

Teodor glared at the Ispolini, shaking his head. The giant seemed intent on testing his patience. He wanted to believe it was the nature of their race, but he really had no reference. To his knowledge, Tyr was the first Ispolini to travel this far into Maharia. He was still trying to wrap his mind around why the giant had left Tundris Mor in the first place.

Vlaskhorn jerked in effort to sit up, seemingly startled by the roar. He swatted Teodor's and his wife's hands away. His words came in a fit, much louder than before. "I want—to know—what is going—" Vlaskhorn rolled forward to stand on his feet when he saw the state of his chamber. Torn tapestries, splattered blood, destroyed furniture, and the dead gave him pause. He stuttered in an effort to form more words, but they came as an exasperated mess of sounds.

His eyes shifted to Farthr and Tyr.

"Count Frantisek?" Teodor started.

"What are you doing here? What in the Nine Lands have you done?" Vlaskhorn turned on him, shuffling to his feet and backing away. He grabbed his wife and pulled her back behind him. She did not fight him, though her round face was etched with surprise. "You have brought beasts into my chamber and slaughtered my people! Where is my daughter? What have you done with her? Guards!"

"Husband—" Maja tried.

Tyr stood to his full height, dropping the bloodied bolt to a splintered table. He folded his arms over his chest, the strips of cloth still clamped in his oversized hands. His words boomed over the meager voice of the countess. "He speaks as though we haven't been here all day. What is wrong with him?"

"Ispolini," Farthr said, reaching for the bandages.

"What is a giant doing in the east?" Vlaskhorn pointed as Tyr dipped back down to finish wrapping Farthr's leg. "And why have you brought this monstrous, bloodthirsty savage into my home? He belongs in chains." His voice elevated to a frantic shout. "Guards!"

Maja let go of her husband and wrung her hands under her chin. She goggled at Teodor, shaking her head in confusion.

"Count Frantisek, your daughter is safe," Teodor said a bit harsher, pulling his eyes from the countess. He rested his hand on the hilt of his sword. "Tyr Og, son of Enlil, and Farthr of Brannan are each with the Crimson Sun. You have nothing to fear from them. Please sit. You must have taken a heavy blow to the head."

Tyr interjected as he worked. "Bah! We discussed these matters this morning."

"Did we now? You expect me to believe you have been here since this morning, *Master Bacheva*?" Vlaskhorn coughed again, measuring Teodor with familiarity in his eyes. He sputtered and kept rambling, holding his attention on Teodor. "And what reason did the Crimson Sun provide for being in Cavell? You should know as well as any that your people are not welcome here. We are not cut from the same cloth as other Anshedar. We do not hold allegiance to the Kadari or their precious sun god. We do not need the aid of the Crimson Sun. We take care of our own."

"If you recall, I do not worship the Lightbringer either." Teodor pointed at his breastplate, underscoring the carving of a horse head, the sign of Gero, the god of trickery. Tyr rumbled in his throat behind him, likely irritated in hearing the repeated rhetoric from when they first met with Count Frantisek earlier.

Vlaskhorn scowled at the image.

"Cavell is no place for thieves. Your father has made a name for himself in all Maharia; I have no interest in being involved in his eternal quarrels, no more than I want to be involved in the dealings of the Crimson Sun," the count said. "Whatever problems you have should not affect me, my daughter, or Cavell. Now, where is she?"

Teodor sighed, blinking slowly. He initially was sent by Ivarr because of his unique faith, hoping the count would be willing to listen to someone apart from the sun god. However, the morning had resulted in hours of debate about trust and loyalty and truth, as well as convincing the count that he was not a thief like his father; he had zero interest in tiptoeing through the same dispute again. It had been hard enough to convince the count to be reasonable the first time. The task would be a score more difficult sitting among the wreckage and the dead, with his daughter leagues from her home.

"For the sake of brevity, let us take a moment and let your memory return, Count," Teodor said. "Repeating our dialogue is not the best use of time. You need to trust me."

"Trust you! These are dead men at our feet. I am going to have to explain to their families how they died with honor. Czern's breath! I cannot even explain why you are here!" The count spoke through bared teeth, stomping his foot against the ground. "You are employed by the Crimson Sun, which means you work for my brother and, therefore, the vexatious Kadari. For all I care, you could have a deity sitting on your shoulder; it would change nothing. Your loyalty would remain to those putting silver in your coffers, and I will remember nothing. By the gods, I can remember nothing more than going to bed last night."

"Ask your wife. Let her be your memory," Teodor said. "She was with us this morning."

"I was," Maja agreed.

Vlaskhorn waved her off. "While her reassurance is heartening, I cannot know how you may have swayed her."

"Husband," Maja interjected. "They have done nothing to me. I am of my own mind."

"I have yet to see my daughter," said Vlaskhorn, raising his fist as though he might hit someone. "So if Nitalia is safe, bring her to me."

"Bah! She is on the road to Gaetana to be placed under the protection of the king," Tyr grumbled, tying a final knot over

Farthr's wounds. He gave the count a side glance. "She was taken with your permission. Do you really remember nothing?"

Teodor tensed. He wished Tyr could keep his mouth shut like Farthr and let him do the talking.

"They are speaking the truth, husband," Maja said, resting her hand on Vlaskhorn's shoulder.

"You sent my daughter away?"

"*You* sent her away. She needed to be kept safe from the Dusk Legion," Maja said.

Vlaskhorn's face turned purple. "*Assassins?* I do not see any assassins. Only a thief pretending to be a mercenary with beasts among his numbers, all of which are much too far from home. We do not need them. If assassins are coming for Nitalia, we will protect her. We have always taken care of our own."

Teodor gritted his teeth. "Look at the dead men in your chamber. Clearly you were not prepared to face these cutthroats."

"Neither were you," the count snipped.

Tyr snarled, stomping over to the fallen assassin's body. He grabbed a handful of her clothes, lifting her by the shoulder to be displayed before them. "Right here, you can see we killed one of them. Open your eyes."

The count squinted with caution, studying Tyr and the woman's body. He peered down at her, and then after a moment asked, "Who is she?"

Teodor bit his inner cheek. He mentally relaxed his muscles, speaking as calmly as possible. He briskly walked over to Tyr. "*She is one of the assassins.*"

"And how do I know that?" the count blustered, throwing his hands in the air. "I have never seen this woman in my life. She looks too old to be an assassin."

"Every member of the Dusk Legion has a triangular scar carved into the base of their neck to prove their affiliation. Look, you can see her—" He turned her head and lifted her dark hair to reveal her bare neck. *She was not with the Dusk Legion.*

Teodor choked on his own tongue trying to find his words. Instead, he fumbled for an appropriate curse. "*Sard!* Gero's yard!"

"She does not have one?" Farthr asked, scrunching his face at Teodor's language while struggling to get his four limbs back under him.

Vlaskhorn folded his arms over his stomach.

A stifled grunt from one of the fallen soldiers behind Teodor kept the count from saying whatever was on the edge of his tongue. His guard's black armor rattled as he made his way to his feet. His eyes rolled back, his hand touching the side of his face where a reddened lump swelled from his ear to his chin. The thin black hair on his head, as dark as the armor he wore, was matted to his forehead as though he had been drenched in a bucket of water.

"Tomas!" Vlaskhorn cried, turning his back to Teodor. "You are alive. Glory to the Grey-Clad. Maybe you can tell us what in the Nine Lands happened here? I want a full report."

"My lord..." Tomas awkwardly dipped his quivering chin, rubbing his head. His light eyes scanned the chamber as he regained his senses, looking to a bloodied sword near his boots. His hands shook in front of him, caked in dried blood. "I-I don't know. I remember the doors opening...and now *this*. My blade...I... am drenched in blood... I-I do not recall anything."

"Czern's breath!" Vlaskhorn screamed. "What dark magic has been wrought?"

Teodor sucked in a breath, trying to find a way to convince the count of the truth. One of the assassins recognized him; they had to be from Lonmere. "The Legion was here, Count. I am sure of it. They came to kill your daughter. They must have found some way to block your memories."

"What of the girl?" Vlaskhorn pressed, nodding at the woman in Tyr's hands.

"A sellsword?" Teodor suggested. "Maybe?"

"You think the Legion is hiring killers?" the count scoffed. "Unbelievable."

"What...what is the confusion, my lord? We *were* waiting for the Dusk Legion to come," Tomas slowly offered. Vlaskhorn's eyes widened at him. "We weren't sure they would, but we thought they might. You asked us to ambush them here in the chamber. We spent most of the day waiting here after the mercenaries took your daughter to Gaetana."

"And why would the Legion send men to kill my daughter? We have never had any dealings with them. As far as I am concerned, they could be on the edge of the world. They are as far from Cavell as Tamarri, where the lot of you should have stayed," the count said, pointing his finger at Teodor and the others. Holding his tongue, Teodor had no answer for the count. He was still in shock that the woman was missing the mark of the assassins guild. Vlaskhorn blew air through his nose. "I cannot believe I would send Nitalia away."

"You did, husband," Maja said.

"You did," Teodor assured him. He turned to the Ispolini. "Tyr, you have lived among the Stuhian people in Lairhein. Could the dragon-man have placed him under some spell?"

Tyr frowned, staring at the dead woman. "I have never seen anything like this before. You will have to ask Eisliev."

"What dragon-man? Who is Eisliev?" the count asked as his wife neared his side again. Teodor noticed him clasping her hand and patting it with reassurance.

"We have a Stuhian in our company," Teodor sighed, combing his beard with his fingers. "He and Seigfeld are with your daughter right now, taking her to your brother as swiftly as the road will carry them."

Vlaskhorn shook his head. "The road to Gaetana is not safe this time of year. Beasts are thick during the Season of Frost." The count pursed his lips. "Whatever was agreed to before is done. You will bring them all back here. We will discover the identity of this woman lying dead in my chamber, and you can go back to Tamarri. If there is danger, my daughter will be protected by her own. She will stay with her family."

"It is not safe here either," Teodor argued, reiterating the logic used that morning against the threat of *beasts* in the Dyndaer. "The Legion could be waiting for her return. Your brother's forces will outnumber the cutthroats'."

"The *Legion*, if they are involved, could also be chasing her down on the road while you stand in my chamber," he threw back. "I would rather have her face men than monsters."

"If they are giving chase, you would turn her around only to have them cross paths in the woods. What chance would she have facing professional killers?" Teodor scoffed. He motioned to the scattered bodies. "She was better off not being here for *this*."

Vlaskhorn curled his lip. "I do not know what is going on here. For all I know, this may be some intricate scheme by the Kadari or the Crimson Sun. You said it yourself. You have a dragon-man in your company who could have very well cast a spell on us all! You will bring Nitalia back!"

"You cannot be serious," Teodor said. "We were sent here to keep your daughter from harm."

"Husband—"

"She is safest at home. That will be the end of it," the count commanded. "Tomas will go with you and see that it is done."

Chapter V

TYR, *The Crimson Sun*

Tyr observed the shadowy visage of Castle Frantisek on the rise behind them. The castle and its towers were a monument to the hamlet's craftsmanship, its thick walls shielding it from the rest of the town. Though compared to the underground city of his home, Almdalir, hidden away in Mount Dvargen on Tundris Mor, Tyr would have guessed the town to have been constructed by children.

Jammed between a river and the towering trees of the Dyndaer, Cavell was poorly placed. While timber was plentiful, the ground was worthless for crops, primarily entailing tangleweeds, lichen plants, and marshlands. Tyr could not believe the Frantisek family had maintained the place for almost three hundred years; at least, that is the history Teodor had shared with him on their way down to Cavell. He wondered if it was dumb luck that kept Cavell safe. Even now, with the war to the south growing deadlier every day, Cavell sat untouched in the depths of this forest. As he examined the hamlet, he reckoned nobody cared to seize a pile of—

"I am well enough to travel alongside you," Farthr insisted, interrupting Tyr's thoughts. The Svet moved unsteadily through Cavell's open gates, favoring his injured foreleg. The single guard stepped quickly to the side as though the centaur might take his head in a single bite.

Teodor noticeably eyed the dark strips of cloth wrapped around the Svet's injury. The bandages were soaked with blood from the wound, but Tyr was sure the bleeding had slowed since exiting the chamber.

Despite the pain, Tyr took note of Farthr holding his head high. His hands swung on either side of his human-like torso, where the waist blended with the body of a stallion. His thick hooves clopped loudly against the dusty road.

Teodor crossed his arms over his breastplate. "I know you are well enough to come along, Farthr, but I need someone to return to Tamarri and tell Ivarr what has happened here. Besides, you are the only one who can journey through the Hyaendi Hills without causing a disturbance. Tyr or I would have to stick to the coast or risk being ripped to pieces by your brethren."

Tyr rubbed his nose at the thought of fighting off the roaming centaurs in the hills. From what he gathered, the strange Svet were as ferocious as the Ispolini but less refined. Regardless, he was glad not to return to Tamarri and speak to Ivarr Gauthus, the head of the Crimson Sun. He had met the older gentleman a couple of times when he signed on and found him to be more of a noble prick than Teodor.

Teodor looked to the guard at Farthr's back, not waiting for the Svet's response. "You are positive no one has exited this gate in the past hour?"

The guard, a man who had barely sprouted hair from his chin, shook his head. "Nothing, Master Bacheva. It has been quiet."

Farthr twitched his ears, stepping close enough to Teodor to draw his attention back to him. The noble took a step back, eyeing the centaur and crossing his arms. "If I am to see Ivarr, what should I report?"

Tyr snorted. "Say that coming to Cavell has not helped us rid our confusion over the warning." He mirrored Teodor's stance. Before the noble Anshedar could scold him for his poor humor, Tyr went on, "The princess is safe and people are dead, but we have no idea if the Dusk Legion was involved. Nor do we know why they would want the princess dead to begin with. In fact, we cannot be certain the princess was ever the target."

"The Legion was behind this. No matter what marks were or were not found on that woman," Teodor said. "I do not doubt it. They were skilled in combat, enough so that they were able to clear a room of guardsmen and contend with us."

"We were outnumbered," Farthr said.

"The Crimson Sun is always outnumbered," Teodor said. "The fact that one of the assassins recognized me is also important. They knew my father."

Tyr scoffed. After the past few months, he did not know Teodor well, but even he was aware of the man's relationships in the north. "That does not tell us anything. You and your family are known through most of Maharia. Anyone can put on a dark cloak and recite information about your family."

Teodor shook his head. "No. This was different."

"What do you want me to tell Ivarr?" Farthr growled, seemingly irritated by asking a second time.

Teodor unfolded his arms to stroke his beard, speaking slowly to the centaur as though he were choosing his words carefully.

The pompous attitude made Tyr want to crush the man under his fist.

"We are going to stick with the facts until we can verify the rest," Teodor said. "Tell Ivarr that Cavell was attacked, but we have not confirmed the identity of the assailants. You can provide specifics of the battle in the castle and let him know that we are moving forward as planned."

"What do you mean?" Tyr dropped his jaw. "Are we not bringing the princess back to Cavell?"

Teodor shook his head. "Of course not. Whether she is the intended quarry or not, she cannot be protected here. Look how many are already dead."

"You are going to deliberately disobey the orders of the count?" Tyr raised an eyebrow. Teodor was known for his dutiful nature and trustworthiness. Even if he worshipped a god of lies, telling lies was unbecoming of him.

Teodor moved away from the guards at the gate, hissing to Tyr under his breath. "I have been ordered by Ivarr to take the princess to the king. That is my commitment. Not to some little brother overseeing a half-town in the middle of nowhere." Teodor flicked the underside of his signet ring with his finger. "I intend to see our task through and ensure the princess is protected. If the count has a problem with it, he can take it up with Ivarr once we are done."

Tyr adjusted the long-reaching axe on his back and looked back at the hamlet a second time. Residents roamed the winding roads in the dim light of the hanging lanterns, sneaking glances at them through the open gates. As expected, many had never seen a Svet or Ispolini before. He noticed a couple children pointing and giggling, pulling at their mother's skirts and shouting for their father's attention. Once the adults took notice, they were no more respectful than the children.

Tyr cared little to be a spectacle, but he was used to the bizarre treatment. Even during his time among the Stuhia of Lonmere, long-time allies of the Ispolini, he felt like he was on display for their amusement. Few had ever ventured far enough to meet with his kind on Tundris Mor, and they preferred not to leave their secluded island.

Although he did not see the guard from the chamber roaming the streets, he turned his back to the citizens and lowered his voice. "What about Tomas? I do not think he is going to come along willingly if we are defying his lord."

"We will think of something. The guard hardly has the means to make us do any different," Teodor said. "I imagine we will spend some time trying to catch up with Seigfeld and Eisliev anyway. They should be half a day ahead of us. We have plenty of time to consider our options."

"Bah!" Tyr grunted. "As long as you don't plan on drowning him in a swamp or leaving him helpless in these woods. Been enough death today and I don't think he could contend with a simargl."

Teodor scrunched his face at the mention of the oversized winged wolves. "We are not killing him."

Farthr adjusted the crossbow hanging at his side and turned from them, walking off into the Dyndaer without another word. Tyr watched him for a moment, realizing he was taking his leave without saying farewell.

"I think you insulted him." Tyr lifted his chin toward Farthr.

"The injury the Svet people received during the Second War brings more insult to them than anything I could say in passing," Teodor said, giving little context to his statement. Tyr was not too familiar with Anshedar history, but he was aware the Svet were defeated by the humans and enslaved by them. The few that were free stayed in the Hyaendi Hills, except Farthr, who somehow managed to be pulled into the protective folds of the Crimson Sun.

Footsteps sounded on the road, causing Tyr and Teodor to turn simultaneously. Tomas advanced at a slow pace with a pack slung over his shoulder, a torch in one hand and a polearm in the other. He led three horses behind him by ropes.

Teodor leaned closer to Tyr and whispered, "I am doing Farthr a favor by sending him back home. Seigfeld only released him from the Shade Fells a few months back; the story is that he had been trapped by demons. I am not sure he has yet recovered." He clicked his tongue on the roof of his mouth. "Besides, I am not sure what prejudices he might face out here." He squinted at Tomas, who approached. "The Svet are not exactly welcomed into the company of most Anshedar."

"The Witiko captured him?" Tyr squinted an eye at the human with disbelief. "Since when have demons held prisoners?"

"I do not know the full details. You might ask Seigfeld," Teodor replied, "but I know the memory lingers, and such an experience would be haunting."

"We are all haunted by something." Tyr scowled, his mind replaying segments of his past year.

He had watched his sister brutally mauled by a bear, murdered another Ispolini to defend her honor, and was banished to the Deep where he was overwhelmed by the demons like those that captured Farthr. If it were not for crossing Eisliev and his own father, he suspected he would already be worm food.

The guard neared.

"Glory to the Grey-Clad. I do not think we have been properly introduced," said Tomas, adjusting the pack over his shoulder. The young man cleared his throat. "I am Tomas Ethelred, son of Tallis. Count Frantisek agreed to provide a few horses to speed up our travel." He looked to Tyr and tightened his face apologetically, the expression looking rather odd with the swollen bruise on the side of his face. "I am sorry we do not have any large enough to carry you."

"I do not need a horse," Tyr said.

Teodor slapped Tomas on his shoulder in greeting, rattling the iron armor encasing his body. "I am Teodor Bacheva, son of Gaspar. We are glad to have you join our company. I am looking forward to hearing what you might recall from the battle in the castle."

Tomas looked dour, nodding hesitantly.

"And I am Tyr Og, son of Enlil," he said, keeping his arms folded. "If introductions are done, we should be on our way. They had horses too, meaning they are already leagues ahead of us. If we travel all night, we might be able to catch them by morning."

"All night?" Handing off one of the horses to Teodor, Tomas bobbed his head with eagerness. "I am already keen on returning home."

The three of them traveled well into the night, speaking cordially to one another until exhaustion began touching the corners of their eyes and the desire to make conversation faded. The enigmatic forest was haunting to travel through, no matter the time of day. With the thick treetops blocking any evidence of the sun, moon, stars, or even the light of the sky, the time of day was difficult to distinguish, especially with the current season keeping the skies cloudy and the weather relatively chilled.

Of course, the Season of Frost in Maharia was nothing compared to the brutal winters on Tundris Mor. Tyr's skin may have been cold to the touch, but he felt warm, even when he wore nothing more than his brown-colored feminalia, a fitted knee-length pair of pants made from the ibex that roamed his home island. Shirts, tunics, and boots were rarely fashioned for the Ispolini, unless one held position among the Council of Elders or hoarded coins and commissioned specialized garments.

They stopped a couple of times to let the horses rest or to relight a torch, but otherwise they maintained a steady pace through the forest. To their fortune, no beasts roamed in the immediate vicinity of Cavell; even after the path leading from town was overtaken by brush and vines, they saw little movement among the trees. Tyr suspected they frightened off most creatures with him floundering through the bushland and Tomas's clanking armor. While most creatures lingering in the Dyndaer would not be instinctively fearful of any one of them, he assumed the sound of their brazenness was more likely to trigger caution than curiosity.

After a time, Tyr found himself rubbing a pink blemish on his right arm. He hated the scar, a lifelong reminder of the white bear he fended off to protect his sister, Maruda. The effort had been in vain, only to have her fall from the cliffs of Tundris Mor during the battle. He hardly needed a scar to remind him of his failure; the memories were constantly with him.

The two of them had been searching for the Blood Cascade, a fiery aura of souls, at the direction of their father, who hoped they could resurrect their mother. Tyr remembered little of his mother, who was slaughtered by the Witiko when he was a young child. Regardless, he now was in constant search of the Blood Cascade for both his mother's and sister's sakes.

Tyr rumbled to himself, the sound of Maruda's scream echoing in his ears, the last sound heard from his loving sister. He doubted he would ever be free of the nightmarish noise. He had promised to protect her in the same way she had saved him from demons when he was a boy—moments after their mother died—only to fail her in the same moment the promise was delivered. He should have been the one taken.

His life was a chronicle of misery.

"You look like you could use a drink," Tomas nervously laughed, nudging Tyr and presenting him a flask. "I would hate to know what thoughts cause a man—er, giant—to scowl so."

"I was thinking of home." Tyr winced, nearly looking eye to eye with the man on the horse. He reached out and accepted the flask. "A good ale, I hope."

"The best I got to offer," Tomas shrugged.

Teodor, riding a horse in the rear, wiped his mouth with the back of his hand, indicating he had already taken a swig while Tyr was caught up in his thoughts. "Sard," he cussed. "Tastes like watered-down piss."

A smile tugged at the guard's mouth as Tyr tilted the flask to his lips. "It's true."

The liquor burned the back of Tyr's tongue and his nostrils, holding the flavor of spoiled oats. He nearly spit it from his mouth. "Bah! That is terrible."

"Another nine or so and you might get a good hum going. Won't even taste it anymore. Been awhile since I lost track of my footsteps." Tomas grinned. "The wife does not like seeing me botched beyond reason."

"Best put it away, then," Tyr said. "You don't want to be losing track of your feet out here anymore than at home."

"That is why I ride a horse." Tomas chuckled, looking over his shoulder as if to see whether Teodor was laughing too. Their party leader simply turned his head the other way. Tomas turned back to Tyr. "You said you were thinking of home. If you miss it, why don't you go back?"

"I did not say I missed it," Tyr said.

He felt the muscles in his shoulders tense at Tomas's innocent suggestion. Of course, the young man could not know that Tyr was banished by the Council of Elders in Almadir on the same day his sister met her end. The rage that consumed him upon returning home—after losing so much—made his head spin as he looked at the guard.

He did not at all remember the brawl that led to him murdering several Ispolini, save how much blood had been spilled. He should have been thrown to the lava pits and burned alive, but one of the elders, a friend of his father's, convinced the council to mercifully cast him to the Deep. To his fortune, he found Eisliev and his father roaming amongst the demons.

None of that mattered now, though, as the guard continued to run his mouth.

Tomas tilted his head. "I suppose I imagine everyone misses their home. We have barely left Cavell and all I can think about is my wife and child."

"I do not have anyone back home," Tyr snarled. He was being truthful, considering his father, Enlil, lived among the Stuhia in

Lairhein now and not on Tundris Mor. Tyr did not see any reason to be specific or attempt to bond with the talkative guard. He wanted the conversation to be over and hoped his abrasive tone would end it.

"Oh." Tomas breathed in. "Do you plan to have a family again someday? Like a wife? Or a son?"

Tyr turned to face the Anshedar, feeling the heat touch his ears. The guy could not take a hint. His vision reddened. "To think, it was I who opined not to drown you in the swamp."

"Wha—"

"Tyr!" Teodor snapped.

"My-my... I am sorry. I did not mean to upset you." Tomas gulped. "I was only asking questions to pass the time. I thought—"

Tyr sneered. "If you have any more questions, I promise you I can carry you through the Dyndaer on that pike stick of yours with the same efficiency as your horse."

He almost missed Teodor's darkening gaze, which he caught from the corner of his eye.

"You will apologize and behave in accordance with the Crimson Sun code," Teodor demanded. When Tyr did not immediately respond, he roared his name with authority. "Tyr!"

He spent many years of his life having others bark orders at him, whether it be his clansmen or the Elders back home in Almdalir. If his father had not sent him to join the Crimson Sun with Eisliev Kluk, he would have long ago carved another path for himself. He was not in the mood to hear Teodor's demands.

Facing forward again, Tyr lifelessly muttered, "I am just letting him know his options."

Tyr heard the ale churn in the flask as Tomas took another swig. The guard, after numbing his tongue with liquid courage, spoke again, trembling. "Tell me the truth, did you kill the guards at the castle?"

"Sard, no!" Teodor spluttered. Without facing him, Tyr imagined the distraught look on his noble face. "The Crimson Sun keeps peace; we do not incite wars or kill innocents."

"Woah!" Tomas hollered at his mount, pulling on the reins, abruptly ending their talk. The torchlight caught the edge of a bloodied scene smeared across the forest floor. Guts and entrails, ripped flesh, and chunks of some animal colored the faded foliage. The smell of death had not yet touched the shredded carcass, overwhelmed by either the nearby mire or the onset of cold weather.

Flaring his nostrils at the guard, who nearly stilled his heart with the needless shout, Tyr asked, "What is that?"

Tomas swung a leg over the horse to dismount, keeping the torch steady in one hand and his polearm in the other. His horse whickered, undaunted by the graphic scene.

Tyr heard Teodor dismount as he neared the gore with Tomas. He peered through the shadows curling around the piercing yellow light, but he could not see anything moving. Teodor soon approached, his footsteps crunching against the hardened ground.

"These are Eisliev and Nitalia's horses," Teodor said, pointing to chewed-up cadavers that had been pulled into the brush. One horse's head was mauled, the legs gnawed through, and the belly completely gutted, but Tyr could see the faint shape of a mare. Tyr twisted around, looking into the pitch of the forest, while Teodor addressed Tomas. "Nine Lands. Give me your torch."

Tomas handed him the blazoned stick, covering his mouth with his free hand. His words were muffled behind his fingers. "Simargl did this. They have been killed and dragged off."

Jeering at Tomas, Tyr shook his head. Were the Anshedar not trained to track? Could they not recognize signs of multiple animals? If Tyr hadn't learned, he'd never have been able to eat. Tyr gestured at the large footprints of the winged wolves. "There are no signs of struggle," he said. "Looks like they abandoned the horses, using them as a distraction to escape the simargl."

"Right," Teodor said, running the torch along the ground following the smeared blood. "Nothing has been dragged too far. Looks as though the beasts had their meal, maybe wrestled it a bit, and left."

"Our own horses are not spooked," Tyr agreed, touching the blood on one of the carcasses and then rubbing it off on his britches, "but this is recent. If they are alive, they cannot be far."

Teodor whipped the torch between two bushes to reveal a spoor evident by small broken branches, smashed grass, and footprints. "They went this direction."

Handing off the torch to Tyr, Teodor joined Tomas in returning to their mounts. Tomas looked to the torch for a moment, seemingly slighted by having his immediate access to light and warmth kept from him.

Tyr led them through the brush, staying on the path with ease. After pursuing everything from deer to dragons on his Tundris Mor, following the trail of his fleeing companions was too easy. Although sleep tugged at his eyelids—a proposal the ice-cold forest urged him to resist—Tyr stayed alert. Little time passed before a familiar voice called out to him, the unmistakable accent giving the hint of condescension with every word.

"Tyr, is that you? Nine Lands, the lot of you are louder than a brigade of soldiers."

"Eisliev." He pinpointed the Stuhian circling around a thick oak, shielded in his thick red robes. A hanging hood masked his light eyes and red hair. Tyr advanced to meet him with Teodor and Tomas at his back. He was careful not to show too much interest in Eisliev despite his desire to drag him off and speak in secret. Even with their newfound positions among the Crimson Sun, neither of them had any interest in the company's trivial missions. With the war growing in the south and demons flowing from the Netherworld, he and Eisliev were aware of greater dangers than the life of a single princess. Yet their own ambitions were not to be shared with their companions.

Seigfeld and Nitalia skirted from behind the trees to join them.

Tyr pinched his brow together and ran a hand through his hair. "Is everyone alright?"

Forming a steeple with his fingers, Eisliev said, "Our horses are dead or run off. Simargl are prowling in nearly every known direction. But we remain without injury."

"Praise Czern, you are alive," Tomas said, halting his brown horse.

Nitalia Frantisek, almost old enough to be wed and bear children, stepped lightly around Eisliev, looking up to Tyr with an innocent gaze. She was dressed in a white chemise, the sleeves just reaching her elbows, and a dark yellow kirtle that fell to her ankles. The tunic-like garment was laced tightly on the side-back to display the elegance of her form, her small bust supported by a black bodice stiffened with bone. Over her shoulders, she wore a purplish hooded cloak of the best cloth.

Her attire alone hinted at the luxuries bestowed on the noble class. Even the back holster that sheathed her paired double-edged billhooks was made from the finest leather. The eight-inch smooth wooden handles were decorated with crescent-shaped pommels resting at an angle above either shoulder blade.

"What are you doing here, Tomas?" She blinked rapidly against the hazy light, her golden hair shining against the glimmer of light. Her boots were soft against the ground as she took another step closer. "By the gods, you have been injured!"

Tomas covered the bruise on his face, forgetting to answer the first question. A boyish smile split his lips. "I will be fine, my lady."

Seigfeld tilted his head at Tyr, his brown hair waving over his light eyes. He held his weight on his weapon called a sovnya, a five-foot wooden pole with a two-foot curved blade extending from the end.

Tyr admired the fighter, Seigfeld's reputation preceding him long before they met on this mission to retrieve the princess. The number of tasks that Seigfeld had successfully completed for the Crimson Sun was countless, marking him more of a god than a man among the mercenaries. His name was whispered among the streets of Tamarri as frequently as the king's. Though he was not noble, he often carried the same authority Teodor possessed on this particular mission. Therefore, Tyr was not surprised when the famed warrior spoke with a commanding tone.

Seigfeld waved a doused torch in his other hand at them. "Where is Farthr?"

Teodor answered. "I sent him back to Tamarri to deliver a report to Ivarr."

"You ran into trouble in Cavell, then?" Seigfeld raised an eyebrow.

"The Dusk Legion attacked as we were told they would—" Teodor said.

"We think," Tyr slipped in.

"The assassins killed the guards stationed in the great chamber. They were violently slaughtered," Teodor continued, paying no mind to Tyr. Nitalia gasped, slack-jawed, reminding Tyr of the countess's mien when she viewed the remnants of the battle. "Your parents are well, save your father's lost memory," Teodor was quick to add.

"What do you mean?" Seigfeld pressed.

"We cannot explain it," Teodor said. "Tomas cannot recall the battle, though he was present during its entirety, and Count Frantisek does not even remember us coming to Cavell and offering protection for his daughter." Teodor eyed Nitalia warily. His breaths quickened, and he forced a chuckle. "He requested that we bring her back to Cavell, where the assassins are likely lying in wait."

Nitalia took a step back, her eyebrows knitting with concern.

Tomas cut in, rushing to face Teodor. No humor lines marked his face. "He did not request anything. He *instructed* she be brought home."

"What did the count say exactly?" Eisliev remained where he was as Seigfeld neared.

Tyr saw Eisliev gesture to him ever so slightly with a bob of his head, hidden in the shadows beneath his hood. Not needing to hear any words to understand the meaning, Tyr moved behind Teodor and glared down at Tomas. The castle guard met his fierce gaze and took a step back, bumping into Seigfeld's broad chest.

"What he said is not important." Teodor tightened his jaw, his forced smile staying on his lips. "We must do what is best for the princess and think for ourselves. We came to Cavell in good faith. The Dusk Legion has undoubtedly placed Count Frantisek under some spell with the intent of us bringing Nitalia back to them. We have the advantage out here and should keep it. She will be safest in Gaetana."

Tyr bit his tongue, desperately wanting to point out the flaws in Teodor's reasoning. Not only were they lacking proof of the Dusk Legion's involvement, but they could not be sure Nitalia was the target of an attack.

"You are asking me to commit treason?" Tomas looked at Tyr again, fear etching his face.

"Teodor," Seigfeld said, lifting his strong chin, "we cannot go against the command of Count Frantisek. We already have enough problems being trusted by the nobles in the Dyndaer. We were lucky to even be granted an audience."

"Our duty is to protect her," Teodor said. "In good conscience, I cannot lead her back to Cavell. If we go to Gaetana and the king wishes her to return home, then so be it. We should keep to the original orders given to us by Ivarr—*and* the count's original agreed course of action, don't forget."

Seigfeld turned to Nitalia, standing with her mouth in awe at the exchange. "Let her decide. Her command can hold sway over her father without compromising the Crimson Sun or binding this guard to subversion."

Though Nitalia's bright blue eyes were lined with water, Tyr noticed that no tears dropped. "Master Bacheva, is my father in danger?" Her honeyed tone overflowed with surprising strength and confidence.

"I do not believe so, Princess," Teodor answered. "If the assassins wanted to kill him, they would have done so before we reached him in the chamber. I suspect they will wait a while longer and, when we do not return, eventually attempt to chase us down. We can use the time to put distance between us."

"You mentioned a spell," Nitalia said, pushing a strand of golden hair behind her ear. She lifted her small nose in the manner of her father. "How would assassins gain access to magic? Are the Kadari working with them?"

Tyr moved away from Teodor, edging his way closer to Eisliev, who perked up at the mention of the spell-slinging faction of religious zealots. He pulled his hood back, tangles of red hair bobbing over his ears and eyes. "Were the Kadari there?" he asked.

"No. Certainly not," Teodor said. "A dragon-man was among their numbers."

"How did you survive?" Seigfeld asked.

Tyr shrugged, trying to keep his eyes from Eisliev. "I have been asking the same question. He was certainly a Stuhian, but he did not contribute much to the battle."

"A coward?" Seigfeld scrunched up his face.

"A tactician," Eisliev corrected. "A dragon-man among assassins would have been away from Lairhein for a long, long time. We would be wise to stay clear of him."

Nitalia lowered her voice to a whisper. "Could he have stolen my father's memory?"

A light flashed in Eisliev's blue irises, looking to Teodor and then Nitalia. "It is possible," he finally said.

The princess gulped before pulling her purple-colored hood over her head. "We will continue to Gaetana, Master Bacheva. Tomas will not give any argument."

"As you wish," Tomas said.

"I am glad to hear you say that, Princess," Teodor said. "Let us find a safe place to make camp for a few hours and then continue down the road."

As they set off in an orderly fashion, Tyr neared Eisliev. "Can a Stuhian really erase a man's memory?"

The red mage looked up at Tyr with a sly smile and said, "Of course not."

Chapter VI

KREL, *The Dusk Legion*

One sellsword was dead. He hoped the other two would survive until they cut down the princess. Chances were they would need the extra bodies when fighting the Crimson Sun, if for nothing else but to shield him and Brenn from flying cross bolts.

Thunder rolled overhead. The late autumn rain drizzled through the branches, soaking Krel's cloak and clinging his beard to the underside of his chin. He tugged at the strands of wet hair and flared his nostrils, sucking in the scent of the damp forest. He knew the princess was being taken to Gaetana but finding the path through the oversized forest was easier said than done. He searched the woodland ahead for any sign of what direction they might have gone.

By mid-morning, the diminishing prints of several horses venturing westward, soon to be washed away by the raindrops, were found snaking through the trees. He splashed forward through a small puddle, leading the two men and woman at his back.

"Bad omen, it is," Rehor remarked after a short distance at Krel's back, "having rainfall this late in the year. We will be frozen solid by evening, hmm?"

Krel did not bother turning around. Rehor had looked for an excuse to start conversation several times since leaving Cavell as though the taste of their defeat did not satisfy his tongue and needed something different to whet his palate.

Krel swung his arms as he walked. "Then we will have to keep moving to stay warm. We should have left last night when we saw them exiting the gates." He tried to keep the bite from his tone. "They have almost a day on us and horses too. The chances of us catching them before they reach the king's city are growing slimmer by the moment."

"We made it beyond the walls as soon as we were able," Brenn said, the torch in his hand fighting to stay lit through the increasing precipitation. He matched Krel stride for stride, his brown cloak having a surprising amount of bounce for the water it held. "Might be better to catch up to them outside the forest anyway. This place gives me the creeps. But we need to be honest with ourselves, Krel. Are they worth catching? Maybe we should just head home."

"I am not in the mood for your humor. You were the one who wanted to attack her in the forest to begin with, remember?" Krel pressed his beard and moustache together in a mound of fur. He twisted his frame to look back the way they had come. Cavell had completely disappeared in the array of trees and scattered brush. Although morning had come, little light descended from the heavens to the forest floor. While the overcast offered little help, Krel knew the Dyndaer rarely received any natural light. It was a wonder that anything grew in the hodgepodge of swamp weeds and tangled vines.

"I wanted to ambush her in the forest before anyone knew an attack was coming. Face it, the mission has been thwarted. We—" Brenn cleared his throat, pausing to look at Taryn hanging in the back. Krel trailed his gaze to the younger sister. Her eyes were glossed over, staring blankly through the lofty trees. She sidestepped to avoid running into whatever tree fell directly in her path, but otherwise, she shuffled along with the fervor of an old ox. Krel could see that her eyes were bloodshot from crying, matching the rosy complexion of her cheeks. She long ago stopped wiping the salty drops from her eyes and the clear snot sliding from her nose. He had no idea what to do with a girl crying over her sister. Her constant crying made him uncomfortable. Brenn finished his sentence, whispering, "We left a body."

"Quinn cannot be tracked back to us. I made sure of it." Krel curled his lip, turning from Taryn, and tapped the purse of coins under his robe. He was not dumb enough to flee the chamber without dropping a few Gaetanean coins next to her body. Whoever inspected her body would question her origins and hopefully be steered far from Lonmere. The fact that the sisters were from the town of Mecka on the outskirts of Gaetana only served them better.

Brenn widened his eyes, glancing at the two sellswords. "How?"

"I did not hesitate when the opportunity struck," he replied. He then rubbed the triangular scar on the back of his neck, an echo of the one cut into Brenn's flesh, the sign borne by any member of the Dusk Legion. "The Stuhian's suggestion is sensible. We will murder the princess and pass the blame to the Crimson Sun. The death will still pit the Frantisek brothers against each other, distracting them from the war. In doing so, we will earn favor with the Uvil and appease the senate. This is not over."

Krel noticed Brenn eyeing Taryn again, twisting his face with concern. "Defeating the Crimson Sun will demand vigilance," Brenn said. "A handful of them matched us in the castle. We can safely assume more are in the company of the princess."

"We do not need to fight them," Krel said. "We need to kill the princess while she is under their care. If we are not seen, we won't be held accountable."

"They saw us in Cavell," Brenn maintained. "If anyone ends up dead within twenty leagues of this place, we will be to blame."

"No one saw us but those we intend to frame."

"The Crimson Sun is a bit—" Brenn shook his head, lifting his forefinger and thumb to Krel, "—more trusted than the Dusk Legion. If it is their word against ours, we will be on the losing end."

"They will have no proof." Krel looked from Brenn's outstretched hand until he dropped his arm. "We have no choice. What can we do but claim innocence and let the chips fall where they may? One way or another, they are not going to start a war against Lonmere based on hearsay. Nitalia's death will still serve to make the distraction the Uvil need to advance into the Gaetanean Kingdom."

"I am sure that wars have been started on less than hearsay." Brenn's head did not stop shaking from side to side as he gawked into the woods. Clutching his arms to his chest, he offered in a quiet voice, "How do you plan to do this?"

Krel gritted his teeth. "There are several among their number. I am sure dissonance exists among them; we only need to select the right target and make it look as though they are responsible."

"The Svet," Taryn forced in a hollow tone. Her voice quivered with ire, repeating herself. "The Svet. Blood and spit. I want to see him ripped apart by his own."

"Look there." Krel gleamed. "Taryn has the right mindset, even after undergoing her loss."

Rehor whistled through his teeth, saying, "I do not think she speaks from a place of devotion." Krel snapped his attention to the dragon-man, his hand falling to the hilt of the long knife at his belt. Rehor tracked the movement and knitted his eyebrows. He looked back at Krel with a smile widening on his face. "Though I admit that I share Taryn's enthusiasm." He jabbed his fist into the air playfully. "Let's get the princess, hmm?"

Brenn consented. "Fine. We will do it your way."

He nodded offhandedly to Brenn, unconcerned over the man's acquiescence. He would have gone on to kill the princess regardless of Brenn's approval.

Fixating on the Stuhian, Krel was incapable of hiding his frustration any longer. "Rehor, what do you think we are paying you for?"

The Stuhian scratched at the wet mop on his head, blinking sluggishly at Krel. "Going to tell me, I suspect you are, hmm?"

Krel sneered, checking the path ahead. "I want to know why you did not assist in the fight against the Crimson Sun."

"Is this another effort to tease the redhead?" Rehor slanted his head, squinting at Krel. His tone was absent of his usual joviality. "Spent an evening of your life in that little battle, you did. I wasted a couple *weeks* of my life wielding *Koldovstvo* for you."

At the mention of the ancient magic, a word which Rehor emphasized, Krel's throat tightened. The dragon-man could turn him inside out if he so desired, but Krel would not let him evade the question.

He halted the party and faced Rehor.

"You used that ring on your finger against the sentries. Why did you hold back against the Crimson Sun?"

Brenn interjected, "What ring? What are you talking about?"

Watching Rehor tuck his hands inside his brown robes, Krel stepped into his space and stopped him from advancing. He lifted a finger to Rehor's nose. "He has a silver ring that gives him the power to control men's minds. I watched him use it against one of the guards."

"The one who turned on his own?" Brenn gasped, distancing himself from Krel and Rehor. "How is that possible?"

Taryn had the opposite response, visible only to Krel at Rehor's back. What color lingered in her cheeks fled. Her brown eyes protruded, chin lifting, with a growl emanating from her throat. She stomped forward, pushing Krel away as she sandwiched herself between them and grabbed Rehor's robes. She nearly slipped in the mud but had enough momentum to shove him backwards. He flew from his feet and slammed back into the sludge. Thick mud splattered over his clothes and visible skin. Krel heard the faint clanking of the glass vials in the pouch at his belt.

Taryn screamed, "You let my sister die when you had the power to stop it!"

"I could stop nothing." Rehor's tone softened, raising his hand at the young woman. The silver ring on his finger was exhibited for them all to see. "Faegrim works on the minds of those who cannot touch Koldovstvo, but its magic does not have any effect on the Svet or Ispolini. Constructed differently than that of other mortals, their minds are. Any simpleton can see the differences."

"Liar!" she bawled. "Even without the ring, you could have ripped that Svet to pieces with your magic."

"Perhaps. At the cost of my own life, I could rip you all to pieces, hmm?" Rehor dropped his head back to the mud and closed his eyes. He waved his hand haphazardly in front of him as though he were painting, pointing roughly at each one of them. "I could disembowel you, or wither your skin until your eyes pop out, or have you hump a tree until nothing remained but a bloody corkscrew of a cock, hmm?"

Krel mirrored Brenn's example and stepped away as Rehor's finger tapped the invisible space between them, a dangerous grin splitting the redhead's lips.

Rehor popped his eyes open and worked his way up to his elbows. He crossed his legs as though he were making himself comfortable in the muck. "Our contract involved me tagging along to kill a princess. Said it yourself, you did. I'm not part of the Dusk Legion. I'm not your partner. I'm not your friend." He pointed at Krel and then Brenn. "And to my understanding, in order for me to get paid, only one of you has to survive this insane excursion."

Krel gritted his teeth. "Perhaps you should be on your way if you are not committed to—"

"Oh, no, no, no." Rehor shook his head. "I have spent weeks of my time, and even more of my life, to travel down here and see this done. Made a contract, we have. We *will* see it done."

Taryn sniffled at Krel's side. She dropped her eyes from Rehor, chin quivering.

Brenn wiped the collected water on his brow, offering a hand to Rehor. The rain seemed to intensify, splashing in puddles forming at their feet. "What about the swordsman?"

"You mean Master Bacheva?" Rehor clarified, licking his lips. He paused for a moment, admiring Brenn's hand extended toward him. Without immediately accepting it, he said, "For one, you are paying me to kill one noble, not two. Second, nobles are noble for a reason. Nitalia is the daughter of a count who is brother to a king. The bounty is great, and the risk of being tracked down is slim. Teodor, however, is the son of Gaspar Bacheva, master of the greatest thieves guild to ever exist in Maharia. I would wager they will be more difficult to outrun if one of their own is killed, hmm? That is a lot of risk for no bounty."

Krel heard Taryn's muffled sobs through the cascading rain as she turned her back to all of them. He was not certain if Rehor was a madman or not, but he made some sense. "You fear someone will survive the battle and hunt us?"

Rehor took Brenn's hand, allowing himself to be pulled to his feet. He adjusted the herb pouch, opening the flap to inspect the vials before answering. "I have lived long enough to know that someone always survives to tell the story of a battle. The center of campfire tales, I personally do not wish to be." He loudly clicked his tongue. "And I happen to like Teodor's father."

Chapter VII

KREL, *The Dusk Legion*

Rehor Malankov knew Gaspar Bacheva.

The thought haunted Krel to the point that the rows of elm and hawthorn trees seemingly vanished around him. He listened to the soft squishing of their boots against the forest floor, trodding behind the others while weighing the threat of the dragon-man among them. Revering the Guardians of Gero, even though they were the rival faction of the Dusk Legion, was not a crime, but it certainly threatened everything the Legion had set out to achieve in coming to the Dyndaer.

Krel's mind rattled with the questions of why Rehor knew Gaspar and how he and Brenn happened to bring him into their mix. Even if he had not infiltrated their band at Gaspar's instruction—which Krel doubted was true—Rehor choosing to reveal the Legion's hand would devastate the Lonmerean Kingdom. Defending against rumors was one thing but silencing an eyewitness to the events in question would likely leave them at war against the greater nations of Anshedar.

Even in the protective folds of the northern mountains, Krel knew Lonmere could not survive a war against the other kingdoms.

In the end, the answers to any question he could fathom mattered little. The chance of Rehor escaping his and Brenn's wrath and spilling the truth of their mission was not worth the risk. He was glad the plan to kill the sellswords had not changed.

The need to ask Brenn his position on Rehor was unnecessary. Anyone with half a brain would understand that eliminating Rehor was a priority. The conclusion was not remarkable considering what power the dragon-man held and how he chose to wield it. Based on what Krel heard, to their fortune, he resolved that Rehor was not the type to viciously slaughter them—despite the threats—though he did not have faith the Stuhian would keep them from harm either.

The comment about only needing one of them alive especially dawdled in Krel's mind. And the faint clinking of the containers in Rehor's bag while they walked did not keep his imagination from playing through scenarios that would result in his death. He was not an expert in *what* secreted concoctions in his bag did what, but he deduced that Rehor could craft a poison where the draught would not reach its full potency until sometime in the future. For all he knew, they would die from sickness long after the mission was over, ignorantly believing it came from natural causes instead of being fashioned at the hand of the Stuhian.

Grinding his teeth, Krel stepped over a sodden patch on the ground. He and Brenn needed to regain control of the situation. Swiftly. Every moment wasted was another chance for the dragon-man to escape or otherwise gain the upper hand.

As he turned to give Brenn a leveled look for what might have been the hundredth time since daybreak, Taryn blurted out, "Look at that." She gestured over Brenn's shoulder to the northwest; the consternation in her voice was unmistakable.

Krel followed her dainty finger. Hours ago the rain dispersed, leaving the Dyndaer dank and reeking of mildew. With the fetid swamps nearby, he was surprised that an additional foul smell was able to reach his nostrils.

Taryn directed them to a collection of trees much like the rest. Dispersed plants highlighted the ground between them, riddled in a motley of ferns. In the center of it all appeared to be several half-eaten pieces of some animal. The distance was great enough that Krel was not sure he would have seen anything without Taryn pointing it out.

He eyed her curiously.

A wind whipped through the canopy of trees, almost stealing away her question. "Is that blood fresh?"

"Yeah. I think so," Brenn said.

Krel neared the scene of carnage slowly, surprised to find any sign of activity in the forest. Despite the coming of winter and the icier weather, no wildlife had stirred since leaving Cavell that morning. They may have seen a handful of jackrabbits or spotted deer on the road from Lonmere, but today he had not come across so much as a bird hopping through the branches above.

Brenn weaved ahead of him, his eyes darting through the thick trees and back to the bloodied mess. They stopped together to inspect the assortment of animal parts. It did not take long for Krel to realize these were not the leftovers of forest animals.

He smiled. "These were horses."

"Only horses." Taryn bent her neck at Krel's left. She weaved her hands into her hair and pulled the strands with aggravation. She clearly was eager to find a human torso amid the slaughter. She muttered, "I guess we need to keep going."

Rehor chirped behind him, "Our work may have been done already for us, hmm?"

"These must be their horses," Krel agreed, sneaking a glance at Taryn. Turning back to slaughter, he curled his lip. "But I only see horses."

Brenn said, "At least we are on equal footing. We can pick up the pace and hopefully catch them."

Without warning, Taryn emitted a yelp of fear in Krel's ear and stumbled away. Unsure what to think, he turned to her with a frown. She motioned deeper into the forest before twisting completely away from them and scurrying to the nearest tree. Incapable of seeing much farther into the Dyndaer, he blindly scanned the outline of trees against more trees, nothing but shadows fading into darkness.

"What?" he mumbled.

"I don't know," Brenn said, squinting in the same direction. He lifted his hand over his eyes as though it would help in the already darkened forest. "Taryn, you want to use words?"

Rehor's foot crunched against a bone as he copied Taryn's movements.

Krel almost cracked a smile before turning to see the young beauty's face turn ashen. "Simargl." She frantically grabbed the low branch of the nearest tree and began to climb.

A growl rang out from the direction she had pointed, pulling Krel's attention to a singular spot. Almost a hundred feet away, masked in gloom, two cream-colored eyes shined back at him. The beast stalked forward, one large paw after another, until its silhouetted frame emerged as a black wolf with two leathery wings tucked on either side of its elongated body. Krel doubted the creature flew with the wings, but he heard tales of them gliding down from great heights to capture their prey.

With its long shaggy tail tucked behind its hindquarters, it folded its ears back against its oversized skull and growled again, bearing its canine teeth. Krel suspected the simargl's mass was greater than Brenn, Rehor, and him combined.

Brenn scurried around Krel, fleeing past Rehor to join Taryn in the tree.

"We cannot hide," Krel said, looking at his long knife. Like Taryn's blades, he would be lucky if the dagger pierced deep enough to do any harm to the beast. He reached for his crossbow and a quarrel; the weapon would only be slightly more effective. "We need to kill it and be on our way. More will come if we wait around."

"I am not about to punch it to death," Brenn said, pulling himself up to another branch.

"You should have brought something besides your fists." Krel stiffened his jaw while Brenn ignored him and made his way farther into the branches. Looking at Rehor, Krel hoped the dragon-man would give a sign that he was with him.

The Stuhian swatted the red curls from his eyes and then lifted one shoulder from beneath his hefty brown robes, conceding with a quiet *hmm*.

The simargl lurched through the trees at them, and Krel fired a quarrel from his crossbow, striking the beast under the muzzle. As expected, the hit barely penetrated the coat of fur, eliciting no more than a short-lived whine.

Sixty paces. Forty.

A lightning bolt ripped through the trees from the heavens, tearing through the flesh of the simargl, exploding the earth and dismantling a smaller tree in its wake. The crack of light knocked Krel off his feet, sending him spiraling onto the dead horse's meat. With a ringing in his ear, he immediately scrambled into a crouch, hearing the simargl's gravelly wail as its feet balled up under its body, skin and black hair splattering. The beast crashed against the forest floor and skidded into the trunk of an ash tree.

Elevating its head, the simargl snapped once at nothing and then crumpled to the dirt to die.

Krel's mouth dried as he stumbled to the beast twitching on the ground. Crimson blood dotted the exposed seared meat, seeping sluggishly from an incision near the spine, reaching down to the heart, where the magical fire had ripped through the flesh.

"Nine Lands," he said.

"You're welcome." Rehor pulled his shoulders back and displayed a wide grin.

Brenn's shout was wordless as he abruptly fell from the branches and landed with a thud at Rehor's feet.

"No!" A scream tore from Taryn's throat. "Blood and spit! Get back!"

A warped, wrinkled hand retracted around the trunk from midway up the tree—from where Brenn had been pushed from his perch—as a lumbering *thing* no bigger than Taryn advanced along a thick limb toward her.

Its bent back was lined with visible bone-thorns distending along the spine from the bark-colored skin. The taloned creature inched along, resembling something between an elderly man and a forest fiend. A stringy brown beard and mustache scarcely covered its thick black lips and slippery, salivating tongue that zipped in and out from between pointed teeth.

Taryn kicked, striking between the short, thin antlers angled from its oval head, and screamed again. A reptilian-like membrane slipped over the murky eyes momentarily before the monster continued its approach.

She reached for her dagger as it stretched for her.

Krel readied his crossbow again, moving away from the dead simargl. Lining up the bolt, he asked, "What is that?"

"A bauk," Rehor responded, "which means the chort are here too. You can injure him, but do not kill him yet."

"Brenn, are you okay?" Krel blurted before hearing the full of the Stuhian's direction. He lifted his weapon to take aim, then snapped his head to Rehor. "What? Why would we not kill it?"

Brenn coughed, his blue eyes watering as he tried to regain his breath. He croaked, "H-hold on. What is a chort?"

A ghastly howl rang from a nearby hemlock, giving the impression it discharged from the tree itself. Another sounded from the adjacent grouping of pine, cypress, and hawthorn.

"Get behind me," Rehor directed, the smile leaving his lips. He darted his blue eyes between the trees.

"What about Taryn?" Brenn asked.

Krel pulled Brenn to his feet with a single hand and yanked him to Rehor. Before anyone could say anything about Taryn, who continued to shout at the bauk, a beast unlike anything Krel had seen literally materialized from the base of the hemlock.

Whether it emerged from the ground itself or from the trunk, the chort did not solidify until its form was beyond the other physical elements of the forest. The faun-like hind legs were thick, holding the bulk of a boarish body with muscular arms and clawed fists. The thickness of its neck supported a monstrous head adorned with curled ram horns, a snarling snout with black eyes on either side, and a third in the center of its flattened forehead.

The Stuhian began to weave magic at the speed of thought as more chorts emerged from all sides. Fear gripped Krel, seeing the dragon-man reveal his true power. Twisting the ground ahead into a boiling black pit of sludge, he caught the first chort in it. The beast screeched like a rat thrown into the fire, clawing at the air uselessly before sinking from sight.

Silver bolts of chained lightning hurled into the reddish-brown flesh of the encroaching creatures. Fire scorched others that hoped to flank them. Roars issued from some throats, grinding barks of pain and anguish emerged from the throats of others; some throats were no longer intact. Rehor was a master of his craft, his face etched in concentration.

Krel raised his crossbow in hopes of firing one shot but was spellbound by how Rehor changed while he cast his ancient magic. The few spells he wielded up until now showed no visible signs of aging, indicating he was drawing more Koldovstvo amid this fight than any before.

As wrinkles lined Rehor's upper lip and the corners of his eyes, strands of grey peppering his crimson-colored mop, Krel fought back the curve of a smile. If the dragon-man killed himself outright or even aged to the point that he could not defend himself, he and Brenn could forever be done with Rehor Malankov.

He lowered his weapon, turning to Brenn at his back to find the other assassin was gone.

"Let go of the limb!" Brenn shouted to Taryn, who hung suspended from the branch by one hand. The bauk was standing over her. She swung with her dagger at the creature with her free hand. Brenn yelled at her again. "Come on!"

Krel noticed blood dripping off the girl's elbow. A closer look revealed several gashes along her left arm.

Taryn released the branch, falling twenty feet to Brenn. He grunted, catching her small frame easily in his outstretched arms. Krel did not hear her groan above Rehor's destruction, but he noticed the mixed look of pain and appreciation as she rolled into Brenn's chest. He let loose her legs and stood her upright, eyeing the bauk scurrying along the limb above them.

Krel fired at the fiend, missing wildly as it raced above them. He reloaded.

With an abysmal growl of savagery, Rehor formed orbs of darkness and swept them toward the few remaining chort, engulfing them. The ethereal spheres devoured the creatures' flesh before the beasts could make it within striking distance.

Rehor fell to his knees.

The dead chort lay in grisly piles around the dragon-man, hemorrhaging blood and convulsing. None had come close to touching Rehor or anyone else.

"Rehor," Brenn said with a tinge of concern, "you nearly killed yourself."

Krel adjusted his stance behind the Stuhian so that his crossbow bolt was pointed at the back of the redhead's skull.

He could end this right now.

Rehor did not notice, tilting his chin to acknowledge Brenn and Taryn. The dragon-man smiled at the dark-eyed girl. The youthful color was faded from his skin, his cheeks were sunken, and he had more grey hair than red dotting his scalp. "How awful do I look? Be honest."

Taryn grabbed her arm to slow the bleeding. She turned her head to see the bauk leap to another branch and backed closer to Rehor. The bauk hissed at them, shaking a distorted finger. She said, "I would sooner sleep with you than him."

Krel met Brenn's eyes, tensing his finger on the trigger of the crossbow. Brenn widened his eyes in shock and shook his head disapprovingly.

What? Did he not understand the threat?

Krel hesitated.

"Sounds like we are negotiating," Rehor replied to Taryn, unaware of the silent exchange. "But first—"

In the clip of a bird's wing, the Stuhian waved his hand at the bauk. The hunched creature was yanked from its roost with some invisible strand of magic, landing at Rehor's feet.

Taryn screamed in terror while Brenn and Krel both leaped backward. The creature was more horrendous up close than Krel could have imagined.

Krel dropped his crossbow, letting it hang by its leather cord. "What in the Nine Lands are you doing?"

"What did you want him for?" Brenn echoed.

The bauk shrieked as Rehor continued to cast Koldovstvo, ignoring their questions. Its legs and arms were pulled stiff. Mounds of earth roiled over its limbs to encapsulate its feet and hands, binding it to the forest floor. Rehor stroked his wrinkled face and squinted at the ancient creature before him.

He did not look at any of them, though he addressed them. "I may not be a legionnaire, but I think we can probably keep this part of our adventure secret, hmm?"

Countless ash-colored tentacles, like a mist hanging over a greensward, crawled from Rehor's body to the bauk beneath him, burrowing into the crux of the creature. No sound was made as energy pulsed from the bauk to Rehor, restoring the years of the dragon-man's life.

"*No*," Krel uttered in a dull breath, watching the smoothness return to Rehor's cheeks and the color to his hair. He shuddered and stepped away, seeing the lifeless body of the bauk wilt and decay. In a matter of moments, the dragon-man shed his middle-aged features and returned to his more formative years.

"Now, where were we?" He turned to Taryn with a pleased smile. "Ah, yes. I remember. Negotiations. Let us find somewhere a bit quieter to talk." Rehor chortled to himself, stretching his arms out to the sides with satisfaction. He ignored Brenn and Krel, winking at Taryn. "In the meantime, you should consider whether you prefer to be on top or bottom, hmm?"

Chapter VIII

BRENN, *The Dusk Legion*

Krel jerked Brenn by the arm, pulling him to a nearby tree, while tensely searching the woods around them for Rehor and Taryn's return. Trying not to fall over, Brenn did not fight when Krel pulled him close—too close, nearly burning him with the torch in his other hand. His hot breath hung by Brenn's nose. As he fought the urge to gag, words emerged with Krel's sour breath. "He's dangerous."

"This forest is dangerous," Brenn countered, leaning back to escape the rancid smell. He rubbed the back of his neck, looking for Taryn and Rehor too. The two had surprisingly scampered off when Krel had stopped them to rest. Brenn thought the back and forth was for show—a tease, especially when considering Taryn had shoved Rehor to the mud earlier that day—but after a few whispered words, the two did not hesitate to duck off into the shadows. "Who would have thought all those stories about the Dyndaer were true?"

"Do not change the subject. We should have killed Rehor when he was weak." Krel's voice was barely audible, even at the short distance. "We will have few chances to overpower him. I need to know you are with me. We will have to strike fast next time." Krel tightened his hold on Brenn's arm. "Are you listening to me?"

Brenn pulled away from Krel, raking his eyes over the other assassin. Cracking his knuckles one by one, he took his time answering while studying Krel's face. His high cheekbones and the taught skin beneath them took on a harsher look with his serious and frustrated demeanor. The man's eyes were bloodshot, suggesting exhaustion was finally taking its toll. The fatigue must be the reason he was ignoring the madness they had endured.

"Everything changed when we were at the castle," Brenn said. The cross look Krel gave him matched the deadly expression he held after the fight with the chort when holding the crossbow at Rehor's back. Brenn's bones chilled. "Our focus needs to be on killing the princess, not the sellswords."

Krel gave a pained stare, curling his arms up over his head. "Do you hear yourself? Nothing has changed except recognizing that Rehor is a real threat. I should have taken my shot."

"He risked his life for us back there." Brenn pointed off in the direction they had come. "You think you should have thanked him by putting a bolt in the back of his head?"

Krel's nostrils flared. "He was saving himself. We had nothing to do with it."

Brenn was unsure how to respond to Krel. "He has a good reason to keep us alive. He thinks he is receiving a sack of silver at the end of all this."

"Do you really think he cares about coin? No Stuhian cares about money," Krel said.

Breathing steadily through his nose, Brenn wrung his hands together. He typically enjoyed poking at Krel, but he could see that this was a fire he needed to douse before the man did something stupid. He could not remember a time when Krel had been this determined to cut a throat.

He wettened his lips. "How do you not understand this? You insisted that we complete the mission. Well, we have no way of defeating the Crimson Sun without him beside us, let alone surviving this forest. We should consider ourselves lucky we found him in Egis, or we would be dead ourselves."

"Do you think he is going to fight with us?" Krel snapped back. "He barely raised a finger against the mercenaries at Cavell. We lost Quinn because of him." He glowered, faintly hearing groans of pleasure deriving from somewhere in the enfolding forest. "And now he is out there humping her sister. What is wrong with that girl that she would spread her legs for the man most responsible for Quinn's death?"

Brenn could not help but smile. He, too, was amazed Taryn was laying with Rehor, but he did not expect Krel to be torn up about it. The man sounded envious, resentful.

"I never thought his jest would have come to transpire," Brenn admitted. The rumpus of Taryn and Rehor's copulation grew louder and louder before resulting in what Brenn guessed to be their combined climax. "Especially so soon."

"This is not a matter for joking," Krel rumbled. "You heard him. He is allied with the Guardians. The likelihood of him scampering off and blabbing about our being here far outweighs the chances of him being loyal."

Brenn gave Krel a hard look, trying to understand the man's desperate need to murder Rehor. With their plan to pin the murder of the princess on the mercenaries, he did not think they would even go through with killing the sellswords. He had almost been relieved by the thought.

"He said that he respected Gaspar Bacheva. He never said he was allied with him. I think we can agree that Gaspar is an impressive man with plenty of characteristics worthy of admiration," Brenn said. "One way or another, Rehor is a hired hand. He only needs to be loyal until we are done with him."

"Exactly!" Krel smacked his hands together. "He could do anything to us afterward. It is like you are intentionally ignoring everything I am saying. He can disappear in this forest at any moment. If he tells the Guardians that we killed the princess, it would ruin everything."

"Taryn could too," Brenn said, hearing the two in the woods gear up for another round. "Are you planning to kill her right now too?"

"Why not? That was the original idea."

"You are acting like this is the first time we have had sketchy sellswords on a job. People who agree to kill a princess for silver are not *normal*. We should expect them to be eccentric, but you and I will come out on top. We always do. The fact is that they are holding their own. You kill them now and we are severely outmatched against the enemy. Cock and pie!" Brenn ran a hand through his long hair, shaking his head in disbelief. "Are you really convinced Rehor is dumb enough to betray the Legion? I mean, no matter what I say, you are an assassin. You do not need my approval to kill him."

Krel hit the tree with the side of his fist. "You really think we need him against those mercenaries? We have done hundreds of jobs without hired hands."

"Not when facing the Crimson Sun. These are not regular sentries or ordinary ruffians," Brenn argued.

"We were going to kill them anyway." Krel raised his voice. "If he gets away, killing the princess will not matter."

"You are overreacting." Brenn hesitated in an attempt to make sense of Krel's conclusion. "He may be bizarre, but I do not think he is in league with anyone. Why would he tell anyone what we have done down here when he has done more than any of us? I really don't think we need to kill either of them anymore."

"What? The senate told us not to leave behind any loose strings." Krel spit out words quicker than Brenn could make sense of them.

Brenn looked away. "I know."

"Nine Lands!" Krel smashed his beard to his mustache. "We have no idea who Rehor really is, and after seeing what he can do… You cannot be serious, Brenn. How can you be comfortable keeping him with us? Why are you protecting him?"

"For the same reason you don't like him—because I saw what he can do!" Brenn replied with a guffaw. His mind swirled, overflooded with thoughts, likely from exhaustion. He withheld the urge to point out how Rehor controlled a guard with Faegrim, erased the count's memory with his herbs, and single-handedly fended against a horde of monsters. "I am less interested—personally—in traveling through the rest of the Dyndaer without him. If the Crimson Sun doesn't kill us, the creatures in this cursed forest will. We are out of our element."

"You're scared," Krel said, a slight edge in his tone.

Brenn looked back at him, slack-jawed. In an attempt to attack him, Krel seemingly told the truth about himself. His partner was afraid of fighting Rehor alone because he knew he would lose.

In the distance, another elevated moan of fulfillment pricked the air. Taryn seemed pleased.

Slapping his partner on the shoulder, Brenn chortled between his words. "What kind of gibe is that? Yeah, I am scared. I mean, maybe you knew the Dyndaer had imp-men crawling through the leaves and demon-goats sprouting from trees. Where I come from, regular men made of flesh and blood are the greatest threat."

Krel lifted his finger. "Do not play stupid. You knew the stories about this place held some truth to them."

"I was aware of the simargl and maybe a couple other beasts," Brenn admitted, holding his smile, "but nothing like what we just saw. The gods only know what else lurks in this mirewood."

Branches crunched in the distance, signaling Rehor and Taryn returning from their tussle.

"Are you with me or not?" Krel asked.

"No. No, I am not with you. If you want to kill Rehor after we are done with the Crimson Sun, I won't stop you, but I am not raising a hand against him or Taryn, for that matter." Brenn rocked back on his heels. "You are mad if you think you can contest his magic. Cock and pie, Krel. You saw how he ripped the skin off those chort…sucked the life from the bauk. You want to be flayed alive with black magic searing through your bones? Be my guest. As I said, I do not see any reason to kill either of them anymore."

"We could do it together," he nearly pleaded.

Brenn waggled his head. Seeing movement from the corner of his eye, he whispered, "Swine don't stampede into a wolf den for a reason."

Rehor waved at them as he neared, adjusting his robes and satchel with his other hand. "What are we talking about?"

"Nothing." Krel pushed off the tree toward the two of them.

Rehor took a breath, puffing his cheeks, and studied Krel for a moment in an awkward silence.

Pointing at Taryn cupping a fresh bandage on her arm, Brenn redirected their attention. "How is your arm?"

Rehor replied before Taryn had the chance. "Lucky for her, I had some paste to help it mend. Sadly, it broke open again while we were *exploring* the woods. We had to patch her up again." Rehor rolled his eyes over to Taryn, giving her a playful smirk that made Brenn want to vomit. "I apologize if I was a bit rough."

She leered oddly at Brenn and Krel before batting her eyes at Rehor. "You were perfect."

"I am not paying you to hump in the woods." Krel scratched at his beard. "We are wasting time."

"I have not been paid anything yet. And you stopped us, hmm?" Rehor said. "We cannot be blamed for taking advantage of the moment."

The sneer on Krel's face even made Brenn uncomfortable. He clicked his tongue, saying, "Well, I hope you saved some energy for the road ahead. We still have a princess to murder."

He stomped off through the brush.

"Oh, I cannot wait," Rehor chirped, following after Krel.

For the remainder of the day and beyond nightfall, Krel kept a quickened pace, eating away the miles with their constant stride. Despite the cold, Brenn was soon sweltering beneath his wool shirt and cloak. He could even feel the moisture in his boots from droplets of sweat building around his aching feet. The rows of trees soon started to look the same, giving the impression they were roaming in circles. With the sun's light diluted by the trees above them, Brenn could not say whether they were heading in the right direction or not. In fact, he would not be surprised if they soon strolled back up to Cavell's gates.

Krel refused to stop again, save when Rehor paused to pick a few edible berries for them to chew on while they walked. Krel, not surprisingly, refused to put the bit of fruit in his mouth until he saw Rehor swallow it. Rehor noted Krel's caution, waggling his eyebrows at Brenn; yet he said nothing.

On the other hand, Taryn's behavior had flipped from uninhibited bouts of anger and sadness to unhinged aloofness. She sporadically would tease Rehor when he made a lewd comment toward her. but most of the time, she walked in silence with her thumbs tucked in her pants, eyeing the Dyndaer. The tears had stopped, along with her sniffling, as she meandered on the edge of the group. She reminded Brenn of a caged animal, defeated and broken.

Growing weary of the march through the woods and finding no sign of the Crimson Sun, Brenn drifted back to Taryn, matching her stride for stride. After his and Krel's discussion, he realized how overshadowed she was in comparison to Rehor, but in truth, he was not interested in killing her any more than the dragon-man. Regardless of whether he was losing his edge or the thrill of the kill, he knew he pitied the woman. Her sister was dead, and she was marching with a team of assassins to slaughter another woman for a bit of silver. He suspected she did not think the exchange was worth the price anymore, but she remained with them.

Whether her mind was on the nature of death, the nature of life, or simply revenge, he hoped to offer her some kindness.

They walked a short distance before he finally murmured to her, "How are you holding up?"

Her round brown eyes looked up at him, lips parting and then closing again without any words. As though his inquiry had sent her to the verge of tears, she looked ahead again.

He fumbled looking for something more to say, blurting, "Your eyes are incredible." He gulped after hearing his bizarre comment, hurrying to add, "I don't mean that as a come-on. I just have never met anyone with brown eyes before. It is, um, remarkable."

"My mother said my father gave them to me," she said, keeping her chin forward. "Only thing he gave to me."

"You never met him?" Brenn asked.

She shook her head and mouthed the word *no*.

Brenn scratched his head. His attempt to be kind felt more like he was pestering her, but he did not want to simply walk off either. "What else did your mother tell you about him? Did she like him?"

"Blood and spit. Are you planning on unraveling the mystery of his identity before the night is done?" Taryn retorted, pushing a strand of dark hair behind her ear, only for it to fall over her cheek again. "Or is this simply small talk before you ask me to join you in the woods too?"

"Sorry." Brenn clicked his tongue. "I did not—I thought—"

Taryn cut him off with a look, scrunching her nose as though she were studying his expression. "My mother was raped," Taryn said, "by some jackhole in the middle of the night while Quinn's father was drunk and wandering the streets. She did not know what he looked like, let alone his name. If you want to search Maharia for him, she said that he smelled like wet dog."

"Nine Lands. I am sorry." Brenn pressed his tongue to the roof of his mouth, unsure how to respond. He would be kicking himself later for even talking to her.

"Did you hump my mother? Why are you apologizing?" Taryn peered at him and then leaned into him, lifting the corners of her mouth in a smile. He flinched slightly with thoughts of escape; his fingers grew cold. She took a long sniff and then blew the breath from her nostrils. "Nope. No wet dog. I guess you are safe."

The humor sounded odd through her sharpness.

"You needn't have worried anyway. I knew from the beginning you were not a god. Ruled you right out," she added. "Don't beat yourself up over it. While most men think they are gods, none are. It won't stop them from spending their lives searching for a woman who will call them one, though."

He lifted a single eyebrow at her. She did not pause long enough to realize his bemusement.

"Oh yeah," she said. "My mother concluded that it was one of the gods—Wolos or Gero—who planted a seed inside of her. Can you imagine either of them seeing a poor tart, the wife of a drunk, and saying to themselves, *she will bear my gift.*" Taryn tittered with amusement. Her acidic tone changed to being coyer, but he was not sure if it was intentional. Her seductive tone seemed to be more wanton than anything purposeful. "She told anyone who would listen that I was blessed by the gods, a child of light. Come to think of it, you should probably kneel, just to be safe."

"Could we postpone?" Brenn forced a smile. He rubbed his thigh, the tense muscles burning into his lower back. "My legs are killing me right now. If I go down, I am staying down."

Taryn chewed at her bottom lip with her perfect white teeth, raking her eyes over Brenn again. She most definitely was not upset any longer. "Don't make promises you can't keep."

Glancing over his shoulder, Rehor said, "I will share her for your cut of the silver."

Taryn squinted at him, suddenly wrapping her arm around Brenn's waist. "I am not yours to share, *dragon-man.*"

Brenn fought the urge to pull away, his hands clamming up. The awkwardness that had been there a moment ago quickly returned. He looked to Krel for help, but his partner did not even turn around. He simply picked up the pace to distance himself from them. Brenn opened his mouth to protest.

"*Ooo,*" Rehor howled loudly, silencing Brenn. "I like a woman who knows what she wants."

Krel cursed ahead. He spun around to shush them, his face already twisted into a snarl.

Pulling away from Taryn's clasp, Brenn sprang past Rehor to his partner. "What is it?"

He pointed through the trees. "We found them."

Chapter IX

TEODOR, *The Crimson Sun*

"What was that?" Tomas asked, lifting his polearm protectively and trudging over to stand beneath Princess Nitalia. She twisted around on the white mare, cheeks flushed from the cold, placing her hand on his shoulder and searching the shadows.

Teodor followed her gaze, seeing nothing beyond the glow of torchlight. The smell of pine needles and snow on the air, mixed with the dirty scent of the mire, tickled at his nose. He waved the torch in the air illuminating the towering trees next to them. The radius of light appeared dim in such a great breadth of the forest.

If anything stirred in the dark, they would not see it coming until it was already on them.

Seigfeld spoke with authority. "We should not have stopped yesterday. The assassins likely did not wait as long as you expected." The frown on his shaven face darkened along with his blue eyes, grasping the lead rope of the princess's white mount. The animal snickered and snorted, nuzzling forward to search Seigfeld's hand for a treat that did not exist. For leagues, Seigfeld had been coaxing the animal with dried apple slices that he had originally brought for his own war mount called Jab, which he regularly spoke of and had fled during the encounter with the simargl. Although there was no sign of the horse, Seigfeld swore Jab was alive and would find them. Nevertheless, the apple slices helped convince the mare to be led through the enigmatic woods.

"We cannot walk the entire way without sleeping, Seigfeld," Teodor said from his cohort's left. He signaled Tyr to watch the thick array of trees behind them, even though he knew little could be seen in the encroaching darkness. The Ispolini pulled each of the remaining two horses by a long rope. The brown and grey mounts whinnied in a similar fashion as the white, bound by the strength of the giant instead of being bribed with treats.

"If that *howl* was the assassins," Nitalia said, "they would have traveled nonstop to reach us. We have rested. We hold the advantage."

Teodor checked the trees to his right for movement, keeping his voice low. "We are lucky we did not turn back for Cavell. We would have crossed them sooner, and they may have caught us by surprise. You are right, Princess. We have the advantage now."

"We also could have run the chance of making it home and having the full guard with us. We have no idea what their numbers look like," Tomas said. He listened closely, angling his head. The wind whistled through the brush. He pulled his blade free as though the airstream would bring their enemy.

"Bah! They are but a handful," Tyr said. He went on as though they were sharing stories over a fire. "If you forget about the Stuhian with them, we have little to worry over. And Eisliev will be able to deal with him without much effort."

Teodor left Seigfeld at the head of the group and shuffled past Nitalia and Tomas, keeping the torch outstretched. He could not see anything in the midnight shadows but knew Eisliev was at the other end of the princess's horse. "Can you defeat him, Eisliev?

Tomas's tone was scathing as he passed. "We are defenseless out here."

"Might be best if this other Stuhian and I stay clear of this fight, or we might all end up dead," Eisliev said as Teodor approached, poking his head around the rump of the white mare. He had kept quiet for most of the trip, walking alongside the princess shrouded in his red robes. His blue eyes twinkled in the firelight. "The last thing you want is us two battling to the death in the middle of the Dyndaer. We will draw every beast you can imagine from leagues in every direction."

"Sard! You will do as you are told," Teodor said, staring down the Stuhian. Tyr's comments about the dragon-man not being committed to their charge rang in his ears. "Princess Nitalia will be kept from harm at all costs."

"I know why we are here," Eisliev said, grimacing, "and I am saying she might be placed in greater danger if fire and ice start falling from the heavens."

"I would only ask you to use your magic defensively, or not at all, if you can help it, Master Kluk," Nitalia said with a warm smile as she twisted around to peer down on them from her horse. "I would not ask you to waste the years of your life for my benefit, no matter what Master Bacheva requests from you."

"He is an affiliate of the Crimson Sun. That is why he is here." Teodor scowled at the girl. She was hardly old enough to be called a woman and was telling him how to manage his men. "I would ask you to leave the battle tactics to me."

Nitalia elevated her chin all the more, despite the fact that she already looked down on him from her hoisted position. "Master

Bacheva, I am not fond of your tone. You and I are not going to bicker about this, especially here and now. My position grants me authority to command any who have sworn to protect me—"

"No one swore—" Teodor tried but was cut off.

"Do not mistake me for one of your men. I chose for us to continue our journey to Gaetana. Therefore, I will dictate how we get there. Attempt to govern me and you will deal with my uncle at Gaetana."

Tomas was quick to respond. "Well said, my lady."

Pinching his eyebrows together, Teodor clamped his mouth shut and studied Nitalia. She may have been royalty, but she had little understanding as to where he held allegiance. If he did not have the mind to listen to her father, he certainly was not going to be ordered around by her.

Seigfeld met Teodor's eye at the front, motioning with his head for them to continue. "We have been dawdling here long enough, and far worse roams this forest than assassins. We were lucky to have escaped the simargl. Let's not press our luck by standing here like a target."

The horses suddenly quieted.

Teodor flinched as a bolt zipped between him and Eisliev, striking the croup of the white mare. Another foot higher and the quarrel would have planted itself in the princess's back.

Nitalia's startled cry was almost silenced by the screaming horse as it reared back. She clung to the reins and braced down in time for the animal to hurtle past Seigfeld and bolt into the woods.

Teodor reached out helplessly as Seigfeld soared off his feet and crashed against the wet grass and mud with a pained grunt. His sovnya sprang from his grip and flew into the immediate foliage. Stunned, he scrambled to retrieve the weapon, choking in his attempt to regain his breath.

"Princess!" Tomas cried, steadying on his feet next to Teodor.

At the same time, Tyr growled, "The Dusk Legion is here!"

Eisliev snarled, looking in the direction from which the bolt came. Before Teodor could say anything, Eisliev's voice resounded, carried by the magic of Koldovstvo. "I am Eisliev Kluk, son of Maelili—" Teodor noted how he mentioned his mother's name and not that of his father "—the Arkhon of Lairhein. If you are Stuhian, *Eretik* or otherwise, you will step down from this battle and stand before me in *Klukas*."

Teodor jerked his head to Eisliev along with Tyr, having no understanding of the words the Stuhian was bellowing. Arkhon. Eretik. Klukas. The forest was suddenly alive with Princess Nitalia's screams persisting, stampeding hooves of the horse fading, and stifled arguing coming from the trees as a result of Eisliev's demands.

"What in the Nine Lands are you doing?" Teodor turned on the dragon-man.

"Nitalia!" Tomas shouted with less fervor, fretfully glancing to Eisliev, who neared Teodor.

"I am buying you time," Eisliev rustled, waving Teodor off and gesturing to Tomas. "Take him and get the princess."

Teodor tensed at receiving instruction from the dragon-man. But the sound of feet smashing the foliage somewhere behind Teodor, giving the impression that one of the attackers was pursuing Nitalia, broke him from his urge to flaunt his authority.

Tyr swelled his chest, pulling the other two horses behind him. His concerned gaze fell to Eisliev. "This is no time to go to the spirit realm. Any one of them could cut you down. Another bolt could fly at any time."

"Then you and Seigfeld better guard me. If the Eretik is reasonable, this will not take long," Eisliev said.

"What if he is not?" Teodor asked, trying to make sense of what the two were rambling on about.

"Then no one is going home alive," Eisliev replied.

Teodor gritted his teeth and backed away, gesturing for Seigfeld to stand. The warrior grabbed his shoulder and mumbled something unintelligible.

"Watch him," Teodor grumbled at him, pushing Tomas in the direction Nitalia had gone. "We are going this way."

Taking the torch with him, he left the other three in the gloom of the Dyndaer, unsure what exactly Eisliev was scheming. As much as he wanted to trust the Stuhian, there was too much at stake—and too much unknown—to think Eisliev had their best interests in mind.

"Nitalia!" Tomas called.

Teodor clenched his fist around the torch to keep from striking the man. He pulled his sword from its sheath and said, "Gero's yard! Do not give away our position."

Tomas set his jaw, looking at the torch in Teodor's hand. "You're kidding."

From the shadows, the wide-shouldered assassin from Cavell jumped forward, throwing his iron-plated fist into Tomas's nose with a crunch. Tomas rocked back, blood spurting. He grunted as a second jab struck him in the side of the skull.

Teodor sidestepped as Tomas toppled sideways, hitting the ground at the same time as his polearm. He showed no sign of standing again.

Teodor loosed a primal yell, thrusting his sword at the assassin, who dodged the attack with ease. He then swung the torch in a wide arc and stabbed at the air again. The assassin only distanced himself from the attacks, holding a familiar smile on his face.

"I expected better from the son of Gaspar Bacheva," the assassin said. "You fight more like a noble than a thief. I give you permission to fight dirty. We are not having an honorable combat. We have no audience."

"I am *not* a thief," Teodor growled.

"Say what you like. The world will define you however they see fit," the assassin smirked.

Teodor shifted his eyes to the guard and back to the assassin, holding the torch to the side so the light would not blind him. "Did you kill him?"

"He will be dead before morning," the assassin admitted, circling around so the body was between them. Nitalia's horse whinnied in the distance behind the cutthroat. The assassin did not bother to provide any honey to sweeten the truth. He simply spit it out like it was poisoned ale. "You cannot do anything to save him. He is bleeding in the head."

Teodor fought the urge to lunge at the killer. He leveled the sword at a downward angle and put distance between them. "Tell me why the Dusk Legion wants the princess dead."

"Why would I do that?" he replied.

Teodor squinted at the assassin, measuring his tone. From what he could gather the man was admitting to being part of the Dusk Legion. Though he had no explanation for the dead woman at Cavell who did not bear the mark. "Because hiring sellswords to do your work can get messy. In fact, I am surprised the Lonmerean senate agreed to it. Are you positive there is not a better way to see your ambitions accomplished?"

The assassin took his turn to retreat a step, folding his arms across his broad chest. "Put all that together on your own, did you? Should I expect you to offer aid? The Crimson Sun is going to align with the Dusk Legion, then?"

"We cannot know if you do not tell me why you are doing this," Teodor hurriedly responded, although his mind raced with details the assassin had ignorantly confirmed. They had hired hands helping them, which meant they needed expendable people who had no connection back to their home city. This offset their chances of being targeted if the plan went awry. And whatever they were doing was sanctioned by their senate, meaning this dastardly pursuit was backed by the highest officials of Lonmere. They would start a war between the four kingdoms whether they wanted to or not.

"You may not have inherited your father's legendary prowess with that weapon, but you did gain his mind," the man said, dipping his head with what may have been appreciation.

Teodor heard a rustle behind him, suddenly realizing the assassin was keeping him talking and not the other way around. He twisted to the side, catching the edge of a dagger across the hardened side of his iron breastplate. Without his movement, the smooth tip may have slid into his gut.

The dark-haired tart rotated away almost as soon as she emerged, lifting her dagger at him. He pointed his sword at her, waving the torch between the two assassins.

"You were supposed to slit his throat," the man said.

"Not until he answers me. Where is the Svet?" The woman pulled a second dagger from her belt. "Where is the savage that killed my sister?"

Teodor gritted his teeth. Faint movement caught his eye behind the man. Golden hair shimmered behind a tree. *Nitalia!* Teodor shifted his attention to the dark-eyed woman. "He is gone. He went home."

The curved blade of Nitalia's billhook caught the male under the leg, lifting him into the air and sending him heavily to the ground. Her swiftness even surprised Teodor as she kept her movement fluid and carved the air in front of the female. The second swing appeared to be more for show than to inflict damage, keeping the woman at bay, for a second rotation brought both billhooks across the center, aiming for their attacker's pretty face.

The assassin girl was nimbler than Nitalia, rolling under the obvious attack. Teodor lurched forward and slammed his sword down, using its blunt side to stop the female from stabbing a dagger in Nitalia's thigh. Keeping the momentum, he drove the torch into the girl's chest, igniting her clothes.

She cried out and rolled away from him.

With the light gone, Teodor could only hear the muscular man's breaths as he scrambled toward them. Even his footfalls were nearly silent. The first two punches, although wild, landed against Teodor's breastplate: one in the gut and one in the side, having little impact on him. The third swing whooshed inches from his jaw and a fourth by his ear.

Not wanting to swing his sword aimlessly in the dark, Teodor grabbed the weapon like a stave and shoved with all his strength. He connected with the body in front of him and soon regretted the decision. The assassin, a man far more skilled in close-range combat, used the momentum to pivot and reposition himself behind Teodor. In one moment, he felt pressure against his blade, and in the next, a heavy strike to the back of his head that rocked him forward.

Dots sparked his vision.

He faltered, fighting to stay conscious. He assumed the assassin would be on him again at any moment, but the scuffling at his back told him Nitalia interceded. The sound of metal on metal clanged. Again. A deep-throated grunt followed by a shrill cry. He then heard the thwack of a crossbow. A woman's surprised shriek. Blades crossed again. Another grunt.

"Nitalia!" Teodor struggled to see anything in the pitch black. His eyes could not adjust to the complete darkness of the forest. "Run to Seigfeld. Go!"

Footsteps stamped closer, hands awkwardly running along his torso. Nitalia panted. "Not without you. Come on."

They ran blindly through the woods in what Teodor hoped was the direction of his companions. Brush scraped against his pant legs and slapped him in the face, despite his hand defensively raised over his face. A third voice behind demanded that the assassins give chase.

The soft glow of orange light materialized in the trees ahead, irradiating a bizarre sight. The magical orb floated over Eisliev, his hood pulled back, while the redheaded man from Cavell kneeled in front of him offering a trinket in his hand. Tyr stood protectively by Eisliev, holding to the reins of their remaining two horses. He peered at the enemy Stuhian as though he was about to tear his head from his shoulders.

Seigfeld stood like a sentinel at a nearby tree, searching the forest until he saw them racing in his direction. His hand hovered over his shoulder. "Praise the Lightbringer you are safe. What happened out there? I thought I heard shouts but…" he looked back at the two Stuhia, "…I could not gauge which was the greater danger." He twisted back as Teodor reached him. Nitalia huffed behind him. "Where is Tomas?"

"Dead." Teodor forced out the word. Seigfeld shifted his stance, raising his sovnya as though the assassins were coming on their heels.

"You are hurt, Princess," Seigfeld said.

The blood dribbling behind Nitalia's ear to her neck had already started soaking into her golden hair. She gripped the billhooks in her left hand, reaching to the wound with her right. "I am sure it is nothing but a scratch. I swear that woman could see in the dark as though it were day."

Teodor gritted his teeth, trying to examine the wound closer in the awful light. The cut did not look deep enough to cause serious injury. There was nothing he could do right now anyway. He could hear the Dusk Legion nearing. "We need to go." He motioned to the Stuhian men talking in soft voices, and he looked to Seigfeld to answer his question. "What is this?"

Seigfeld tugged at his ear. "Nine Lands if I know, Teodor. We watched him *pray* for a bit. When he finally stood that guy came out. The way they have been acting, I assumed they were lovers."

Teodor scrunched up his face.

"What? I heard the Stuhia do not hold themselves to men or women." Seigfeld shrugged. "The guy is kneeling and offering a ring? What would you make of it?"

"Kill them!" A shout sprouted from the darkness behind them. "Kill them, Rehor!"

A bolt buried into a tree by Nitalia's head while a dagger struck her in the back. She cried out and fell into Seigfeld's arm. He pulled her away with a mighty grip.

Teodor sheathed his sword to help Seigfeld pull Nitalia along. "Get her on a horse."

They only made it a few feet before Tyr intervened, picking up the princess in his arms. "I have her."

Teodor nodded, springing onto one horse while Seigfeld climbed onto the other.

"Eisliev, let's go," Seigfeld said, laying his weapon across the saddle and extending his hand.

The red mage slipped the silver ring on his own finger and reached for Seigfeld. With a firm pull, Eisliev joined Seigfeld. He brightened his light so Teodor could find a path ahead.

"Ho!" Teodor cried, kicking the horse.

The enemy Stuhian in brown robes remained on his knees, looking up to Eisliev. "Thank you, Arkhon."

Chapter X

TYR, *The Crimson Sun*

Tyr turned as Teodor drew the dagger from Nitalia's back. Even as strong as the young princess was, she could not stop the girlish wail from leaving her lips. She clung to the ground, a slodge-podge of mud and wettened leaves in her fists, until her knuckles were as white as her cheeks. Her second moan brought back images of Maruda's death.

Seeing the princess hurt upset Tyr more than he was willing to admit. His sister's screams pounded inside his skull along with the low growl of the white bear that he fought against before she died.

He echoed the growl, folding his hands in front of him. He tried to focus on the task at hand instead of being swept away by the past. Thinking of Maruda would only bring forth his wrath. He snarled through grated teeth. "The bastards are going to keep coming until we stop them. We cannot keep on like this through the whole of the Dyndaer."

Seigfeld grumbled in agreement, squatting next to Teodor. "No, we cannot."

Tyr twisted his neck to see Eisliev tie off the two horses. The mundane task was easier to watch than the princess squirming against the small ridge where he laid her down moments ago. The thick trees on the bank hid her from any searching eyes.

"Lucky you were wearing this armor." Teodor struggled to speak as though he were looking for the right words. "We cannot wait here for long. Nobody get too comfortable."

Making the mistake of looking again, Tyr saw blood seeping through Teodor's fingers as he put pressure on the wound. While the gash was unsightly, he guessed Teodor was most shaken by the encounter with the cutthroats. With Tomas dead, Eisliev's encounter with the dragon-man, and Nitalia injured, the situation was anything but a victory.

Teodor adjusted the straps on the side of the armor, loosening it so he could lift the back and gain access to the wound. "Seigfeld, I am going to need bandages, and then we need to get moving. Eisliev, can you do anything to restore the vitality of the horses?"

The red mage lifted his eyes and shook his head. "It is not in my blood to touch the primal element."

Teodor lowered his eyes in thought, clearly having no understanding of Koldovstvo or its practice. Tyr sighed to himself. After spending the past several months in Lairhein, he knew too well the eight cruxes of Koldovstvo. Elemental magic was accessible to all the Stuhians, but the specialized magics were distinguishable by bloodlines. Tyr could not remember all their names, but he knew Eisliev's line allowed him to manipulate time and space.

After digging through a pack on his back, Seigfeld handed several strips of clean cloth to Teodor. "I do not have much, but this should keep her well until we reach Gaetana. How bad is the cut beneath her ear?"

"Eisliev?" Teodor flicked his gaze upward.

The dragon-man moved the ball of light down to Nitalia and augmented its brightness. "Any brighter and we will be a beacon in the woods. You are going to have to work faster. Unless the assassins are bleeding out too, I suspect they are close behind."

"Sard! I know. We are trying." The swordsman, their leader, tensed his jaw as though he were holding back his real thoughts from Eisliev. He pushed Nitalia's hair to the side and grimaced, answering Seigfeld, "The bleeding has stopped. Looks worse than it is, I am sure."

"I will be fine. Wrap my back and I will readjust my armor so we can be on our way," Nitalia said. The concern in her voice was more believable than what the men seemed to be able to muster. "Master Bacheva, were you injured?"

"I might have a dent in the back of my skull," he answered dully, "but I will survive."

She flinched as Teodor pressed a bandage against the gash. In the orange glow, Tyr could see the blood staining her olive skin. Again, images of the blood lining his sister's pale flesh masked his vision.

Shadows tinted the edges of Tyr's vision. He shook his head to shake away his manifesting wrath.

He heard Nitalia forcing her next words through the pain. "How did Tomas die? His wife will want to know."

Teodor waited a moment before responding. When he did, his voice sounded distant. "Honorably."

"Listen," Tyr paused to control the shakiness in his voice. He was powerless to push the thoughts of his sister aside. Being near Nitalia was not helping. The heat of anger burned from the back of his skull to his fingertips. If he did not crush something, he was going to lose his mind. "You and Seigfeld should continue on with Nitalia. Get her to Gaetana posthaste. Eisliev and I can stay back to stall the assassins." He ignored the Stuhian's cold stare from the horses and shook his wooly head in an attempt to focus again. He repeated himself. "We cannot keep going on like this with the Legion on our tail."

"Not a bad idea," Seigfeld said, "if they can manage to hold them on their own."

Teodor handed the bandages over to Seigfeld, standing to his feet. Small cuts lined his face, barely visible through his dark beard and moustache. "Tyr, I do not know what happened back there, but I am admittedly a bit reluctant to grant you this request, even as good as it sounds."

Tyr rumbled. "Why?"

"Ivarr granted your station as mercenaries among the Crimson Sun less than two months ago. I infer his interests lay in your unique faculties. Truly, a giant and a dragon-man are rare in the civilized eastern world." Teodor faced Eisliev. "Ivarr's ruling is law, but I do not know either of you or your true interest in being affiliated with our faction. Seeing you bark orders at the enemy and somehow managing to have one of them bend the knee is more than concerning. How could I overlook that?"

"I told you I was causing a diversion." Eisliev rubbed his teeth with his tongue from beneath his lips.

"Gero's yard! I want to trust you, Eisliev," Teodor said, "but you expend more energy spitting out fancy words to distract from the truth than ever saying anything worthwhile. If we are being candid with one another, it is exhausting."

"Bah! Tell him who you are, Eisliev," Tyr said.

Again, Eisliev scowled at Tyr. He folded his arms inside of his red robes, and after Teodor offered an expectant look, he said, "I *was* the Arkhon of Lairhein, but I relinquished my position to my half-brother, Petr Hamus." He looked off into the forest as though the topic were of no interest. "The matter is nothing for you to concern yourself over, *Master Bacheva*. To our benefit, the other Stuhian believed I continue to hold the position of Arkhon."

"And what does that mean? What is an Arkhon?"

"A king," Tyr clarified. "Eisliev is the king of Lairhein, er, was…or might be again, if he so chooses it."

"You are royalty?" Seigfeld looked on Eisliev with stiffened posture, crinkling his brow. Even Nitalia was silent, captivated by the revelation. "You do not look like royalty. Why have you not said anything?"

Eisliev's orangish orb faded, dancing over them as he spoke. "An Arkhon holds no power in the lands of the Anshedar, and as I said, I handed the title over to my half-brother. I have my own footpath to follow, which does not involve the ruling of a nation."

"This is…sard!" Teodor cursed and covered his mouth, tilting his head in thought. "This is huge. The Anshedar have never had any success in contacting Lairhein. Outside of the few Stuhia who travel east, little is known about the culture, the rules of engagement, the path to diplomacy… Do you realize what this could mean? The Crimson Sun could close the gap, unite the northern kingdoms. With your help, we could bring forth a treaty of peace."

"The Stuhia governed over themselves long before men came across from Kalamaar," Eisliev declared with a snooty gaze. "Your people live too passionately, too recklessly to coexist with my people. I promise you that the *civilized* Anshedar have nothing to offer the free people of Lairhein. The Shade Fells separate dragon from men; hear me when I tell you that it is for the best."

"You are employed by the Crimson Sun," Teodor said. "Your interests should align with our own."

Tyr winced at Teodor's tone.

Eisliev lifted his hand to silence the man before he could say anything more. "The Crimson Sun aims for peace and prosperity for the four kingdoms of men. That is their axiom. You will have neither if you start knocking at the gates of Lairhein." He signaled to Tyr to follow him. "We are your allies, Master Bacheva, but we are not puppets. Now take the princess to Gaetana and we will deal with the Dusk Legion."

Tyr nodded to the princess and Seigfeld and then Teodor before balancing the axe on his back with a single hand and following Eisliev into the forest.

He heard Seigfeld mutter, "There goes our light. I will get set on making a torch."

"You are not a king here," Teodor called after them.

"No, I am Eisliev Kluk," Eisliev replied over his shoulder. He then spoke in a hushed tone so only Tyr could hear him. "Kings will tremble at my name."

They walked a distance, well beyond earshot of the Crimson Sun, when Eisliev folded his arms. "What was that about back there? Are you trying to destroy everything we have worked to achieve?"

Tyr shook his head. "I could not stand being around the princess any longer. She reminds me of my sister."

"Your sister?" Eisliev shook his head, kicking at the dirt. "I doubt she is even half the size, you oversized lout. Enlil sent you with me to help, not to make matters worse."

At the mention of his father's name, Tyr reached around and touched the axe he carried, a final gift from his father. Enlil remained at Lairhein with the intent of living out the rest of his days with the Stuhia, protected by Eisliev's kin, Arkhon Petr Hamus Kluk. In the meantime, Tyr aided Eisliev so he might eventually come across the Blood Cascade and restore life to his family or join them on the other side of this life.

"Touching your axe again, I see," Eisliev said. "I keep wondering what you are compensating for by carrying such a large weapon. It is hardly practical."

"You know my father gave me this weapon," Tyr snapped at Eisliev. "The Uvil made the blade in the south, stronger than anything found in the north. Bah! I would think you would find some value in that."

Eisliev angled his brows at Tyr. "Keep barking at me and I will bend you over, right here, and make you wish your father imparted you an axe with a smaller handle."

The fire in the dragon-man's eyes gave Tyr pause.

Eisliev stepped around a bush that split their path, saying, "Need I remind you that the war is escalating between the Anshedar and the Uvil? We already know sellswords from the Lilitu are being brought in by the Anshedar to defend against the Uvil, but the effort is wasted." He inhaled. "The Uvil are too headstrong. They live as though their prophecies can shape rivers and move mountains. The king will soon have no choice but to call on the Kadari to aid him in the war."

Tyr sucked in the cold air of the forest. "The Lilitu are many. They could be a wall against the storm."

"No, Tyr, they will not," Eisliev said. "Their society is a caste system. Their empress determines the function of every member, and few will be granted permission to step outside their regular role unless King Frantisek dumps his coffers into the pockets of the Lilitu. Not only will he be uneager to bankrupt Gaetana, but the other kingdoms of men will never agree to it. The Kadari will be left to defend Maharia. They will be pulled from their island and sent through the desert to the front lines."

"I do not get your fascination with the Kadari," Tyr said. "You abandoned your people to seek them out."

Fire flashed in Eisliev's eyes. "I do not care about the Kadari! I am tracking Dagmar Kaligula, who was last seen with those half-blooded rogue mages. I would think you would know something of vengeance?"

A breath caught in Tyr's throat. He grunted in response that he understood, knowing he would not get a word in edgewise once Eisliev started speaking about the Kaligula family.

"They slaughtered my family," Eisliev was practically shouting, "stole our rightful place in Lairhein, and are the reason demons have come to haunt this world. Do you remember the dead we crossed in the Shade Fells? How could you forget?"

"I did not forget," Tyr managed.

Eisliev kicked at the dirt. "When I was a child, my mother's final words were delivered to me. I remember when the grey-haired woman walked through the gates of my family estate. I was standing by my father, thinking my mother had returned home with my lost uncle. She knelt and told me that my mother was dead, and she wanted me to *beware of the Kaligulas*." Eisliev looked to the canopy of trees above them and sucked the air through his nose. "I swear, Tyr, I will tear Dagmar limb from limb. The Crimson Sun is our path to the Kadari, and they will lead me to Dagmar."

Tyr plodded along beside the dragon-man. "First, we have to prove ourselves, Eisliev."

"You don't think I know that?"

"What if we end up being sent to fight in the war or to battle against demons in the hope of saving Maharia? I can see the Crimson Sun being called on before the Kadari."

Eisliev glowered. "We will do whatever it takes, but the Crimson Sun does not have the numbers to face the Uvil."

Tyr's mind was peppered with thoughts. He did not know all the details, but he remembered Eisliev telling him that the Kaligulas murdered the Horned God, the God of the Dead. Though he could not fathom how such a thing was possible, he could not disregard the demons that poured from the Deep. His own nation had been battling demons since before he was a child, resulting in thousands of deaths, including that of his mother. He supposed he should be furious at Dagmar Kaligula too, but he had no evidence beyond Eisliev's word.

"If Dagmar dies," Tyr began, "will it undo whatever the Kaligulas did? Will it make the Witiko and the other demons stop coming from the Netherworld?"

Eisliev narrowed his eyes. "Are you still thinking about the Blood Cascade?" Tyr nodded rather sheepishly at the comment. "I know you miss your sister and mother. I do not know whether killing Dagmar will end what is happening, but I do know when the Blood Cascade returns, you will have the chance to reunite with your lost loved ones."

Tyr hummed in agreement, imagining the dancing lights of the coveted aura of souls. He had searched so many times for the Blood Cascade, first with his sister, then to bring her and their mother back from the dead. It was not until Tyr met Eisliev that he realized the Kaligulas stopped the wonder from appearing with their dishonorable deed.

"Alright," Eisliev said. "You convinced Teodor that we were going to fend off assassins. Should I expect you to fall into one of your infamous blood rages and kill them all? Because I am not about to waste my life killing the Anshedar."

Tyr shrugged. "As long as you keep their Stuhian off my back."

"Rehor Malankov will not bother you," Eisliev said.

"Bah! You may be safe from his magic, but how can you be sure he won't burn me alive?" Tyr asked, ducking under a low-hanging tree branch.

"He will do what I tell him," Eisliev said in a soothing tone, keeping the light floating over the giant's head to illuminate the forest floor.

Thinking of the eight cruxes of magic, Tyr scratched at his head. "What type of magic does he wield?"

"He is an Eretik. The death magic of Marheena is in his veins."

"The Frozen Witch?" Tyr gasped, recalling the little history he learned while in Lairhein. "I thought they were all banished thousands of years ago at the onset of the Ninth Council."

"They were," Eisliev said. "Almost two thousand years ago, the Carian Council took control and banished the Eretiks from Lairhein."

"Nine Lands, Eisliev. We cannot trust him," Tyr said, rubbing the back of his skull. "No matter what he claims, he must have some loyalty to the Dusk Legion."

Eisliev exposed his small finger and the silver ring that adorned it. "You do not understand, Tyr. He has given me his most prized artifact."

"What is it?"

"A gift."

Tyr frowned at the cryptic response. "What did he give it to you for?"

The Stuhian sniggered. "So he might regain entry to Lairhein. He has been roaming Maharia since the breaking of Lairhein. He just wants to go home."

"Well, are you going to let him?"

Obviously finding hilarity in his honest question, Eisliev grabbed onto Tyr's arm, fighting for air between disorderly bursts of laughter.

Chapter XI

BRENN, *The Dusk Legion*

When Brenn was a boy, his father took him and his younger brother to shoot at crows with the bow and arrow. Neither were too good, fighting to pull back the string and rarely hitting anything more than a random shrub or a patch of grass. Though at the end of his first day, Brenn remembered striking one through the wing, taking it to the dirt. The animal writhed clumsily for only a few moments with the arrow, keeping it from soaring off again.

Brenn's father instructed him to shoot the bird again instead of letting it suffer. Being obedient, he hurried to nock another arrow and fire. As quick as he had been, his brother was swifter, reaching out to protect the crow from death. Brenn hardly knew what happened until he saw his arrow lodged through his brother's hand.

Taryn's injury was no different from Brenn's brother with Krel's bolt spearing her palm.

"Pull it out! Quickly!" she squeaked in a half-scream, snotting and sniffling with her words. She rocked on her buttocks, gripping her thigh with her free hand, grabbing wildly at the air every few breaths. "By the gods, do not slide it through slowly."

"It might cause more damage. You might not be able to throw daggers again," Brenn explained, gripping the smooth end while holding her quivering hand over his leg. How she threw the final dagger with her other hand and struck the princess on the Crimson Sun's exit was beyond him. Nevertheless, once he pulled the quarrel free, he knew she would be left with a mangled, gaping hole. She would live, but she probably would never hold anything the same way again. She glared at him through watered eyes, a telltale sign of how little she cared about chucking daggers in that moment. "Okay. Okay," he took a breath, "but we need Rehor to be ready to stop the bleeding."

"I am almost ready," Rehor said, forming a white goop with herbs from his satchel in a mixing bowl he carried with him. An orb of light floated over him to give light. He whistled through his teeth at them. "This will help with the pain too, hmm?"

"Can you not heal her with Koldovstvo? I mean, we all watched you…become young again. Surely there is something you can do," Brenn said.

"No," Rehor replied. "I am not a healer. If I could wield sacred magic, I promise I would not be out here with you. Tucked safely away in Lairhein, I would be, hmm?"

Brenn squinted at the dragon-man. He had plenty of questions about how Stuhian magic worked and why Rehor was so far from home anyway. He silenced his questions for the moment.

"I might be able to stop the bleeding once the bolt is removed," Rehor offered, "but like it, you will not."

"He just fired, Brenn," Taryn said.

At the mention of his name, he looked for Krel, whom she obviously referred to. Seeing his partner was still by himself, off scouting in the woods, Brenn turned his attention to Taryn. Krel had marched off the moment the Crimson Sun galloped away on their horses, thinking they might circle back to finish them. The way the mercenaries were moving, Brenn guessed they were another league closer to Gaetana already.

Taryn persisted as though she were speaking of a dream she was trying to remember. "He did not care that you or I were standing in the line of fire. I saw him lift his bow and shoot toward the sound of battle."

"Krel could not see what was happening. None of us could," Brenn said slowly.

Taryn dipped her head, shuddering. "I could see just fine. The princess would be dead if he hadn't shot me."

"How could you?" Brenn asked, leaning down to see her brown irises. He had battled many times in the cloak of night, attuned to the sound of movement and breathing to help him be an effective assassin. Though he did not deny that blackness shrouded him. "There was no light. The torch was—"

"Because I can! I can see everything." Taryn shivered in the cold air that whistled through the trees.

Brenn searched for some rational reason for Krel's feckless shot that would ease her tension. Taryn was too emotional. Delirious. Irrational. "He may have thought the odds were favorable."

"Your argument is that Krel totally forgot any of us could be in the line of fire?" Taryn shook her head at him, scowling. Her hand trembled in his. "Would you say that if you had the bolt sticking from you instead?"

"Okay, you are right," Brenn said. He repositioned his grip to hold her hand steady and checked Rehor again, who observed them with wide eyes while mashing the dried plants.

Brenn recoiled under Rehor's unblinking stare. He wished the Stuhian would offer some input to ease Taryn's wild rationalizations, but he only sat looking at them as though they were speaking in a foreign dialect.

Breathing in, Brenn caught the scent of burnt leather, drawing his attention to Taryn's upper body where the mercenary had extinguished the torch.

"How is your chest?" he asked.

"Blood and spit! I am not talking about my chest right now! Will you get this bloody thing out of my hand?" she snapped at him. "Rehor was right. Gods, I knew he was right." She jerked her head to the dragon-man. "You were right."

Brenn shot another glance at Rehor. The Stuhian avoided eye contact this time, his movements becoming more irregular. He scrambled to his feet and stumbled over to them with the fiery magical light bouncing over his shoulder. "I am ready."

"What do you mean he was right?"

Rehor shuffled to their side, squatting down. "She is—"

"What do you mean?" Brenn demanded, not letting Rehor change the topic.

Taryn trembled from her shoulders to her knees, the pain apparently searing through her body. She leaned closer to Brenn. "You and Krel were never planning on paying us to kill the princess. Not a single silver coin." Her jaw trembled. "You do not care my sister is dead. I am nothing but a body shield to you."

Rehor sat in silence, frozen stiff with his crushed paste in his hand. His blue eyes shifted to Brenn and then Taryn.

"That is not true," Brenn garbled, twisting his neck to keep them both in his sights. Last thing he needed was them revolting against him, here and now, with Krel roaming the woods. At least she did not say anything about their plan to kill them. "None of that is true."

"He heard you two talking. He told me," Taryn said softly. "Now take this thing out of my hand, and I will go home."

"Heard us talking? When?" Brenn challenged her with bated breath. "When you two were off romping in the woods?"

"We did not do anything," Taryn strained, her fingers wiggling on either end of the bloodied rod in her hand. "I moaned and squealed a bit while he listened to you have your *little* secret meeting. We know what was said!"

Brenn was stunned, unsure what to think or how to respond to her. To believe Taryn sat in the woods acting like she was in receipt of the greatest humping of her life—all the while Rehor eavesdropped on them—was…admirable. Not to mention, she maintained the lie even after they learned of Krel's intentions. "You know I argued on behalf of you and Rehor," Brenn lastly rumbled. He shot his eyes to Rehor, wondering how much more of the conversation the dragon-man might have heard.

Did he know Krel wanted to slit their throats? If so, why would he only share pieces with Taryn?

He jerked the bolt from Taryn's hand without warning.

Taryn cried out, curling forward and cupping her hand to her bosom. A second, less feral whine reverberated through her throat.

Brenn scowled at them in turn. "I promise I have every intention of seeing the two of you survive this journey."

"Krel does not feel the same way. He will use us as pawns in each fight," Taryn said, unable to keep the indignant sound from her tone.

"He will," Rehor agreed, reaching delicately for Taryn's hand. She offered it sluggishly, shakily.

Brenn's arm muscles quivered. The unjustifiable laugh slipped from between his teeth without rhyme or reason. "I see. You mistake Krel and me for thieves. We do not bind ourselves to the idea that every assassin is of a singular mind. There is no honor among us."

"What are you talking about?" Taryn said, refusing to look at her hand as Rehor examined the wound.

Brenn tripped over his words, trying to find a way to explain without telling the full of it. "I have my own principles. I would stand against Krel as easily as I might either of you if I were so moved. I *choose* to see you both alive at the end of this journey. Neither of you need to leave and go back home. We can still see this done."

Taryn's chin quivered, drawing her free arm close to herself. "My sister is dead, and her killer is far from here. I am not being paid. I have no reason to be here."

"I will…" Brenn choked on his words, hardly believing he was about to make this promise. "If you stay, I will help you track the centaur and kill him when this is said and done."

She did not respond, hanging her head, sniffling.

"How noble," Rehor smirked.

Brenn turned on the dragon-man. "Was it nobility that kept you from the battle against the Crimson Sun, Rehor? Or was your most noble moment when you instructed Taryn to crow like a cathouse whore while you spied on us?"

The Stuhian smiled. "One of my finest moments, it might have been, hmm?" Rehor patted Taryn's wrist tenderly. "Give her something to bite down on. Hurt, this will."

Unsure what more Rehor could do besides apply the balm, Brenn searched the ground for a stick. Seeing none, he reached over and pulled Taryn's remaining dagger from its sheath. He then twisted it so she could bite down on the flat, leather-wrapped handle.

"Hold her down." Rehor drifted his hand over the opening, apologizing a second time. Brenn reached out to clasp his arms around the small frame of the woman a moment before fire seared through her hand, cauterizing the skin, blackening the inner wound and the flesh on the surface. She crowed in agony, bucking against him and Rehor as they did their best to hold her steady.

Her perfect white teeth dug permanent indentions into the handle of her beloved blade. Brenn twisted his head away, avoiding the sight of the tears racing down her cheeks.

At that moment, he saw Krel bow behind a tree. He could not guess at how long his partner had been hiding and listening to them. Brenn held Taryn tighter, her shouts intensifying, when Krel poked his head around again. They looked at each other for just a moment while Taryn and Rehor remained distracted. He gave Krel the subtlest of nods before Krel raised his finger to his lips to remain quiet.

Rehor ended his magic, pulling back while Taryn shivered in Brenn's arms. Her eyes fluttered, fighting to stay conscious through the pain. She spit the dagger from her mouth. "Th-th-thank you," she stammered.

Brenn screwed his head back so he would not give up Krel's position.

"Gods," Taryn said, "it hurts."

"Done, we are not," Rehor said, reaching for his balm and bandages.

"Why are you here if you know you are not getting paid?" Brenn asked Rehor.

He smiled. "To become a legionnaire, of course."

Brenn grimaced, unable to believe the lie. He had to know there was no chance of him joining the Legion. The Stuhian's unadorned hands caught Brenn's attention. "What happened to Faegrim?"

Rehor darted his eyes to Brenn and then back to his work on Taryn's hand. "I gave it away."

"You mean to the other dragon-man, the one who is traveling with the Crimson Sun," Brenn accused, rubbing the back of his neck. "You gave away a ring that will allow him to control our minds?"

Rehor said nothing, rubbing the white paste on Taryn's hand. Her teeth chattered. "It is so cold. The pain is going away."

"I have some milroot powder for you to swallow too," Rehor said, reaching in his pouch and handing her a folded parchment. "Heighten your senses and numb your pain for the rest of the day, it will."

Brenn could feel Krel's eyes on his back, causing him to shift where he sat. Narrowing his gaze at the Stuhian, he pressed, "I am asking you to explain yourself. I expect you have a good reason for ignoring Krel out there and falling to prayer—or whatever that was—and giving up our most powerful weapon."

Rehor relaxed his shoulders. "Faegrim was mine, and mine alone to give away, hmm? And I did not pray, I went to Klukas, the space between this world and the next, to speak with Eisliev Kluk as he requested. Every Stuhian can travel to the shadow world at will. You might be glad he did not cast spells against you. He has one of *the* most powerful, if not the most powerful, bloodlines among the Stuhia."

Eisliev Kluk. Hearing the name again reminded Brenn of the words the dragon-man shouted at them before he raced after the princess. "Who is he exactly? Why would you give him Faegrim?"

"Over all the Stuhia, he rules. As far as I know, his family has been in power for over a millennium," Rehor said.

"Are you saying the Crimson Sun has a king fighting for them?" asked Taryn, shooting daggers at Brenn under her dark bangs. Rehor looped the bandages around her hand. She barely noticed, glaring at Brenn with what might have been loathing. "What have you dragged us into?"

Brenn blinked rapidly. He could not process everything that was being said and asked of him. "I don't know."

"How in the Nine Lands did they come by more horses, huh?" Krel boomed, emerging from the trees like a fox startled by hunting dogs. A crooked, fake smile twisted across his mouth as he approached. "We better get moving before they travel beyond our reach."

"Right away," Rehor beamed, helping Taryn to her feet. He smiled, whistling between his teeth. "So close to becoming a legionnaire, I can taste it."

Despite Krel's insistence to travel through the night, they bedded a few hours before sunrise. Brenn was glad to convince the man that the chances of them making it another league without collapsing from exhaustion was slim; not to mention, they would do poorly in any battle if they did not rest.

He woke before any of the others at the sound of Krel's snoring. He was pleased to find the morning was warm. It was probably the last warm morning of the year. Behind the clouds was a pale yellow sun barely hidden, offering specks of sunlight through the falling leaves. The light was so far above the fading trees of the Dyndaer he could have guessed it to be part of another world.

The forest was quiet, all life fleeing from the cold season. Autumn and winter were dangerous months no matter what area of Maharia one lived. Marheena, the Frozen Goddess, was unrelenting; the snows would be thick, the winds nipping. Even now, the tallest wood swayed gently in the smooth breeze, full of moisture, ushering his departure from the secluded encampment. As he wandered away alone, he noticed the taste of dew on the wind, threatening to turn to snow in the months to come. Soon, he found a batch of scattered wildflowers dotting the wilting grasses and sat to think.

His fingers traced the triangular marking on the back of his neck. His loyalty to the Dusk Legion had been unwavering for the past decade, fighting alongside Krel most of the way. Yet this assignment had more moving pieces than he was used to handling.

Murdering a princess among the Gaetanean nobles to aid a foreign government in their war effort was challenging enough. Having the Crimson Sun from the Tamarrian Kingdom involved, as well as the possible ruler of another nation, set up Lonmere for absolute destruction. Like Krel, Brenn was interested in seeing Lonmere grow and expand its borders, but he could not understand how they could accomplish their charge and not be held accountable for the princess's murder.

At the same time, he knew Krel would not withdraw from the task given. Brenn could not blame him wholly, knowing neither of them had ever failed at a job, which he guessed was the primary reason they had been chosen to kill Nitalia Frantisek. Their record was flawless. Yet Krel's devotion to Lonmere was deeper than anything Brenn ever wanted to hold. The burning hate Krel reserved for the other nations of men could evaporate the sea.

Brenn refused to be swayed by his passion.

Furthermore, being born in a place like Lonmere taught him that reputation was everything. He completely understood Krel's need to kill this princess and return home the hero; if they were to go back to Lonmere—if they chose to return with the deed undone—they would lose all reverence. The port city, veiled in the northern mountains, was isolated from most human civilizations, and although the city and its inhabitants were often criticized for their wicked culture, Brenn knew the rest of the world was no different. Those from Lonmere were simply wise enough to recognize their nature and use it to their advantage.

Brenn remembered the look on Father's face when he told him he had been accepted into the Legion, an organization bonded eternally with their own king and the Lonmerean senate. Proud would not describe the joy his father expressed, especially when considering the immediate advancement of status for the whole of Brenn's family. He could not imagine what would be taken away from them if he failed now.

"I wondered where you went. I did not expect to find you out here."

Brenn lifted his head to see Taryn walking between the trees to where he was sitting. For the first time since they left Cavell, her eyes were no longer bloodshot or puffy from crying.

"I could say the same," he responded. "You should rest while you can. Krel will likely not let any of us sleep tonight."

She smiled widely, protectively holding her injured hand near her stomach. "Cannot say I feel too safe sleeping next to him anyway, knowing he might fling me in front of the first arrow coming his way. You promised to keep Rehor and me safe last night, but already you are hiding away in the forest, leaving us to fend against the wolf."

"I am sorry. I had a lot to think about." He folded his arms in his lap.

"How did that go?"

"I don't know yet," he answered truthfully.

"*Hm.*" She lowered her eyes to the grass. "I am going to be straight with you. I am hurt that Quinn is not here…I am hurt. I am angry. I am confused. But I do not want to die too, you know?"

"I know," he said. His eyes fell to the wildflowers.

She fell to her knees and grabbed him by the cloak with her good hand, pulling him close with surprising strength. Her lips were wet, soft, connecting with his. Her long fingers let loose from his clothing and wrapped into his curled locks forcing him to kiss her back. His mind went wild. Was she using him, making him care for her to ensure his protection? Or would she soon plant a dagger in his back?

His eyes remained open, looking back at her tightly shut lids, tears slipping down her cheeks. Brenn did not know how to react; it had been too long since anyone had touched him intimately. Instinct took over, and he interlocked his lips with hers. His large hand settled on her cheek to catch the tears and wipe them away.

When she pulled away and reached for the string on his pants, words flooded from his lips. "What are you doing? We cannot do this."

He gripped her wrist to stop her.

"I just need to forget right now." She bit her lip, avoiding his gaze, as though her own words were hard for her to hear. Perhaps they had sounded more sensible inside her head.

The sweet scent of honey blossoms coasted on the wind. He examined her olive skin, her intent brown eyes, equally full of innocence and wherewithal. He let go of her hand and sank into the wildflowers.

She pulled free the front of his pants as he tried to keep himself from appearing utterly puzzled. She looked at him again and smiled her beautiful wide grin.

Chapter XII

KREL, *The Dusk Legion*

The rain came again without warning, drenching everything in the forest.

Krel's fists knotted as he watched the dark-haired beauty stroll ahead of him with Brenn and Rehor on either side of her. The lot of them spoke to one another in hushed voices, further hushed by the rainfall. While Rehor and Brenn would regularly twist their heads to check his position, Taryn kept her head forward, almost as though she knew his position without seeing him.

He unraveled his fingers to touch the smooth handle of the crossbow knocking against his thigh. Her hips bounced side to side, almost mockingly, knowing he was the only one traipsing behind her. It had been a full day since he woke to find her and Brenn returning from the forest together. The two had not even bothered slinking back in from different directions. He refused to ask Brenn what had happened, having no interest in putting his partner in a position to lie.

Taryn surely blamed them all for Quinn's death and would use her womanly ways to twist them against one another. She had lain with Rehor and now Brenn; he assumed it was only a matter of time before the tart tried to seduce him too. The thought surprisingly warmed him. He would bend her over, have his way, and then flip her around to look into those guilty brown eyes before slitting her throat. She would soon learn that he was not easy like the other two men, stooping down to her level because she was some grieving, two-timing tit-sack.

With every passing moment, he was more confident in thinking he and Brenn needed to bury these two in the Dyndaer. Trusting them was a mistake he was not willing to make. He would have already shot them down if he did not think he needed them to finish the mission. His partner did his duty by killing the guard, but they were still outnumbered.

Taryn tittered at something Brenn said, placing her uninjured hand on his shoulder. He glanced back at Krel with an unreadable look. Krel could only shake his head, hoping Brenn was not buying the woman's act.

For ten years, the two of them had traveled through the north snuffing the marks given to them by the Dusk Legion or the senate. Each target came with their own problems, but none matched the scope of their current dilemma. Krel found little reprieve in thinking Brenn was relying on their historical success for this assignment to be completed without a hitch. To some extent, Krel understood why Brenn would not act against Taryn, especially with her sister dying recently, and even Rehor, knowing he had some relation to the Guardians. But Brenn must be brimming with doubt now, knowing Taryn was only interested in going home and Rehor outright refused to fight the enemy.

Nine Lands, the bastard gave Faegrim to their Stuhian?

Brenn had greater restraint than Krel had ever given him credit. With all the questions circling their company, the younger assassin engaged with the two hired hands while keeping a smile on his face. He even managed to get the trollop to spread her legs for him. Brenn's level of dedication to the job astonished him.

"Did you find any trail of the Crimson Sun when you searched the forest? Brenn mentioned that you thought they might turn back, hmm?" Krel almost jumped out of his skin, realizing Rehor had slowed his pace to join him in the back. The hint of arrogance hanging on the Stuhian's tongue made Krel want to punch him in his mouth.

Although Rehor did not touch him, he drew close as though he were proving that he was not intimidated by Krel.

"No," he replied gruffly, pushing his wet bangs from his eyes. "The horses' tracks went north and west, indicating they headed directly for Gaetana."

"Catching them is near impossible, then?" Rehor hummed, rubbing water droplets uselessly off his brown robes. If anything, the dragon-man may have leaned farther inward, causing Krel to angle his trajectory so they did not collide with one another.

"Lucky for us, the road is long yet. We are not going to stop until we finish what we set out to do," he said, frowning at Rehor. The Stuhian met the scowl with a wide grin, having his magical light dance spiritedly in front of them. Without a doubt, he was attempting to get a rise out of Krel. Even with the heavy rain, he found this area of the forest was not as dark as the rest, so Rehor did not need the magical light.

Krel had not been privy to catch much more than the tail end of the conversation the night before when he was meant to be scouting the forest, but he heard enough to understand Rehor was undoubtedly working against them. He could not see any other reason for the Stuhian's unexplainable behavior. He challenged authority. He philosophized instead of acted during battle. And he made threats instead of pacts. Whether aligned with the Crimson Sun or the Guardians of Gero, Rehor was their enemy.

Krel held no doubt.

"Your diligence is inspiring," Rehor cooed, a soft chuckle escaping his lips.

"Is it?" Krel challenged, stepping casually around a forming wet patch. "Are you so worried about receiving your silver that you must check with me to ensure the plan has not changed?"

"My pockets are indubitably happier when they are lined with silver," Rehor said.

Krel grimaced, impressed how the man answered a question without saying anything. "Your concern comes as a surprise, considering you did not raise a hand to finish the job when the opportunity presented itself."

"I am not sure that the chance we are looking for has come," he replied. "Unlike the mishap at the castle, the happenstance in the forest did present the princess," Rehor clapped his hands as though he were congratulating Krel, "but severely outmatched, we were."

"Faegrim might have single-handedly finished the job if you would have used it. Yet I am to understand you handed it off to the enemy," Krel said.

"Please," Rehor laughed. "Kept Eisliev Kluk from obliterating you, I did. How can you not see that I entertained the most powerful of their group, while you failed to seize the advantage? Faegrim would not have worked on him in the same way it will not hold any threat for me in a battle."

Heat rose in the base of Krel's neck at the proposal that he carried the fault. Realizing that his left hand was clutching the handle of his crossbow, Krel released his grip. He snapped at the Stuhian, "Are you expecting us to trust that you will protect us when Eisliev turns our minds to mush with Faegrim? What happens when he turns us against you amid battle?"

Rehor lifted his shoulders to his ears. "I expect you to trust me when the time is right."

"And when will that be? You conveniently avoid every battle at *every* turn!"

"Taryn!"

Brenn's cry overpowered Krel's, steering all attention to the woman who jerked her dagger free of its sheath and turned on Krel. The blade rotated through the air twice before burying itself halfway into Krel's chest.

He inhaled sharply, dropping his chin to see the base of the blade and handle sticking out from his leather armor. His skin tingled at first, a flush of adrenaline surging through his body. His hand trembled to touch the hilt of the weapon. The sharpened iron was probably a finger's length into his flesh. His breath hitched, reaching for his crossbow. The tip of the blade scraped against bone with the movement, causing him to shiver.

He would kill her. He would kill her and Rehor right now.

The Stuhian grabbed him from the side. Krel fought against the man's grip momentarily before hearing Rehor's frantic tone. "Stop! Stop! In her own head, she is not. Look!" He directed Krel's attention farther into the woods where Eisliev and the giant stood in the faint light.

"Krel!" Brenn yelled, backing away from Taryn. The woman swung at Brenn only to be deflected with ease. She was weaponless with her last dagger thrown, the other having been lodged in the back of the princess. She punched at him again, wildly, with a feral scream.

"Take her down," Krel ordered, surprised his words came without restraint. The blade in his chest must have missed his lung and heart.

Thunder rumbled overhead as Brenn slugged Taryn across the jaw, dropping her to the ground. The bellow of the giant carried across the distance. Krel looked up to see the monstrous Ispolini strutting toward them, unstrapping the large axe on his back. Barefoot and bare-chested, he looked to be fearless in the frigid rain. The red mage at his back folded his arms, apparently having the same nonchalant attitude as Rehor.

Krel grasped for his crossbow again and yelled in agony, the pain surging through his shoulder and arm. Even if he fired the bolt already loaded, he would not be able to draw the string back for a second shot.

He and Brenn might be able to defeat the giant, but they would never be able to contend against the dragon-man, especially with him holding Faegrim.

Krel turned to Rehor. "Kill him. Hit him with lightning like you did the simargl."

"Harm these two, I cannot" the Stuhian replied, slinking back from him. Rehor glanced at the blade in Krel's chest, and then sprang open his pouch to pull out two folded pieces of parchment. "I will kill anyone else, save Teodor too, of course."

"Mother's milk! You are useless!"

"Not completely," Rehor said. "Take the milroot. It will subdue the pain and invigorate you in battle."

Krel winced, eyeing the packet as though it were poison. With a grunt, he grabbed the pouch and tipped its contents into his mouth. If the Stuhian slew him in the forest, he hoped Brenn would avenge him.

Almost immediately the sharp burn in his chest faded despite the knife still sticking out of him. His heart thumped. He felt like he was on fire, the milled magic surging through his muscles. Thoughts ran over themselves, words flooding from his lips. "What have you given me? By the gods, I feel alive." He turned from Rehor before the Stuhian could answer him. Krel stepped over Taryn's body and motioned for Brenn to follow. "Come on!"

"I am not sure this is a fight we can win, Krel," Brenn said. "You are hurt and…" His partner looked down at Taryn's limp body and then met Krel's gaze. "I can't get that blade out of you now." He glanced at the enemies ahead.

"Where are we going to run, Brenn? Are you going to outrun an Ispolini?" Krel shivered, unwilling to see the full damage to his chest. Rainwater soaked him. He yanked the long knife from his belt, careful not to disturb the dagger in his chest. His blade glistened in the rain. "If we are going to die, let's do it in battle. Not running off like cowards."

Brenn slowly nodded, pulling his cestuses out and slipping them over his hands. He gulped, raising his eyes to the charging Ispolini. "Okay. We will do it your way."

Krel slipped through the trees with Brenn at his flank, moving through the rain like a weaving arrow, never taking his eyes off the target. The giant was nearly three hundred paces and closing. The leather chest piece kept Taryn's dagger firmly wedged in his flesh. The pressure in his chest was unavoidable as his feet slammed against the ground but, with the milroot in his bloodstream, the pain was distant.

As though one of the dragon-men called on the Nine Winds, rainwater sprayed through the trees, covering them in a clouded mist. He pushed the wet bangs from his eyes as he ran in the sludge, fortunate that his feet held steadfast. The ground was becoming slicker by the second. The rain soaked into his cloak, weighing down his movements. Without much thought, he loosened the string at his neck and let the fabric fall away from him, lost to the Dyndaer. It was better to be chilled than carrying the extra weight of wet wool when battling the giant.

Krel's blemished armor clung tightly to his frame. It would do little against the might of the Ispolini. He used to joke with Brenn that he was unkillable. Krel never knew the thirst for glory, but he knew battle. This battle would be the test of his claim. All truth needed testing.

"Your blood will stain my axe," the Ispolini roared, stopping in the sludge. A madness filled his blue eyes as Krel and Brenn came within striking distance. The giant stepped sideways in the small outcropping of rocks among the lofty trees.

"We will see," Krel said.

The giant grunted, swinging his axe at a downward angle toward his head like he might split Krel in half with one blow. Krel sprang back as Brenn crashed forward from the shadows, well-nigh hidden in the shield of rain. Brenn leaped in the air and met the giant with a fist to the cheek that knocked him straight to the ground, spitting blood. Brenn did not waste any time, running forward and springing onto the giant, swinging again and busting the Ispolini in the side of the head.

Nary was there a doubt—Brenn was born to fight.

"Get on your feet, Tyr!" A shout of disbelief from Eisliev sounded like a trumpet against the song of the storm.

Tyr snarled, letting go of his axe to block another punch from Brenn. He returned a blow with a fist three times the size, hitting Brenn in the chest. Krel watched as his partner flew to the side, his body twisting against the sharp edges of a stone. Brenn rolled to his side with a belated moan.

Krel took his turn, rushing Tyr as he scrambled to his feet, his armament already spinning in his six-fingered hand. The straight blade of his knife met the curved blade of the axe, and Tyr shoved Krel back several feet with a beastly growl. Krel could not match Tyr's strength.

Keeping his affected arm at his side, he vaulted at the Ispolini, his own blade dancing, thrusting, and cutting through the air, dangerously close to deathblows. The giant dodged and met each attack with equal proficiency, using the handle and the strange silver metal of his blade to defend against each strike.

Gritting his teeth, Krel readjusted his grip, the pressure in his chest intensifying with every hard movement. Brenn stumbled back to the battle, his foot scraping on a rock behind the giant.

Tyr turned to the sound and charged, catching the other assassin in the chest with a broad shoulder. The stunned expression barely formed on Brenn's face before he flew back into the rocks a second time.

He slumped against the rock, his wet hair plastered over his face.

The giant disregarded Brenn and turned on Krel again, clearly intent on obliterating both of them without the aid of the Stuhian standing farther back in the forest. Krel moved left and right, cutting Tyr's forearm and bicep with his weapon. The bulk of the giant kept coming, slinging his axe to one hand, then pummeling a fist into Krel's cheek and chin.

Krel kept his balance and ducked the next blow, landing a weak counter against the giant's midsection with his knife curled into his fist. He hurried with a secondary bash against the ribcage. The crack that sounded was barely noticeable, possibly imagined. Krel cursed at himself for not flipping the dagger forward to stab the Ispolini. He lifted his head to appraise the impact, only to catch another fist to his jaw.

He flew back, landing harshly on his rear.

Either the Ispolini was carved from stone, or Krel's fists were feathers.

Brenn came from nowhere again, dodging the powerful blows that Tyr unleashed as though he had learned Tyr's fighting style. He was bruised and bleeding, protecting his ribs with one hand, but he was miraculously standing. He sprang into the air, connecting an armored fist with Tyr's eye.

Blood gushed.

The Ispolini raged, shoving Brenn to the side with the handle of his long axe. Krel took the place of his fellow assassin but caught a knee to the chest, a hair beneath Taryn's dagger. He toppled into the mud, blood spewing from his chest wound. His insides felt broken, blood overflowing from his gaping mouth. His chest suddenly burned like fire, his focus hazy. He fought against the blackness, keeping his eyes on Tyr, who approached for a finishing blow.

He strained to push himself to his feet.

He tried again.

Nothing.

"No!" he heard Brenn bellow accompanied by the splashing of water. The giant howled as the assassin struck him multiple times.

A louder roar, more savage, ripped along with the crash of thunder overhead. Krel blinked away the fog covering his vision in time to see the black flash of a simargl tackle the Ispolini. Snapping jaws and the giant's roar reverberated through the forest.

Lightning webbed above the trees.

Brenn appeared over Krel, frantically pulling at his arm with one arm. "We have to go. More are coming."

His legs were not working properly, but he eventually hobbled to his feet. "My knife," he managed, searching the slop at his feet.

"Consider it gone. Come on. I cannot carry you on my own. My ribs are broken." Brenn pulled at him.

Krel made it a couple of feet, Tyr's rage-filled roars matching the slobbering snarls of the simargl. Krel coughed up a mouthful of blood, nearly collapsing to his knees. "I am not sure I can."

"I will drag you if I have to."

Brenn repositioned himself, wrapping Krel's good arm over his shoulder. He attempted to hoist him up before falling to his knees with a wounded roar, dropping Krel back to the ground. Krel barely knew what had happened and Brenn was on his feet again, grabbing him once more. Forcing himself to stand alongside his partner, he gripped Brenn's other shoulder to balance his weight.

His eyesight wavered, riddled with the question of who he should eternally hold animosity toward if he were to outlive this defeat. In a single beat of his heart, Krel determined that whether it was Taryn's dagger, Tyr's strength, or Rehor's betrayal at fault, he would choose to hate them all.

Vowing his vengeance, Krel grappled to keep breath within him while—with each step Brenn nearly dragged him—death strove to steal it away.

Chapter XIII

TYR, *The Crimson Sun*

A low rumble gurgled in the simargl's throat, gelatinous drool dripping across Tyr's swollen eye and sliding down the side of his face and neck.

He twisted from the snapping jaws and tufts of black fur, lying against the mushy ground, feeling the pricks of grainy mud sticking to his back and tense shoulders. He anchored his feet against stones, lucky he was as long as the monster wriggling on top of him, and secured his hold on the snout of the beast. The simargl was stronger than him, but he could withhold its bite with enough leverage.

From the corner of his good eye, Tyr watched with ire as the two Anshedar assassins made their escape. The loud bark of additional simargl in the opposite direction told him that pursuing the bastards was out of the question.

Tyr roared against the fury of the beast looming over him, the shaggy black hair nearly covering the dark eyes. Tyr snaked his body underneath the monstrous creature's mass, heaving against the jaws in an attempt to weaken its position over him. With a hand on either side of its black lips, the razor teeth sliced at his fingertips. He was not sure if he could break free on his own, but he could contend against the simargl for a while longer.

On his forearm, he could see blood oozing from a cut inflicted by one of the assassins. He had not felt the injury at the time, but at a quick glance, he realized that the gash could not be ignored. The blood leaked down to his elbow before blending with the rainwater underneath him.

But first, he needed to tear apart these curs!

The simargl were as dangerous as the large white bears—like the one that had killed his sister—on Tundris Mor. Their sheer mass posed a challenge for anyone who did not have the uncontested strength of an Ispolini. If he were thinking clearer, he might have cursed the simargl for not pouncing on one of the assassins, the easier prey, but he knew that he was the better meal.

The weight of the simargl's muscular frame pulled back but swiftly thrust itself against Tyr with the intent to grab hold of his throat. He fought to hold the oversized wolf at bay, seeing its leathery wings stretch out behind it.

The guttural growls of the other two simargl rang from the right. Tyr scarcely could see the large animals amble through the steady downfall of rain, their yellow eyes glowing hauntingly, emerging from the dampened woods.

"Eisliev!" he roared.

The line of fire that came at his request bolted through the air, brightening the unlit forest, striking the simargl pinning Tyr.

The beast lurched sideways from the impact, shifting its body enough that Tyr could gain the advantage. With a snarl, he kicked off with his leg and threw his shoulder forward, toppling the simargl sideways.

Rolling in the opposite direction, Tyr sprang to his bare feet and scooped up his weapon. The simargl was equally spry, clambering to all fours and reeling toward him again. Tyr heaved the weapon forward with immense force, the steel blade cutting through the thick skin of the shoulder with ease. He could have thanked Enlil for gifting him the weapon in that moment; no iron would have cut through the animal's flesh.

A yap of anguish emitted, and the black beast whipped its head to the right from the impact, drawing back and clawing at the fresh injury. A snarl from the second simargl drowned out the wounded one. He spun around in time to dodge its cracking jaws.

Eisliev rained more fire at the second simargl, two bolts singeing the fur and skin. Again the animal barked, revealing rows of white fangs, almost oblivious to the damage Eisliev inflicted. Seeing the ivory against the crimson gums brought forth images of his sister's death once more, pulling at his senses until his own vision was draped in red.

Maruda. He had promised to protect her and failed.

Flipping the axe sideways, he crushed the back against the skull of the simargl with the hope of caving the bone on impact. He rotated the long handle once and swung again at a downward angle, propelling the sharp edge into the fierce mug of the simargl, the long, curved blade splitting the skin from eye to jowl.

Blood splattered across Tyr's vision as the first simargl continued to whimper behind him.

"Tyr!" Eisliev's voice hinted at alarm, and even then, Tyr barely heard the cry.

He ripped the blade free from the second simargl with a mighty pull, seeing movement from the left. He did not bother turning to acknowledge the third simargl that bounded for him and instead, rolled through the muck to dodge the beast's deadly attack. Its jaws snapped where he once stood, tucking its wings back against its long frame, giving the indication it had glided to Tyr to make its attack. No matter, Tyr was back on his feet and charging the beast.

Doing his best to keep his balance in the mud, he spun the axe in his hand and undercut the soft tissue of the neck. The beast tried to howl in protest, but the cutting blade severed deep enough to split its vocal cords. Despite the red blood that oozed, the third simargl stood solidly on its four massive paws. In one smooth motion, it dipped its head low and squarely hit Tyr, sending him back into the second beast.

His weight collided with animal, knocking it sideways and off balance. Tyr shifted onto his back foot, miraculously keeping his balance, and rotated to meet the first simargl head-on. With its shoulder wound slowing its charge, Tyr whipped the axe behind his body and leaped forward, crushing the simargl across the snout with his fist. Its entire head snapped sideways under the might of the Ispolini.

The winged wolf whimpered again and pulled back; no longer showing any sign of wanting to fight for its meal, it unexpectedly ran off into the woods.

With an inhuman bawl that would make thunder sound like a mere drum, Tyr raged toward the remaining two simargl. The one with the split neck was already crumpling to the moistened soil when his axe came down on the cranium, lodging itself in the thick bone. The simargl jolted once and died.

Tyr let go of the handle and stampeded toward the second beast with the split face, having every intention of strangling the simargl until its life was forfeit. He swung into the air as the winged wolf turned tail and shambled off into the forest, only bothering to look back to ensure the Ispolini was not following it.

The squishing footsteps against the mud tugged at the Ispolini's ears, pulling his attention back to the right. He flexed his muscles and spun around with a growl, reaching for the handle of his blade.

"Cool your blood, you brainless turd," Eisliev said as he came near. His red robes flowed behind him, running along the ground. "I swear to the gods if you so much as swell your chest at me, you'll be the tallest Ispolini with the smallest bits this side of the Shade Fells."

Tyr sniffed, shaking the cloudiness from his vision and focusing on the red mage sauntering toward him. "I am the only Ispolini this side of the Shade Fells."

Eisliev shrugged at the remark. "In any case, I will not be the recipient of your wrath. Look at the madness you have wrought by dragging us away from the others."

Dipping his head at the Stuhian's request, he jerked the weapon free from the carcass at his feet. He cleaned it off on the fur of the simargl and then returned the weapon to the holster on his back.

"You are going to have to realize your mother and sister are gone," Eisliev said, standing rigidly in the continuing rain, "and there is nothing you can do about it. Even if the demons are stopped and you find the Blood Cascade, are you really so selfish that you would bring them back to life?"

Tyr clamped his teeth shut to withhold a snarl.

"You made a promise to myself and my father! It is not selfish to reunite them with those whom they love and love them back. Besides," Tyr said, fighting to form his argument while keeping his blood from pulsing in his eardrums, "we all must complete our charge to be allowed into Thrice Ten Kingdom. I would be selfish to keep them from being born again and stopping them from having a second chance to sit before the glory of the highest."

"Who is to say they have not already done their given deed?" Eisliev replied. "Are you really so thick-headed that you cannot understand common reason? Whatever you *could have* or *should have* done is rubbish when compared to what needs to be done now.

Demons are walking among the living. The Kadari are growing stronger every day. Dagmar Kaligula remains alive."

"According to you, these problems have all existed for the last age," Tyr said.

"And they grow worse by the day," Eisliev spat. "We need to track down Dagmar and destroy him. We do not have time to wander off and watch you slaughter dogs when you get sad." He gestured at the simargl lying at his feet. "I have entertained this long enough. You need to forget about your sister and mother."

Tyr flared his nostrils at the Stuhian. "You gave up your kingdom, your inheritance, to an incompetent half-brother because your mother is dead."

Eisliev raised an eyebrow at the accusation. "My mother's death has nothing to do with my purpose. I aim to honor my family's name."

"Nine Lands!" Tyr could not hold back his roar. "You are navigating Aenar, seeking revenge on your mother's enemy. Your grief is as real as mine. Why can't you admit that you have not dealt with the loss? Do you need to hear it again? Your mother is dead too!"

"Yes, she is. I was a child when she was killed while exploring another part of the world almost twelve hundred years ago," Eisliev scoffed. "If I had any memory of my mother it would not be anything more than the taste of her teat. Get it through your head. I have nothing to miss!"

"Bah!" Tyr did not accept the excuse. He could not viscerally feel pain every waking moment while the Stuhian felt nothing. "My mother also died when I was young. We have the capacity to mourn the idea of having a mother as much—"

"Mothers die as frequently as ideas, if not more often. You are pathetic." Eisliev's face twisted into a scowl. "I am *not* you, Tyr Og. In fact, *most* of the world is not you. Not everyone is crippled by the concept of death. We die. It is the one promise given to us by the gods." He lifted his finger to Tyr, shaking his head as he spoke. "We do not think about or react to death in the same way any more than we experience it in the same way. Just as we can live on in the afterlife, some of us choose to live on in this world after our friends and family pass on. Clearly, some elect to curl up and pretend to be dead too. You want to take a guess where they end up after crossing the Kalinov Bridge?"

Tyr's eyes burned as he stared down at the redheaded Stuhian, fire filling his chest. The Stuhian suggested Thrice Ten Kingdom was beyond his reach if he was crippled by his grief. While he was certain some wisdom was in Eisliev's words, he could not hear it. He did not want to. He would rather tear the dragon-man's head off.

"Are we ready to head back to Teodor now? Tell me you have finished your excursion into the forest and released enough tension," Eisliev said. Tyr balled up his fists, attempting to calm himself to respond without shouting. "Can you stomach being around the princess a few days more until we reach Gaetana? Because I am not going to stand out here and waste magic on beasts to keep you alive. My life is not worth wasting on yours, especially when you have no interest in living it."

Tyr looked off in the direction of the assassins, touching his swollen eye. He managed to ask, "What about the Dusk Legion?"

"I do not know how they could be a threat anymore." Eisliev whistled between his teeth. "The girl's jaw is likely broken, one has a dagger sticking from his chest, you completely broke the insides of another, and Rehor is not going to raise a hand against us. If they come back for another round, they are dumber than you look."

Chapter XIV

BRENN, *The Dusk Legion*

The fenlands burned with color on each side of Brenn as he crouched in the fading grasses and waning wildflowers surrounding the quagmire. A cold wind stirred up from the north, nearly bending the trunks of cypress trees. He listened to them crack and yawned hard enough to cause his jaw to ache. Midmorning had transformed into midafternoon, and already the sky was as dark as dusk under the heavy shadow of the trees.

Autumn's bite cut through Brenn's armor—through his flesh—freezing him to the bone as though he were without skin.

And yet, drops of sweat still slid down the back of his neck, causing his dark hair to stick to him like a wet cloth. He did not need to make excuses for the perspiration in the cooled weather. His ribs were cracked, his face was swollen, and his body was ripe with fatigue. If it were not for the threat of the Crimson Sun, he would be fast asleep.

Skimming the terrain for movement, he wondered how long it would take for the mercenaries to track them down and finish what they started. With Krel half-conscious, Brenn did not have them backtrack far before circling wide and using the shadows of the forest to cloak their position. While they had crossed several hollows hidden away in the forest, dug deep into the underearth beneath twisted trees and heaps of stone, he was not brave enough to lead his companions where more fiends were likely to be found; thus, they made camp near the edge of the swamp behind the array of thickets and wide-leaved plants. Nevertheless, despite his effort at concealing their temporary hideaway, the worst tracker would not have taken long to discover them. He began to wonder if the giant and red mage turned back for Gaetana, believing to have run them all the way back to Lonmere.

They would be loath to discover that the Dusk Legion did not surrender so easily.

"Krel is swearing we will be back on the trail by nightfall," Rehor said, plopping down next to him. A slap on Brenn's shoulder jostled him, causing him to catch his breath in his throat. "What he plans to do in another fight, I cannot say. Even with his wound cauterized, he can barely turn his neck."

Brenn was unsure how he had missed the Stuhian coming up behind him. The swish of the robes against the grass should have alerted him. He was not fit to be acting as lookout.

"Did you hear me? The man is after blood."

"I heard you," Brenn muttered.

Brenn beheld Rehor. He was starting to understand Krel's concern and ire for the dragon-man. Even while he was glad to hear Rehor's knowledge of healing with herbs helped Krel, Brenn could not ignore how the Stuhian was the indirect cause of Krel's wounds.

Because of his folly, Faegrim was used against Taryn who, in addition to everything else, now had to worry about being mind-controlled by the enemy when they were encountered again. Krel's injuries would place them at a further disadvantage in any future fight. Not to mention, none of them could trust Rehor to fight against the Crimson Sun. So far, he had all but refused to participate in any fight involving the mercenaries.

Brenn spoke through clenched teeth. "The question is whose blood is Krel after?"

"Ah." Rehor pulled back from Brenn, rubbing his chin. He could see the curve of a smile on Rehor's face. "You mean he plans to kill me before pursuing the princess, hmm? Surprised, I would not be."

Brenn grimaced, eyeing the scrawny man while scraping away the loose strands of hair that had fallen over his eyes. "Do you think this is amusing?"

"A bit," Rehor confessed, "but then again, I find life to be amusing. The way we clamber around each other believing that our pursuits are greater than any other. You assassins are an especially interesting breed, threatening death to any who are not aligned with your self-interests."

"I have not said anything about killing you," Brenn said.

"You were thinking it, hmm?" Rehor replied, holding the smile. "The Dusk Legion comes and goes, silencing those who do not fit their agenda. You play a dangerous game, moving nobles and factions to gain power and intrigue. Yet you judge me for finding the way you play the game *amusing*."

Brenn was growing tired of the Stuhian's mind games. "Are you a traitor?"

"A traitor to whom? To you?" The redheaded man shook his head. "No, no, no. Despite what Krel would want you to believe,

I am not conspiring with anyone against you. Not the Guardians of Gero. Not the Crimson Sun. I have zero investment in your princess-killing quest."

"Then why did you agree to the job?"

"I thought it sounded *amusing*." Rehor blew air from his lips as though he were fighting back a chuckle. "How was I supposed to know the Arkhon would be allied with the Crimson Sun?"

Brenn frowned, unsure whether he could trust him.

Rehor said, "I am an observer, Brenn."

"That much is for certain. You do nothing else unless pushed," Brenn scoffed.

"And who do you help without being enticed? Do not pretend you are as dense as your friend." Rehor clicked his tongue. "I see Krel battling reason with his sense of duty. I see Taryn's struggle in understanding herself. I see your personal war, deciding between what is comfortable and what is right. You are a killer with a conscience, Brenn Dardrogan."

He did not want to process the truth of Rehor's assessment, even though his heart told him to listen to the Stuhian. He knew dragon-men lived to be ancient, increasing the likelihood of wisdom being woven in the words.

"What about you?" he asked. "What is your conflict?"

"Besides joining you and becoming a mighty legionnaire?" Rehor lifted his eyebrows, his voice softening as they looked across the fenlands. "Torn between doing the will of others and living for myself, I am."

"And what do you want for yourself?" Brenn asked, suddenly feeling a sense of sadness for the Stuhian.

"I want to go home."

Brenn slipped the sheepskin blanket from his bag over his legs and breathed in the stale air, his chest shuddering as it rose and fell. He could not remember a time when he had been beaten this badly in a fight.

Pulling his cloak in around his shoulders, he leaned his back against the tree and eyed Krel across the way.

"You sure they are gone?" Krel asked.

Brenn nodded, chewing on something Rehor called *borra leaf* which Rehor promised would help him sleep. It tasted sweet like sugar. He glanced off to where he had been stationed by the bog, hoping the dragon-man would be as vigilant as he promised in taking his watch. He was not sure what to think of Rehor, but he believed he was not actively working against them. He was not helping them, but he was not trying to kill them either.

"They would have found us by now if they were coming," Brenn finally said. Leaves rustled to his left, shushing him and whatever response Krel may have offered. A moment later Taryn's shape appeared in the shadows, slinking down next to a tree she had claimed sometime that prior morning. He knew she had been sitting with Rehor for a while, possibly thanking him for dragging her away from the battle. He watched her lie down, curling herself into a ball. She might have positioned herself to look in his direction. He could not tell.

Once Taryn's identity was clear, Krel repositioned himself with a loud groan. "Good. A few hours' rest and then we can be on our way. With any luck, we can reach the princess and the other two men before the Ispolini and Stuhian."

"How do you think we will accomplish that?" Brenn asked. "They could be half a day or more ahead of us."

"Rehor," Krel said plainly.

Brenn scrunched his face, muttering, "I figured you would have him dead by morning. He abandoned us against the Ispolini."

Krel hissed at him through the dark. "Will you keep your voice down?" Brenn could see him turn his torso toward Taryn, incapable of turning his neck because of the cut in his chest. Krel whispered, "He gave me something during the fight that made me feel like I could run forever. I think we could use it to keep us moving for the next couple of days."

"Do you trust him now?" Brenn asked.

"Of course not," Krel said, dropping his voice so that most of his words came at a murmur, "but I will use him until I am well enough to carve out his heart. Beating him at my best would have been hard enough. Trying anything now would be impossible."

A sharp pain in Brenn's side stole his words away. He knew the possibility of Krel accepting Rehor was as unlikely as giving up chasing the princess.

"You should have stood by me when I told you we needed to act," Krel said.

Brenn cleared his throat as Taryn shifted in the leaves again. "Even if we managed to circle around the Ispolini and Stuhian, the other three have horses. We cannot guess how far they have gone, Krel. They may be beyond our reach."

Krel grunted. "The only way anyone escapes you and me is by killing themselves and fleeing into the hereafter."

The comment made Brenn laugh; he grabbed his ribs. He remembered when he and Krel often joked about the reach of their blades extending to every corner of Aenar.

"This forest is full of dangers to stall them on the road," Krel said, a thin smile stretching his lips. "A bit of chance may save our necks yet."

Brenn asked, "You think we can still peg the murder on the Crimson Sun?"

"We better."

Brenn settled his head back against the tree and closed his eyes, speculating what scheme would leave them blameless. Rehor had laid the groundwork by deceiving Count Frantisek, but too many were now involved for the Dusk Legion to convince anyone the Crimson Sun was to blame. He could only hope that some solution would surface before they accomplished their task.

"Brenn," Taryn whispered, crawling across the ground and reaching for his hand, "will you come with me? I would like to spend some time with you before we leave."

Her fingers interlaced with his own, tugging gently to take him into the forest.

He swallowed hard, eyes snapping open to where Krel sat a few paces away. The borra leaf was taking its toll, pulling his eyelids closed. His body ached, and his mind was numb.

She slipped closer to him, her tongue touching the edge of his ear. "Please."

"Yeah," he said. As he pulled away from the tree, he swore he heard Krel mutter his disapproval and felt his eyes burning into Brenn's back.

Taryn led him through the trees as though it were clear daylight, weaving him back and forth without any hesitation. Certainly, none of them had time to search the forest when they settled, and with the possible beasts that roamed, he was surprised at her confidence in leading.

She did not say anything to him. In his stupor, Brenn's heart pumped with passion, fury, and confusion, knowing he was lusting after the woman gripping his hand but uncertain of how his fondness for her might further rip him from Krel's trust. The thoughts were fleeting as he stumbled along at her heel.

By and by, she brought him to a small clearing where white moonlight cut through the treetops with magnificent force, tunneling into a hovel of rock and earth. Beforehand, he had not known the moon was even in the sky; how she found the spot in all the Dyndaer, let alone near their encampment, baffled him.

Instead of raising the question, his focus was on the blossoming woman. She turned around at the opening of the slanted cavern and fell into his arms. Her black hair seemed to stain her pale shoulders, her cloak pulled back to reveal her loosened tunic.

He searched her over, captivated first by her smooth skin, surprisingly warm against his cold fingers. The puffy welt on her chin where he had slugged her was black and purple, an unspeakable testament to his panic. He swiftly looked away, ashamed by what he had done, and met her brown irises.

Immediately, he was overwhelmed with an eagerness for her taste, wanting to feel her lips on his again. The air circulated her scent.

"Brenn, do not stare at me so," she chortled. Her hand, wrapped in fresh bandages, grazed the long strands of his hair. She pulled him close to her with her other hand so that her breath was on his cheek.

"How am I to look at you any other way?" he asked.

"I do not know," she said. She pushed off her toes to kiss the tip of his nose.

He hungrily kissed her mouth, his mind swirling in a frenzy. She kissed him back without complaint. When he needed a breath again, he pulled back and grinned.

"The night is ours," she smiled. He could not believe how captivated he was by her smile.

"For a while," he agreed. He was finding it difficult to deny her any request.

"Kiss me again," she urged, lifting her good hand to grip a handful of his hair.

Again, he obliged her demand. His tongue licked the surface of her pouted lips, and she spread them slowly to meet his mild suggestion. The kiss was long and searching, their tongues dancing in song. Taryn pulled back to take a breath, and Brenn pressed into her again to reclaim her. Together they kneeled to the softened grasses outside the ingress of the cave.

Taryn moaned intensely, suckling on his bottom lip and then sinking her teeth into him lightly. Soon, she began pulling on the tail of his shirt, the cold evening air gushing against his back. He broke contact with her mouth only to lift the fabric over his head before settling to capture her again with ravenous urgency.

She tilted her head to the side, admiring his bare chest and the muscles in his arms. "Krel does not like us being together, does he?"

His ears barely heard her as his kisses traced from her ear to her neck. "Krel worries over many things. You are safe with me."

"Safe with a fervent boy with boyish desires," she giggled, kissing the side of his head spiritedly.

"A boy?" Brenn looked down on her, gripping her slender hand from his chest and sliding it to his lap. "A boy, you say?"

Taryn bit her lip, her eyes scanning his naked body, outlined with the sores of battle. Her eyes saw everything as she claimed.

Her cheeks rosed in the dimming light. "I sense you *growing* into a man."

He leaned in for another kiss.

She pecked him on the lips briefly and pulled back.

"What is wrong?" he asked.

Taryn pressed a finger to his lips. "I want to know why you hired us to help murder this princess instead of bringing more assassins from the Dusk Legion. You admit to not intending to give us silver. What did you have in mind?"

Brenn nearly gagged on his own tongue, staring at the woman before him. His speech was slurred suddenly as though his words were having difficulty making it through his lips. "You brought me out here to poke at my emotions."

"No, I gave you a chance to loosen your tongue on your own, and you refused." She matched his tenor, her face cold. "The leaves Rehor gave you will make you honest. You cannot withhold it. Tell me."

Brenn stood up, grabbing his shirt with a scowl. Her dark eyes locked on him like death on a grave. Krel was right not to trust them.

The ground spun under him, his vision blurring more and more. "What is this?"

"Rehor said you planned to cut our throats since the beginning. I need to hear it from you," she said. "Were you going to kill me?"

"You were to be slaughtered and made to look like sellswords from Gaetana," Brenn said before he could think what words were coming from his mouth. His muscles were weak as he tried to step away from the woman. He spoke in a haughty whisper. "But that changed when we learned the count was aware of our coming. Everything changed at Cavell. I did not lie to you when I said I would keep you safe."

"What changed…"

"I simply saw no point in it. I like to think my profession does not make me a monster. Though I am discovering I might regret you," he said, trying to focus on her hazy form beneath him. His threat sounded like a child's whining. "Why don't you run off now? Go home before I change my mind."

Taryn shook her head, dropping her eyes. Her tone was full of hopelessness. "Where would I go? I cannot navigate the Dyndaer by myself. I will be dead sooner out there than with you."

Brenn growled through his teeth. "Take Rehor with you. I do not know why he is lingering around anyway."

"He won't go," she replied meekly. "He is strangely invested in killing this princess, even when he knows nothing will come of it. I think he seriously wants to become a legionnaire."

Brenn angled his eyebrows. He had not realized how much the two had spoken with one another. "That will never happen."

Taryn looked up at him. "Can I leave after you have killed the princess? You do not have to hunt the Svet with me. I won't hold you to it."

He turned his back on her, yanking his shirt back over his head. "Yeah."

"Do you swear it?"

Brenn curled his lip. At least, he hoped he did. "I swear it."

She stood and touched his shoulder. The pitched tone of her voice had returned as though she were flirting with him again. "You do not have to leave me right now, Brenn. I needed to hear the truth from you. You must understand. I wanted to trust you."

He swatted her hand away.

"Save your words," Brenn said, clouds moving over the moon above them. A darkness swelled inside him, which may have very well been the breath of the god of darkness who ruled over the Dyndaer. "When this is done, I will see you out of the Dyndaer. Afterward, you're as dead to me as your sister. Do not come to me again." His whisper was barely heard, dry as a shriveled corpse.

He left her standing with tears in her eyes.

Chapter XV

TEODOR, *The Crimson Sun*

Teodor bounded from his horse's side to grab Nitalia and pull her away from the *zilant*. The winged-snake, thicker than the horse and five times longer than Teodor, stretched its fanged mouth around the elongated pate of the grey mount, horrifically staring at him with haunting eyes, daring him to intervene. The horse kicked its legs uselessly against the tufts of grass and mud, enfolded in the twisted body of the serpent, suffocating slowly as the zilant squeezed the life from its body.

A faint wheeze emitted from the mare as it kicked again, a red river of blood dribbling from the zilant's mouth as its fangs inched along.

"It came from nowhere," she said, hovering her left hand above the handle of a billhook sticking upright over her shoulder. She backed away, holding the left side of her back where the knife wound was hidden under her bone armor. The fire they had crafted an hour earlier crackled at her feet.

Seigfeld stepped in front of her, a shield against the zilant, lifting his sovnya defensively.

Teodor watched the brown and green scales of the zilant slowly roil forward as the beast continued to consume the horse. He suspected it would take the afternoon before it finished the chore. "This way, Princess. We do not need to watch it." He pulled at her gently. "Let it have the horse."

"I did not plan on telling it *no*," Nitalia replied. A guttural hiss reverberated through the snake's body as it shifted again.

"I did not know they grew to be so large," Teodor said, looking to the branches weaving above their heads where the oversized snake-creature had sprung from while they were resting. He said a quick prayer that they would not cross another. "I thought it might be too cold for them to be slithering about this time of year."

"It must have been waiting for a final meal before retiring for the Season of Frost." Seigfeld relaxed his weapon, realizing the animal would not be unraveling from the horse and attacking them anytime soon. "You should see the three-headed dragons swooping over the highest peaks of the Shade Fells. Their presence fastens your feet to rock and stills your heart."

Teodor looked wondrously at his companion. As many times as Seigfeld told him the tale of rescuing Farthr from the Shade Fells, traveling through a myriad of tunnels beneath the desolate mountains, Teodor could not believe it. Few Anshedar had ever gone as far as the Shade and returned to tell the story of what they discovered.

The orange glow of the zilant's eyes disappeared as the snake widened its mouth more to take in the mount.

"We need to be on our way," Nitalia said, dropping her arm from its position over her shoulder.

Teodor gestured to the remaining mount. "Would you like to ride while we walk, Princess?"

Nitalia took a final look at the zilant. "No, I'll walk too."

Teodor lit a torch in the fire before snuffing it out and shuffling them away from the winged-snake. He led them cautiously in the direction he hoped was west or northwest. He and Seigfeld were not the greatest guides, especially in the Dyndaer, where the late-season rain and hidden sun kept them from their projected path. Up until this point, Teodor had relied on Farthr, Tyr, or Eisliev to point them in the right direction. Of the three, he had not expected the dragon-man to be an expert in scouting the difficult terrain, but Eisliev had a remarkable knack for being a pathfinder.

Yet with Tyr and Eisliev out hunting what remained of the Dusk Legion and Farthr gone, he and Seigfeld were left to their own devices. Unfortunately, this meant they had become lost. More than likely, they were traveling in circles. Princess Nitalia was kind enough not to ridicule them for their inability to navigate the twisted forest, which Teodor decided was due to her own lack of understanding. Even though she was born among the trees, she too did not know how to pinpoint their location, often reiterating how the wood had no natural path or markings.

Teodor hoped they would reach Gaetana before spring.

As they meandered away from the zilant, pulling the last mare behind them, Nitalia sparked a conversation with Seigfeld, pressing him to tell a story that Teodor had heard once before.

"Is it true you have seen the dragons, Master Brecher?" she asked. She made a fist with her hand as though she were fighting against the pain in her back from the knife wound. Teodor was sure the injury felt no better when riding on the back of a horse. "I have never met anyone who has ventured as far as the Shade Fells."

"Many have not," he replied, pulling himself along with the staff end of his sovnya. He continued to favor his bruised shoulder while traipsing along. "And yes, I saw a few in my adventure in the west. Though I did not dare near the serpents. If you want any specific details outside of their sheer size and color, I would invite you to speak with Tyr when he returns. The Ispolini are known to battle the dragons on the ice caps of Tundris Mor."

"Fascinating," Nitalia whispered. Her blue eyes widened at Seigfeld as she pushed a strand of golden hair behind her ear. Teodor watched her delicate movements, imagining how she might respond in a similar fashion while sitting around her father's long table in Cavell. Her noble mannerisms reminded him profoundly of the qualities his father had hoped to instill in him. Nitalia went on, squeezing by a tree that separated them momentarily, "What were you doing in the west? Were you on assignment for the Crimson Sun?"

Seigfeld winced. "No, my father called me home to Eris—"

Nitalia interrupted, "I thought you said you were from Hleduk? I am afraid I am not familiar with Eris."

"Originally," he replied. "In fact, I consider Hleduk home, but my family moved to Eris after I joined the Crimson Sun. You would not be able to find it on a map, I am afraid. The small hamlet is far in the west, beyond Gaetana, on the northern outskirts of Faldar."

Her mouth formed an oval, cheeks rosy in the dropping temperatures of the forest. "I would love to know more. I have never traversed beyond my uncle's home in Gaetana. Why were you all the way out there?"

Again, Seigfeld took his time to answer, as though the words were difficult for him to speak. Teodor did not blame him for his hesitation, knowing what strain the warrior had gone through in his expedition. While he had returned from the journey a few months ago, he only started speaking of the details before leaving for Cavell.

"My sister, Anneinda, went missing," he said. "My father believed her to be taken by monsters of the Shade Fells. Demons, really."

"Gods," Nitalia gasped again. "Will you tell me the tale? Did you find her?"

"I did not," Seigfeld said. He let loose a long sigh, staring off emptily into the Dyndaer. "I—I found the cave where she was taken, a place without light with lichen that would burn your skin if you touched it. The place was darker than any place I have ever roamed, including this forest you call home."

They carried on for a few more steps in silence, hearing nothing but the rustling of their own footsteps and the clomping of the horse at their rear. Seigfeld looked to be fighting a trembling jaw and watering eyes, of which Teodor noticed Nitalia was mindful. Typically, when Teodor thought of ladies her age, he expected them to be more immature. Thoughtless. Yet, whether it be from her noble upbringing or her general temperament, Nitalia was ever vigilant in her understanding of emotion. He had not given it much thought until now, but he watched her interact with each of them with a certain delicate nature that he imagined was only becoming of a woman of her stature.

Even at a young age, she was…motherly.

Seigfeld went on with his broken tale in a raspy tenor, somehow willing to tell the young princess what he was reluctant to speak to his brothers in the Crimson Sun about for so long. "As assumed, I did find demons—something the Ispolini call the Witiko—in the depths of this dark, interminable place. As Teodor knows, I found Farthr there, held captive by the demon spawn, but my beloved Anneinda…I could not find her."

Nitalia stepped closer to him, placing her hand on his arm. Her words were neither apologetic nor sympathetic, but strangely appropriate, bespeaking the nature of Seigfeld's courageous and honorable character. "Thank you for being here with me to protect me from these assassins, Master Brecher. Your bravery will not be forgotten."

Seigfeld nodded dutifully, her words likely holding more meaning for him than Teodor knew.

Teodor kept his lips sealed, watching the exchange with fascination. Nitalia did not seem to inherit any of the characteristics of her father, who might have insisted the will of Czern, the God of Darkness, allowed Seigfeld's sister to be taken to strengthen him. Instead, she was affectionate. Ever gentle in her response to his turmoil.

The sheer difference in how Nitalia was from her father was uplifting, considering how much different Teodor was from his own father.

"Master Bacheva," Nitalia began, her voice soft and smooth, "my father has heard the rumors of demons emerging throughout Maharia. What does the Crimson Sun know of this? Is it true the Netherworld is overfilled with the spawn of the dead?"

Teodor spoke evenly with the hope of not upsetting her. "We know the Kadari have been battling against these undead monsters for some time now. Recently they asked us to help them find a lost artifact that might end the onslaught. We have some of our most skilled mercenaries traversing the north as we speak, looking for it." Teodor gulped. "But in truth, we know very little of the threat. Seigfeld's account of the demons in the Shade Fells are among the few accounts that are more than spurious rumors."

"Your father has not heard of their insurgence?" she asked.

"I have not spoken with my father in a very long time, Princess," Teodor said.

"Why?" Nitalia batted her eyes innocently.

Teodor thinned his lips behind his mustache. Nitalia seemed to be digging into each of their histories. For what reason, beyond general curiosity, he could not be certain. Regardless, he was not as apt as Seigfeld in sharing the bleakness of his family interactions. His father did not want him anywhere near his business or his estate. Teodor was as welcome home as assassins might be in the city of Eldhaft.

He dipped his head almost apologetically, lying through his teeth. "My duty requires me to be away from Tamarri often, and rarely do I venture to Eldhaft. I am sure he and I will cross paths again."

"I hope you do," she said, "if you wish it."

The three of them traveled half the night in silence on the unmarked path, weaving through the shrubs and trees. The rough terrain slowed their pace, encouraging them to continue until their muscles burned in equal measure to their eyes. Twice they needed to stop to relight the torch, and Teodor inquired whether they should stop for the evening. Yet the fear of having another creature come upon them in the night kept them steadfastly moving through the woods.

Once or twice, Teodor considered letting the brown mare run free, debating whether the animal was becoming more of a hindrance, possibly giving away their position to the roaming beasts. He hoped they would not discover anything more dangerous than the zilant. However, the princess insisted they keep the mare from trotting off aimlessly into the dark woods, where it would undoubtedly die.

At last, when they could not take another step without collapsing, the three of them made camp and rested. The remaining night hours slipped by in a few blinks. Before the sun showed any sign of light in the patchy clouds beyond the canopy of trees, they were marching again.

Seigfeld was the first to notice a break in the trees ahead. "We have reached the end," he sighed, pointing to the thinning hawthorns and black gums. "We will be at the gates of Gaetana within a few days."

"I am afraid not," Nitalia said. "We have only reached the Drayrich Run. Let us hope we have exited near the crossing. Between the pursuit of the Dusk Legion and the onslaught of creatures, we have twisted back and forth enough that I cannot say where we might be."

Seigfeld breathed deeply, his chest swelling as he pushed forward to reach the river ahead. Teodor did not blame him— seeing the clear light radiating beyond the trees was refreshing and invigorating. The sound of the water rushing along the river reached his ears.

Teodor asked, "How much farther is Gaetana from the Drayrich?"

Princess Nitalia adjusted the sleeves on her shirt and smoothed the purplish cloak out behind her. "Equal to the distance we have already traveled. That is, as long as we do not get lost."

Seigfeld turned his head. "You mean to say we have another patch of the Dyndaer to pass through before reaching Gaetana?"

She nodded, pulling the hood of her cloak over her head. "Yes, but do not worry, Master Brecher. Several towns line the opposite side, including Athon and Trinova. You will find fewer creatures on the other side of the river besides the occasional snow hares or red deer."

When they finally stepped beyond the tree line, Teodor expressed his relief. The rays of sun, even when lacking warmth, were a world of comfort.

"Praise the Lightbringer," Seigfeld said with a grin, tilting his head to the sky and sucking the cold air through his nose. "I do not know how you stay in darkness all year round, Princess."

"I could say the same about your strange love for the light," Nitalia responded, shielding her eyes even beneath her hood.

"Withhold praise awhile longer," Teodor groaned, glancing along the churning river. "We have no way to cross."

"Hm. We are too far north," Nitalia said knowingly, twisting southward. She waved at them to follow. "Come along."

Chapter XVI

TEODOR, *The Crimson Sun*

The water was fresh like ice on Teodor's lips, so cold that he barely tasted more than the chill. He rocked back on his heels as the brown mare to his right dipped its head for a second drink.

The river flowed evenly to the south, showing no signs of life beneath the surface. A variety of endless trees—maple, oak, and cottonwood—extended across the other side. Several willows outlined the edge of the forest like a shielded wall. Teodor frowned to himself, not seeing any end to the arrangement of trees. He hoped Nitalia was right and they would be free from crossing any perilous beasts on the other side.

The Dyndaer was immense. He never thought about its actual size until he entered its fold. Traveling in the far north across the lands of the Svet, in between the cities of Tamarri and Gaetana, did not give him much reason to contemplate the vastness of this wood. His business with the Crimson Sun rarely brought him into this forest, laden with tales of monsters and hauntings and death. Besides the hamlet of Cavell and the city of Ariadne farther south, little more existed in the Dyndaer except ruins from days of old, days of wars long forgotten by the memories of men. He heard books chronicling the history were kept in Gaetana in what was called the Highspire. After this short excursion, he might take leave to read those texts—anything to keep him from returning to this damned place.

"Jab!" Seigfeld suddenly cried, robbing Teodor of his thoughts. The mercenary next to him jumped to his feet and moved down the bank, looping around Nitalia where she kneeled. Teodor stood to see Seigfeld half-running toward two humaniform figures who approached them with Seigfeld's familiar warhorse trotting between them. He rushed toward them with such urgency that he left his weapon lying on the ground by the river. Teodor casually picked it up and followed, studying the two on either side of the horse.

The first was a warrior by the looks of him, leading Jab by the bridle. He walked with candor, standing as tall as Seigfeld with enough muscle to wrestle an ox. His black hair was dark and thick, matching the lengthy beard and mustache stretching from his face to his chest. The hair was so thick, in fact, that Teodor could see little more than his blue beady eyes and wide nose.

The second was a female Lilitu, hailing from a place called Haemus Mons in the distant south of Maharia. She was shorter than the Anshedar with smooth reddish-brown skin. She adjusted the bow on her back, the string stretching across the red sash that angled over her small chest. She was scrawny from her neck to her ankles with an oversized head. Her thin black hair was in need of a trim, long and spiky all over her head, but the circular eyes, three or four times the size of any human, is what held Teodor's attention. She looked back at him, unblinking, examining him and Nitalia at his back with equal interest.

Teodor smiled to himself, knowing what joy Seigfeld was experiencing. They all thought his mount was lost.

"By the gods, where did you find him?" Seigfeld said, lifting his hand in greeting to the strangers.

"Good afternoon to you, too," the bearded man laughed, offering the horse to Seigfeld without complaint. His voice carried as Teodor walked up to them with Nitalia at his side. "I found him wandering near the river's edge, calmer than any animal I have come across in years. I figured if we strolled along the bank far enough we would find his owner." He patted Jab on the side, then flattened the fur with his thick hand. "You have a good animal here. Lucky you came along, or I would have been taking him into battle with me. I suspect he would be comfortable among men of war."

"That he would be," Seigfeld agreed. Jab stepped closer and nuzzled Seigfeld's head, snorting through his nostrils with excitement. As if Seigfeld had been waiting for Jab's return, he fished one of the dried apple crisps from his pocket and fed it to the animal. Lo and behold, the brown mare was soon at his back begging for a bite as well. Seigfeld hurried to give the other mount one before it nibbled the cloak off his back.

The behavior of the two horses caused the bearded man to burst out laughing, throwing his head back. He tilted his head to look at the Lilitu behind him while pointing at the horses. She only shook her head at him disapprovingly and crossed her arms.

"Glad to see you are satisfied." Her tone was flat, emotionless. She did not bother to make eye contact with any of them as she addressed her companion. "You have returned the horse. Can we be on our way now?"

"The war is not going anywhere, Hanna," he slowed his laugh, extending his hand to Seigfeld. "Name is Adamus Ebordon from Ariadne. This is Hanna Bretka, daughter of Briv, from Danduher."

Seigfeld took his hand firmly in his own. "A pleasure to meet a hero-warrior from Ariadne. I hope your city is faring well. I am Seigfeld Brecher, son of Stelghar."

"Teodor Bacheva, son of Gaspar." He handed Seigfeld his weapon and then took Adamus's hand, noticing Hanna exhale loudly. She rolled back on her heels, looking over her shoulder as though she might bolt away to avoid the formalities. Adamus, on the other hand, rattled in his throat at Teodor's surname, lifting his eyebrows in recognition.

Someone always knew the name Bacheva, no matter where he went. It was a blessing or a curse, depending on the company.

Before the Ariadnean commented, however, Nitalia offered her hand to Adamus. "Princess Nitalia Frantisek, daughter of Count Vlaskhorn Frantisek, from Cavell."

Adamus's eyes widened at the title, hurrying to take her hand while folding his body in half. He did not stand again until she patted his knuckles with her fingers. "I meant to ask if you three were also responding to the call for soldiers in Raybin, but I did not realize you were among their company, Princess." He looked to Teodor and Seigfeld and pulled at his beard. "Strange for you two to be escorting the princess, isn't it? Not to sound rude, but neither of you are from Cavell."

Nitalia redirected his question in a hurry, her words sweet like a song. "Czern's blessing on you in the battle to come, Master Ebordon and," Nitalia tilted her head to the Lilitu, "Lady Bretka."

"I am not a lady," Hanna said, again with no visible reaction, giving no sign if she was offended or simply stating a fact. Teodor scrunched his face at the Lilitu's cold mannerisms, unsure whether she was being deliberately rude or whether this was the demeanor of her race. He heard tales of the Lilitu and their strange behavior, ever placing their logic above their feelings, but he had yet to travel to their lands, and the interactions at seaside trade ports were limited.

Nitalia politely folded her hands. "My apologies if I offended you."

"I would have to care about your opinion to be offended," Hanna said, tightening her already crossed arms.

Nitalia paused, smiling kindly. "Yes, of course."

Teodor pulled attention away from Nitalia, speaking to Adamus. "We did not hear about a request for hired hands for the war. Was it commissioned by King Frantisek?"

"It was," Adamus said. "Hanna and I were south of Ariadne near the port when the runner reached us. I imagine they will move on to Talastein and ask for an audience with the empress. Though," he eyed Hanna behind him, his smirk nearly hidden in his forest of facial hair, "I cannot imagine they will convince many Lilitu to raise arms against the Uvil."

"You are lucky to have any of us fighting alongside you Anshedar," Hanna said, tightening her thin lips before continuing. "You lack order and logic. The reason the Uvil have not obliterated your species yet is because you spent the last thousand years breeding without restraint and building a city anywhere rocks could be stacked."

Adamus chortled all the louder, lifting his finger at Hanna. "Are you accusing the Anshedar of expanding too far? Lilitu cities stretch across Haemus Mons and into the north, each one being four times as large with eight times the people."

"You are correct," Hanna said. "Take note that the Lilitu do not propagate ignorance and indulgence like the Anshedar, leaving us better equipped to multiply."

"Why again are you fighting for us?" Adamus raised an eyebrow, an unnerved smile visible on his lips.

"Because even if your race is stupid and selfish, your inept king pays in silver," Hanna said, "and he has a great deal of it."

"You are speaking about my uncle," Nitalia said.

"Czern's breath!" Adamus pulled at his beard and stepped in front of Hanna as though his body could make her disappear entirely. "My deepest apologies, Princess. For what Hanna lacks in manners she will make up for on the battlefield."

Nitalia briskly nodded.

Teodor fought to get a word in, finally taking his chance to get some information from the hero-warrior. "Do you know why the king has sent for hired hands? I thought the army was weathering the Uvil at the edge of the Kalinov desert."

"Oh, we are losing this war. Make no mistake of it, Master Bacheva," Adamus said. "The Uvil do not only have better weapons and armor, but their strategists have outwitted King Frantisek at every turn."

Nitalia's womanly gasp drew their attention.

Teodor gave the princess an apologetic look. "War was never his strong suit."

Adamus bobbed his head in agreement. "It is worse yet. Rumor in Ariadne was the Uvil have been causing dissonance throughout Maharia, infiltrating the major cities and manipulating factions to do their bidding."

"What?" Teodor's jaw fell. "What do you mean?"

Adamus folded his arms, nodding to himself as he spoke. "Well, I thought the stories were a farce at first, but sailors arrived at the south port with an Uvil corpse in their possession. Apparently, they captured and killed the man coming out of Halderon. He was turning the local guilds against one another. And I will tell you, we have seen a number of their scouts in the southern Dyndaer near Ariadne."

"Gods." Teodor's mouth dried. If they were reaching Halderon, they could well have made their way to Tamarri to infiltrate the Crimson Sun. He could not imagine what would happen if they dug their claws into the Guardians of Gero or the Dusk Legion.

"Yeah," Adamus went on, "they are well beyond our lines, running amuck through the north. You would think that bluish, pale skin of theirs would give them away, but they find a way to blend in among us. You have to keep your wits about you and a dagger at the ready."

"They are clever," Seigfeld said. "Causing turmoil among factions might lead to conflict among our kingdoms, which would put us at a further disadvantage in the war."

"Indeed," Adamus said, "and so the king is bringing sellswords to the front lines to fight back the Uvil. We are assuming he is planning to send some of the men from his army to the major cities to hold the peace and inform factions of the alleged schemes, but I cannot be certain until we arrive in Raybin."

Teodor nodded dutifully, noticing Hanna shooting daggers into Adamus's back with her eyes. "We will not keep you from your road. Thank you for returning Seigfeld's horse and for the information."

Adamus scrunched his face at the sudden dismissal and then bowed to Nitalia once more. "We will take our leave. Let us hope the war does not reach the gates of Cavell, my lady."

Nitalia tucked her golden hair behind her ear. "To reach Cavell, they would have to march through the Ariadnean Kingdom, home to the finest warriors Maharia has to offer. They would be fools to march an army into the Dyndaer."

"True, they would be," Adamus chortled. He turned around and waved Hanna onward. "There you are, Lady Bretka," he teased. "Now, on to the next order of business. Should we find you a dress before we march into war? Wouldn't want anyone mistaking you for a man."

Teodor smiled as the gruff man gave a final wink and turned back south with the Lilitu.

"How did you find out the Dusk Legion wanted me dead?" Nitalia asked, folding her arms under her breasts.

Teodor scowled, recognizing the princess had come to the same conclusion as he had. "We received a forewarning in an unmarked letter. Ivarr thought it warranted enough concern to send us down to investigate."

"You think the Uvil tipped us off?" Seigfeld asked.

"They warned us about an assassination they set up themselves to pit us against one another," Teodor said. "This is not being orchestrated by the Dusk Legion or the Lonmerian Senate at all. They are all pawns in a greater scheme and likely have no idea."

"I wonder what they think they are getting out of this," Seigfeld said.

"The Lonmerian senate is motivated by power and position. Think of how long they have been stewing in silence, hoping to gain an upper hand against the other three kingdoms," Teodor said. "We need to put a stop to this."

"How?" Nitalia asked. "How do you sway assassins not to murder someone they were hired to kill?"

Teodor folded his arms, turning to the Dyndaer behind them. "We do what they least expect and hope to gain their ear."

Seigfeld shifted his feet uncomfortably. "What are you planning?"

"To surrender."

Chapter XVII

KREL, *The Dusk Legion*

"Nine Lands!" The cauterized wound in Krel's chest stung to the point that even walking was difficult. His muscles were tight from his neck to his thighs. The unbearable ache caused him to totter like a helpless fool. He stopped and leaned against a tree, muttering under his breath. "How much farther could they have gotten?"

"They had almost a day's lead on us and horses. If we catch them before they reach Gaetana it will be a miracle," Brenn replied with a grim look. His partner, who had been keeping pace beside him, signaled to Rehor and Taryn to pause a moment.

"We can keep going," Krel said. "We need more of the milroot powder."

"I am running low," Rehor said.

"Just breathe for a moment." Brenn took his own deep breath as if he was modeling how breaths were meant to be taken, wincing and grabbing at his side. Krel scowled at his partner. Brenn said, "If you fall over dead before we reach them, you will not do anyone any favors. Gather your strength and then we will continue."

Rehor and Taryn ambled off to the side, ducking their heads together. Krel was aware of how the two repeatedly wandered off to speak in secret, likely conspiring against him and Brenn. Since leaving the swampside, their whispers had become more frequent. He suspected they were plotting to run away into the Dyndaer; he swore to cut them down if they tried anything.

Krel glared at the backs of their heads, again wondering who Rehor might be working for, whether it be the Crimson Sun or the Guardians. He could not let the dragon-man tell anyone of their scheme; Brenn, on the other hand, needed to understand the gravity of the situation. One way or another, if the two sellswords did attempt an escape, he knew that pursuing them would be impossible in his current condition. Moreover, he was not sure Brenn had the balls to stop them either, especially when Taryn had him so tightly in her clutches.

"You cannot trust him or her," Krel said, gripping his chest. The wound was sealed with fire, but he was not convinced it was healed properly. For all he knew, he was bleeding beneath his skin. "They are not part of the Dusk Legion. Their interests do not align with our own."

Brenn rolled his shoulders back, stepping between Krel and the two sellswords. "I know. I have my doubts about their motives too, but nothing that tells me they are our enemies."

"You are still planning on letting them go at the end of this? She is clouding your head. How can you not see that?" Krel rocked his head side to side, his fingers digging into the bark of the tree. "We cannot let them leave this forest alive, Brenn. We need them only until the princess is dead. Our best hope is the Crimson Sun drops them in the crossfire, but we cannot allow them to walk away alive. I do not care how scared you are of Rehor or how nice Taryn feels squirming around on top of you. We cannot leave witnesses."

Brenn looked over his shoulder nervously to where the sellswords stood mumbling to one another. Krel followed his gaze, straining to hear a single word of their conversation but heard nothing, confirming that he and Brenn were also safe from eavesdropping.

Krel pulled Brenn's attention back to him with his words. "All these years we have stuck together. By the gods, do not tell me you are being drawn away by a pretty face? I will buy you a dozen trulls when we get back home if that is what you need. You can lock yourself in any tavern room you choose and go wild until your bits burn with pleasure."

"They can both rot in the Netherworld for all I care, Krel," Brenn replied firmly. "I am just not convinced we need to be the ones sending them there."

"Since when did you grow a conscience? Must I keep reminding you that we are *professional* assassins? The Dusk Legion is being paid, as we always are, to see this job done right. Why would we do anything different now?"

He could see Brenn debating with himself before answering. He wondered if his partner was hiding something; he certainly had spent enough time squirreling himself away with Taryn too.

"This has nothing to do with how I feel," Brenn uttered. "The bottom line is we cannot beat them in a fight. Rehor is more powerful than both of us, and you can see what Taryn did to you. If anything, we are lucky they do not leave us dead in the swamp."

Krel did not believe the excuse. Brenn was overwhelmed by his feelings for the girl. "They cannot stop us. Not if we stand together. It is in our blood. We were born to kill."

"We were," Brenn paused, blowing air between his teeth and rustling the hairs on his face, "but I think they were too."

His blood boiled at the response. Pushing off the tree, Krel began to hike through the forest again. He ignored Brenn calling his name and said nothing when he called for the sellswords to follow.

The four of them marched without a word. League after league, Rehor's orange orb bounced overhead, lighting the path as they made their way westward.

After a time, Krel calmed himself. The endless walking helped. As he considered how he might revisit the conversation about ridding themselves of the sellswords, he heard muffled voices and footsteps farther along in the forest. His mind leaped to what horrors may be coming for them in this inscrutable place before seeing the torchlight bouncing through the trees and hearing the soft nickering of horses.

"Have we really caught up to them?" Brenn halted, half-crouching behind Krel. The shadows danced between the trees as those who may have been the Crimson Sun abruptly stopped their conversation and moved closer to them.

"Who else could be out here?" Krel had to turn his whole body to eye the orange orb hanging over them. He pointed at it and frowned. "Rehor."

"My apologies." The Stuhian quickly snuffed the light and faced the sounds in the forest.

Reaching for his belt knife, Krel remembered the weapon was dropped during the fight with the giant and Stuhian. His other option was his crossbow with the quarrel still prepped. He hoped he had the strength in his arm to hold the weapon steady enough to fire it.

The shadowed figures advanced through the column of trees ahead, tugging at their horses to follow. Their torch lifted into the air as though it might give them better sight. "We do not have our weapons drawn!"

"They are telling the truth," Taryn said, crouching to the ground with Rehor.

Krel eyeballed Taryn. There was no way she could see whether they had weapons drawn at this distance, even if shadows had not been clinging to them like fog.

"We came to speak with you and nothing more."

"It is them. That is Teodor Bacheva. I recognize his voice." Brenn scrunched his face so that his beard rubbed against his mustache. "What are they doing?"

Krel pushed his hair from his eyes and shook his head with disbelief. "It might be a ruse. Then again, I do not see any sign of the Ispolini or Stuhian. Maybe they have not returned. They would be helpless against us without them."

Brenn nodded, pulling his cestuses from his pocket and slipping them over his hands. "You are right. But nothing is to say they are not hiding nearby. They may be waiting to get the jump on us."

"I do not see any sign of them," Taryn said.

"Me neither," Rehor said warily, "but I can barely see my own feet."

"We will not get a better opportunity." Krel stiffened his jaw, feeling a sharp pain in his shoulder. He flared his nostrils, attempting to ignore the discomfort. "We can entertain them to get close, and then we end it."

"Are you there?" Teodor called again. "We do not want any trouble. We just want to talk."

"We will talk," Brenn shouted back.

Rehor twisted his head, the faint light revealing a wild look in his eye. "We have finally reached the end, hmm? Tell me, if the princess dies, can I join the Dusk Legion?"

Krel looked to Rehor. The man had to be insane.

Taryn gradually stood next to the Stuhian. "Why would they run all this way to give up the princess?"

Krel led the way. "We are about to find out."

Rehor cast his magical light once more, increasing its glow until it stole the shadows from each of their faces. It was then that Krel realized how rough they looked. Taryn had a dark bruise lining her swollen jawline, and Brenn had a myriad of cuts and blotches of dried blood across his face. Krel suspected he looked to be in rougher straights than either of them. Only Rehor appeared capable of battle.

As they advanced the short distance, meandering between what trees separated them, Krel raked his eyes over the two representing the Crimson Sun and the princess.

As Taryn claimed, each kept their weapons sheathed or beyond reach. Teodor had his longsword on his side, while the princess kept her billhooks in the leather holders on her back. The armored warrior kept his bladed staff bound with a leather strap on the larger mount. The princess was positioned behind the armored warrior, enveloped in her hooded purple cloak and sandwiched between the two horses as though they could be protective battlements on the top of a castle. He did not see any sign of wear on any of them, yet he knew the princess had taken a dagger to the back during their last meeting.

Teodor kept his chin high, examining each of them with equal measure. His eyes remained on Brenn for the longest period, folding his arms over the inscription of the horse head on his breastplate. Teodor's firm expression told Krel all he needed to know. The Crimson Sun would not forfeit the princess.

He tested them anyway, seeing no reason to be secretive about their motives. "If you leave the princess, we will let you leave with your lives. You are welcome to kill her first if you like."

Teodor glanced at him momentarily, scoffing under his breath, and then addressed Brenn. "We know the Uvil hired you to kill Princess Nitalia. I do not know what they promised you, but you should know that you have been deceived. They plan to give you nothing."

Krel held his teeth together until he thought they would crack from the force. Teodor disregarded him like a nuisance child, clearly not recognizing that he oversaw the assignment. "I don't know what you think you know—"

"I know," Teodor cut him off, "that the Uvil have been targeting factions throughout Maharia, pitting them against one another, making false promises to anyone dumb enough to trust them." He raised his voice at Krel. "Tell me the Uvil did not hire you and I will call you a liar."

With a sneer, Krel inched his hand toward the crossbow hanging from his waist. His chest and shoulder were on fire with the small movement.

"Keep your hands from your weapon," the warrior in the back warned. "We invited you to speak. Hold some reverence for the rules of engagement."

"Do assassins have any honor?" Nitalia asked from the rear. The horses whinnied next to her as though responding to the rhetorical question.

"Krel—wait—" Brenn started, wavering under the gaze of Teodor.

"You are the liar here," Krel said, folding his hand into a fist inches above his crossbow, stepping between Teodor and Brenn so he might capture the mercenary's full attention. His breath clouded the air in front of his face. He considered how swiftly they could kill the three and be done with this wasted conversation. He only had to trust that the three at his back would follow his lead.

"We could have gone all the way to Gaetana, to the king, and told him of your treachery," Teodor said. "We came back."

"You cannot expect us to believe you will not go to the king," Krel said. Teodor and the other man exchanged swift looks but said nothing. "You either did not think you could outrun us, or you turned back for your missing men. Surprise—you found us. Sorry to disappoint."

"That is not true," Princess Nitalia said. "He thought you might be willing to listen to reason. How can you not see you are being manipulated?"

"Oh, I can see your ploy easily enough. You should have kept running, Princess." Krel leaned forward, only to have Teodor stop him by placing a heavy hand on his chest. The sudden pain shot through him, giving him no choice but to step away and cringe. He fought through the agony, meeting Teodor's eye and saying, "You are without half your men. You are a fool to turn around and think to deceive us with your words, as though something so trivial could slow our step."

Teodor lifted his voice. His eyes darkened with every word. "To win this war against the Uvil it will take all four kingdoms of men."

Krel yelled. "What care does Lonmere have for the other three kingdoms? Your laws have done nothing but undermine our lands and people, increasing your own prosperity while we suffer. Do not preach to me about politics like some noble lord. I know the truth."

"The woe of the Lonmereans is of their own creation," the other man said. "I told you this was a bad idea. They are delusional. They cannot even admit to what is already known. We should be on our way."

"We are all Anshedar," Teodor blurted.

"You are scum," Krel snapped back.

"Do you have no love in you? Killing Princess Nitalia will bring nothing but nightmares to the north. You will embolden the enemy!"

Krel caught Taryn moving from the corner of his eye. She must have been as restless as him. "No. You are the enemy! Kill them all!"

The mercenaries in front of him jumped, the warrior in the back reaching for his sovnya and Teodor half-drawing his sword. Krel roared, moving backward instead of forward, expecting Brenn and Taryn to rush forward as they had in the battle at the castle. He was shocked when Brenn's counter halted them all.

"No! Nobody move!" Brenn shouted. "We will not raise a hand against them. We will let the Crimson Sun take their leave."

"As you say," Rehor said with wide eyes darting between Brenn and Krel.

"No!" Krel cried out, unable to believe what his partner was saying. He bared his crooked teeth at Brenn, shouting between them. "We are not going to let them walk away to simply chase them through the Dyndaer again."

"We should think over what the noble thief has told us," Brenn said, keeping his eyes on Teodor.

Teodor let his sword fall back into its scabbard, dipping his head respectfully at Brenn.

"Mother's milk!" Krel grabbed his crossbow and raised it to fire.

"Taryn! Hold him!" Brenn directed.

Taryn's slender arms encircled Krel's torso from the rear to stop his movement, her hands joining across his sternum. His mind numbed with anger as he let go of his weapon. Throwing his head backward, he crashed the back of his skull into her face.

She cried out in surprise as Brenn bellowed at the mercenaries, "Get out of here!"

Taryn released him, falling back. Seeing the Crimson Sun mounting their horses, Krel ignored the pain in his body, grabbing at his crossbow again. He barely touched the handle when an invisible rope of air wrapped around him and pulled him off his feet.

Hitting the ground with a thud, a sting shot through Krel's body, his head slamming against the ground.

Blackness clouded his vision.

Chapter XVIII

BRENN, *The Dusk Legion*

Brenn stood over his partner and grimaced, ready to hold him down if needed. Krel had completely lost his mind, unwilling to take a moment's breath and think before acting. He was fortunate Rehor and Taryn were willing to listen to him.

"Let them go," Brenn said, taking the cestuses from his hands and returning them to his pockets. He shook his head at Krel writhing on the ground. "I told you to wait. What is wrong with you?"

Taryn hunched over behind him, holding her nose, eyes full of fire. "He broke my nose!"

Blood, red like cherries, gushed over her lips.

"I am not done. I am going to break every bone…in your body," Krel threatened, clutching his chest with his hand. Brenn had no doubt that the wound was bleeding again from hitting the ground with such force. The man was out of control.

Taryn eyed Brenn worriedly, cupping her face so the blood pooled nastily in her hands. Droplets squeezed between her fingers, falling to the ground.

"You are not touching her, Krel," Brenn said, looking away from the woman and running a hand through his long hair. "We are going to talk."

Rehor puffed out his cheeks, his circular eyes bouncing between Krel and Brenn. "You two never cease with the excitement, hmm? I mean, I really thought we were going to kill her that time. I admit she is prettier than I thought she would be. I don't know how she achieved such a great complexion when hidden from the sun, but she has nice color…a splendid figure too, if we are being honest, hmm?"

Taryn angled her eyebrows at Rehor.

"Whoa! My apologies. Everything from your hips to your tits would put a harlot to shame, but you are looking a bit rough. I do not mean *any* offense. Positive, I am of that." He lifted his hands defensively, blowing air into one of his cheeks again before guffawing. "If you keep your *nose* to the grindstone, Taryn, you will surpass her beauty. In fact, I am sure you will."

Her voice was muffled behind her hands. "You would be wise not to sleep tonight."

Rehor smiled all the wider, winking. "Oh, I imagine we could find a way to stay awake together, hmm?"

Brenn's heart thumped inside his chest, twisting away from them to watch the Crimson Sun ride westward into the Dyndaer. Teodor rode alone while the warrior and princess sat on the larger warhorse. He could hear the faint howls of one of the men urging the horse along.

"Blood and spit." Taryn's curse brought his attention back. She flung the blood from her hands and wiped more from her face.

"You let them go." Krel coughed, fighting to make headway off the ground. His face warped hatefully at Brenn. "We came all this way, and you let them go. Are you conspiring against me? Against the Dusk Legion? I should gut you where you stand."

"Save your threats for someone less capable. You know my allegiance, but we need to talk about what he said," Brenn said.

"Our quarry is running off in the woods and you want to have a debate?" Krel sneered. "There is no debate. We have a job to do, and every single one of you seems intent on delaying the inevitable."

Brenn scowled at Krel's arrogance. "Nine Lands, Krel! Did you hear nothing that he said? There is no sense in killing the princess if we were deceived. Inciting a war with the rest of the north is not going to bring Lonmere to power. We will bring our home to ruin long before the war has reached our gates!"

"He is a two-faced mercenary and thief! Why would you trust that noble bastard?" Krel hit the ground with a fist.

"Because thinking they baited us to be a distraction to draw armies to the north while they continue their advancement in the south is a reasonable suggestion. The other three kingdoms have been waiting for a reason to wipe us from the north, waiting for us to break their treasured treaty. I think killing members of the royal family would give plenty of motive."

"Fascinating conundrum, it is," Rehor agreed.

Krel clenched his crooked teeth, slowly pushing himself to his feet. Rehor backed away to Taryn's side, eyeing Brenn as though he were questioning whether to knock Krel flat again.

Krel did not seem to notice, harshly speaking to Brenn. "It does not matter."

"How can you say that? We kept asking how the Crimson Sun knew we came to Cavell to kill the princess," Brenn went on.

"What if it was the Uvil who told them? We have been set up since the beginning."

Krel said, "None of that matters. The senate gave the Dusk Legion a job and it is our job to do it. We cannot abandon this assignment and return to Lonmere."

"They will understand," Brenn said. "They will listen to us. The senate needs to know they were manipulated by the Uvil."

"Why? So they can join the war with the other kingdoms of the north? Do you think they are going to believe you? Believe the Crimson Sun told you the truth?" Krel's hand hovered where his dagger should have been on his belt. "Get your head out of your ass."

Brenn bit the inside of his cheek. Krel was blindly following through with their charge. He knew the alternative was treason, but the senate would have to listen to reason. "They will not charge us if—"

"Yes, they will." Krel growled under his breath. "If they do not mark you as a traitor and have you stabbed to death, they will tell you exactly what I am going to tell you. The Crimson Sun knows of our scheme and they will tell the king whether we follow through or not." Krel roughly pointed to the west and then groaned, pulling his arm to his stomach and favoring his wound. His words were forced through the pain. "Do you not see them riding toward Gaetana? They are galloping to the king's doorstep regardless of what we do. We have come too far down this path to turn back. There is no removing the target on our backs. And if we do not bury every single one of them out here in the Dyndaer—if we do not place blame on them for Nitalia's death—we lose."

"She has to be dead first," Rehor whispered in the background.

"The risk is not worth the trouble." Brenn clenched his jaw, hearing the logic in Krel's argument. "We can walk away. Disappear."

"You want to try to outrun the Legion? And go where?" Krel fumed. "We are legionnaires. Even talking about desertion is grounds for execution. Speak to me like that again, and I will see you punished for it."

Brenn sighed, noticing Rehor and Taryn watching with fascination.

Silence filled the woods.

Rehor piped up again, rubbing his hands together greedily. "A lot of words and not much to say for a conclusion. If we are voting, I am personally in favor of killing her, considering that is why I am here. You know, to get that sweet, sweet silver and all."

With a low growl, Krel stumbled to his feet and after the Crimson Sun. "We are not voting."

With reluctance and rattled nerves, Brenn followed Krel, if anything, to give himself more time to think. With Krel's logic so entrenched in his head, he could think of little else but killing the princess and leaving the Crimson Sun to take the blame. Though the longer Brenn entertained the idea, the less the probability of success became.

For the rest of the evening and through the night, they pushed forward without rest. The lack of sleep only added to Brenn's irritation. League after league, repeatedly, he would play through scenarios of battling the mercenaries and killing the princess; even in his musings, he did not see himself coming out of the fight victorious. They were too injured, too exhausted, and too divided to contend against the Crimson Sun.

Despite his concerns, he did not attempt to bring up the topic with Krel again. His partner would not hear of it, leading their single-file line through the Dyndaer in silence, searching for any sign of the mercenaries. The only audible sound until they reached the river was Krel's frequent cursing whenever he regularly shot angry looks over his shoulder at Brenn, blaming him for letting the Crimson Sun escape again.

Keeping to the end of the line, Brenn watched Taryn weave in front of him as they walked southward along the water's edge. She mumbled about her broken nose off and on until she seemed to realize no one was going to do anything about her injury. Even Rehor did not offer a remedy for her pain. Instead, he strolled behind Krel with a certain gleam in his eye, showing an increased bounce in his step since they decided to pursue the princess.

Whether Rehor was excited that Krel was no longer attributing their continued failure to his lack of participation, or he was simply thrilled to kill the princess as he pronounced, Brenn could not read the Stuhian at all. It was about the time they finally found a bridge crossing over a river to the west that Rehor broke the silence with a series of questions about the Dusk Legion.

"What do you have to do in order to become a legionnaire, hmm?" Rehor cooed, tilting his head to catch the sun's light between the shaded the clouds, marking the break of morning. After being absent of the sun for weeks, Brenn slowed down hoping to see it in full before strolling into the next patch of the Dyndaer.

Krel passed by cottonwoods lining the bank of the cold river flowing south. His hand was flattened against his chest covering his hidden knife wound, as though it continued to bleed. No one had checked the injury for some time. He turned ever so slightly, giving sight to his pale face, a telltale sign of his exhaustion.

"You do not listen well, do you? You are a sellsword and will not be joining the Legion. Never in my life have I met anyone so broken from reality," Krel griped, eyeing a horse's hoofprint in the mud at his feet. Brenn watched him dip down and touch the soil with his fingers, discovering the track was hard. Next to the mark was an enlarged print of a bare foot. Brenn did not have to near him to see the track could only belong to the Ispolini. Krel flared his nostrils, glaring at the markings. "They are almost half a day ahead of us, and it looks like their companions have caught up to them." Krel curled his lip at Rehor. "You are lucky you have made it this far with us."

"Death has a way of avoiding me." Rehor shrugged, moving uncomfortably close to Krel. "So I am hearing you say that listening is a prime requisite for the position. I think I could manage if given the right incentive, you know? How is the pay with the Legion? Do they pay with coin, power, prestige…"

"He never stops," Taryn muttered under her breath next to Brenn. He shifted his gaze to meet her brown eyes. Moisture glossed her eyes, and her pink cheeks gave the impression she had been crying once more. Brenn hurriedly turned away from her. He promised her that he would keep her safe, but he certainly had no interest in entertaining her commentary, let alone her emotions.

He heard her heavy sigh as he twisted back to Krel and Rehor, who ventured farther into the forest. The Lightbringer rose higher and higher in the sky. His light was infinite, inching across the sky and shining through this portion of the trees like a beacon of amity between him and the world below.

The trickling water of the river faded behind them, leaving Brenn with a feeling of homesickness, missing the sound of the ocean north of Lonmere. Because of the city's location, he could not see the water beyond the mountains, but the salt would always be thick on the air. He would often climb to the mountaintops to think while watching the waves clash together.

Krel steadied the crossbow hanging at his belt and attempted to silence Rehor as he continued to nag him with questions. "Why don't we focus on killing the princess and forget about your fantasy of becoming a legionnaire?"

Rehor widened his eyes at the suggestion and went on. "Imagine that you have the final say in who enlists, I cannot. Are you not just another minion? I think if you put in a good word—tell them how I aided you at the castle and protected you in the woods—work together someday as equals, we might, hmm?"

"Why are you so interested in being part of the Dusk Legion? You are not even from Lonmere," Brenn responded, looking over the smooth water of the river flowing under the bridge. "I thought you wanted to go back home."

"Oh, I plan to go back home. Eventually," Rehor said, wiggling his eyebrows at Krel. "But the Legion sounds like a worthwhile experience."

"Being a legionnaire is for life," Krel said, squinting at Brenn instead of Rehor while he spoke. "You do not get to quit whenever you want. You fight for them until they retire you."

"Retire you," Rehor repeated. His reiteration sounded more like a statement than a question.

"You mean they kill you?" Taryn asked.

"They provide a good life for you while you are alive," Krel said. "We all have to die sometime. Might as well be at the hand of those who gave you everything in life."

"Do you give up your life freely? How do you know who has been sent to kill you?" Rehor asked. "Do you just take them at their word, kneel down, and—" He made a cutting motion across his throat. "Sounds rather anticlimactic, hmm?"

"No, you fight, if you are able," Brenn answered. "If you survive, you could get lucky enough to be shielded by the guild and mature to old age until a natural death takes you. Though they usually send their best to finish the job."

Rehor smiled impishly, winking at Brenn. "How interesting."

Chapter XIX

KREL, *The Dusk Legion*

Krel woke before dusk, hearing Taryn creeping beyond their makeshift camp and into the thinning woods. He tilted his head ever so slightly, squinting through the haze of the gloomy light, watching her skulk over Rehor and Brenn's sleeping bodies. Her footsteps were less quiet as she shuffled northward through the brush.

Sitting up, he gnawed at the frosty hairs on his bottom lip and pulled his crossbow close to check that the bolt was still loaded. In his heart, he knew she would attempt to escape eventually, but he had thought she would flee with Rehor. She had guts trying to navigate the Dyndaer on her own.

Not bothering to wake up the other two men, Krel rolled over and pulled himself to his feet. He would take care of her himself.

As she darted farther into the trees, he silently cursed himself for allowing them to settle down for a few hours of rest. He should have expected her to try once they were on the other side of the river, but even now her fortitude surprised him. The fatigue they each felt was beyond anything he thought she would be able to handle.

He had underestimated her.

The wintry chill stung at his eyes and stiffened his already hardened muscles, but he would be damned if the tart made a fool of them.

By a strange grey glow permeating the trees where the moon hung behind a mist of clouds, Krel followed Taryn. He walked on his toes, careful not to put any weight down before he was certain the land beneath his feet was absent of brush or wood to give away his position.

She slipped smoothly in and out of the trees, a shadow against the brown and green backdrop of trees and foliage. She dipped under branches and slowly climbed over rocks, only pausing occasionally to check the landscape ahead of her. Not once did he see her look over her shoulder.

A bit farther and he would steal her life.

The trees continued to thin the longer he roved behind her, and soon he realized that he might not be able to physically catch her without shooting her down first. Yet he did not want to fire the quarrel without a clear shot. Reloading the crossbow with his injury would be slow. If he missed and spooked her, she would run quicker than he could give chase.

As a small clearing came into view ahead, Taryn suddenly sprinted forward out of sight, the hanging willows bordering the glade blocking Krel's view.

"Nine Lands," he muttered, realizing she must have caught on to him. He stumbled after her, hobbling to keep from jostling his left side too much, and sprang into the grassland.

Moonlight faded with the coming of dawn, lighting up the area enough that he would have been able to see someone running across its length. He gritted his teeth when seeing nothing but half-dead grass.

He stalked forward a few steps with his crossbow held at his waist at the ready. He would pierce her flesh, have his way with her, and then slit her throat with her own blade.

"What are you doing here?" Taryn's tone was without fear, rising from behind him once he made it to the center of the glade. He had not heard a sound and certainly had not seen her approach.

He began to turn around, the crossbow angled to shoot through her at the first opportunity.

"Don't move, Krel. Tell me what you are doing out here," Taryn said, "or I swear to the gods I will plant this dagger in the back of your head."

"I would expect nothing less from a little trull like you." Krel glared at the landscape ahead of him, pausing his movements. "Did you not learn the first time? You need more than a single dagger to stop me."

"Answer the question. Why are you out here?"

"Why are *you* out here?" he snapped back, tensing his fingers around the grip of his crossbow.

"Taking a piss," Taryn snipped.

"A long way to roam to empty your bladder," he replied.

"Not when I have someone following me the moment I step away from my bedroll," she said, her tone almost taunting. "So why are you trailing me? Were you trying to get a peek? Sorry to disappoint, but I am not interested."

"Ha!" Krel relaxed his hand, taking the chance to turn around to face her. Taryn met him from over an arm's length away, her dagger pulled up by her ear and ready to be thrown. He curled his lip, peering into her brown eyes. "I hardly care what you are interested in. You humped Rehor and Brenn in less than half a fortnight. I think it is time for my turn."

He took a step closer, flashing his teeth at her.

"Leave me alone, Krel," she said, stepping away from him. She clambered over a patch of grass and somehow kept her balance. Her dagger hand dipped down to her side as she regained her footing. Her tone pitched. "I am not going to tell you again."

He eyed the dagger, advancing at her with a hungry growl. "You do not have the guts."

Krel hardly registered her movement before the sensation of the blade lodged in his gut halted him, his right hand shakily gripping the hilt of the dagger.

Blood oozed from the wound.

He snarled, instinctively grabbing his crossbow and firing at the wide-eyed bitch from his hip.

"No—" she barely screamed before the bolt ripped through her right thigh. Her body lurched in shock, her slender fingers wrapping around her leg. "Brenn!"

He did not wait for her to finish her cry, shuffling forward. Letting go of his crossbow, he punched her squarely in her broken nose.

Whatever sound that spilled from her mouth was unintelligible but was music in comparison to the crunch of her nose snapping under the weight of his fist. Taryn's head rocked back, lifting her feet from the ground. She crashed against the firm soil, the wilting grasses doing little to break her fall.

She sounded like death on a battlefield, turning her head side to side while covering her face with both hands as though she expected another fist to rain down on top of her. Krel dropped to his knees, releasing the knife handle protruding from his gut. He reached down to spread her legs.

She did not fight him, completely dazed.

"I said it was my turn," he snarled.

He grabbed the underside of her trousers and jerked them toward her knees so that her bare skin was exposed to the cold. The fabric bent her legs up around him and he scooted forward on his knees, unfastening his own pants.

"No. Stop. Stop!" Taryn wept angry tears, her words suggesting her wits were coming back after being stunned by the blow. An arm flailed toward him, misguided and wild, missing him while her other hand attempted to protect herself from being plowed.

She kicked feebly, hitting the side of his shoulder with her heel, sending a shock of pain reeling down his arm to his gut. He fought against the ache searing through him and leaned to the side to avoid her weak attempt at hitting him again.

Grabbing her right leg in his left hand, he trailed along her smooth skin until he found the puncture wound from his crossbow bolt. He shoved his finger into her flesh. The projectile had ripped straight through her thigh. Her scream echoed through the glade until it broke into a hollow strain for air.

"You are going to stop fighting," Krel roared, pushing his finger deeper. She threw her head back, slamming her skull into the ground, crying out again. He could see tears flooding her cheeks in dawn's burgeoning light. He grabbed the dagger and pulled it from his stomach with his free hand, his adrenaline numbing the pain. Blood immediately leaked down his waist and leg. He did not care. She had probably already killed him. He would grant her the same luxury. "By the gods, if you don't stop, I am going to use this dagger instead. Tell me how you want it."

Her perfect white teeth were a prison for her tongue as she lifted her head to meet his eye, withstanding her own agony to glare at him for only a moment.

"That is what I thought."

"You lowlife jackhole," she wheezed.

Krel rocked forward intending to have his way when he suddenly heard the rustling of grass. Heavy footsteps shook the ground under his knees. He did not have time to even turn his head when an iron-plated fist smashed across his cheek.

He somersaulted sideways over Taryn's leg with his own pants wrapped around his ankles. Skidding through mounds of grass and dirt, he finally stopped in a clump with his knees tucked and his ass facing the moon. The injuries in his chest and gut burned, but they were nothing compared to the fire in his mouth as he spit out a handful of teeth from his bloodied lips.

"Taryn," he heard Brenn's familiar tone.

Krel spit out a mouthful of saliva and blood, fighting to stand to his feet. Unable to muster the strength, he fell back onto his painful arm, struggling to pull up his britches with his free hand. He could not get a grip on the fabric.

"Brenn," he coughed. "She was trying to run away."

He eyed his partner, who stood over Taryn. An orange orb of light hovered over his shoulder, and farther behind stood Rehor wrapped in his robes. The dragon-man's wide eyes looked exceptionally white in the dim light of the glade.

"I—I was not," Taryn said, choking on her own tears and attempting to pull at her clothes. Blood stained everything from her upper lip to her chin. Her nose looked permanently crooked. She stifled a moan and grabbed at her leg. "He shot me."

"After you plunged your dagger into me," Krel said, looking to see where the weapon might have gone. When he did not see it, he lifted the tail of his shirt to reveal the gaping gash along his gut. His insides were spilling out.

"You forced yourself on me," she cried.

"You cannot force yourself on a trull," he snorted, looking to Rehor and Brenn with a half-smile, blood dribbling from his lower lip. "Alright. Enough of this nonsense. Kill her and be done with it, Brenn, and we can be on our way." He motioned for Rehor to come closer. "What do you have to fix me up? I am going to need some new bandages."

No one moved. Brenn flexed uncomfortably over Taryn, looking at her and then him. The woman's eyes were laced with fear.

Manipulative bitch.

"Come on," Krel said. "She is nothing. Give her a good crack over the skull and send her to wander the Netherworld with her sister."

"No honor among assassins, right?" Taryn said softly, tilting her head at Brenn, lip quivering.

"What?" Krel angled his eyebrows.

Brenn dipped his chin at her. "Rehor. Kill him."

"With pleasure," Rehor replied with a soft smile.

"No," Krel said, shaking his head. The dragon-man approached, a shadow darkening his visage. Krel shouted at Brenn as he neared. "You cannot do this. We are part of the Dusk Legion. We are partners! Brenn, are you listening to me? Brenn!"

He could see the wide-shouldered fighter kneel to Taryn behind Rehor, ignoring him.

The Stuhian wove his hands in the air, his face showing the slightest signs of aging as he cast Koldovstvo. "Let's give you a taste of what is to come, hmm? Let me introduce you to the *Nocnica*, the hag of the Netherworld."

The fabric of space frayed in front of Krel, a frozen mist fanning from nothingness as another dimension shimmered into existence. His heart quickened in his chest, horror filling him before a ghastly shriek erupted from the other side. The coldness that filtered through stung at Krel's skin as Rehor summoned some ghostly being from the depths of the icy wasteland of the dead.

The wraithlike naked form of a female that emerged from the mist captivated Krel, holding his body rigid where he kneeled against the glade. She was nearly translucent with coils of energy spiraling behind her. The lifeless eyes locked onto him before she fully surfaced into the physical world, the black lips and hollowed nose only adding to the haunting look of the undead atrocity.

He gaped, unable to speak, hearing the muted shouts of Brenn somewhere in the distance. No longer could he see the dragon-man or Taryn; his attention was seized by the Nocnica. Her thin lips stretched large enough to swallow him, shrieking again. He was suddenly on his back on the ground and she straddled him, her breasts hovering over him, a clawed fingertip reaching for his forehead.

Death hurt.

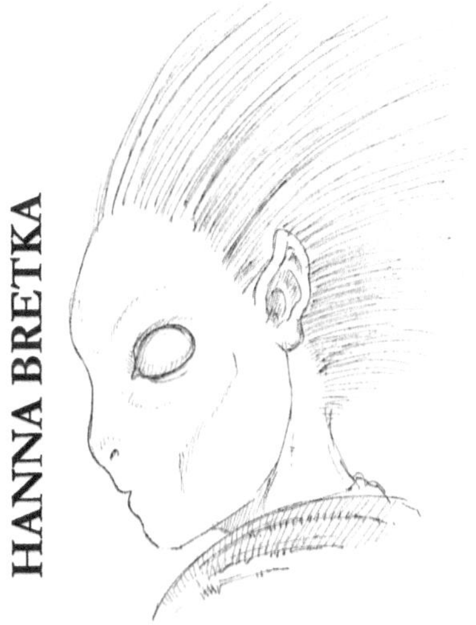

Chapter XX

BRENN, *The Dusk Legion*

At Rehor's command, the screeching Nocnica was dragged back to the Netherworld through a shimmering gateway by some unseen energy, leaving the distorted, half-decayed curled corpse of Krel lying among the dying grasses. The mixture of morning light and night shadows blended in the firmament above, casting an eerie gloom over them as the Nocnica's bloodcurdling scream faded from the glade.

Brenn's instinct was to hurry to Krel, but even at a distance, the twisted corpse of his partner told him he did not want to see the final expression captured on the assassin's face. Even in death, the muscles were cricked every which way, limbs wrapped awkwardly underneath the body, his head bent unnaturally. For a moment, Brenn stared at the whitish color of Krel's skin against his black strands of hair. The demon Rehor had summoned from the other side of the veil had done its part to strip Krel of all life before sending his spirit to the Netherworld.

"Is it gone?" Taryn wriggled at his feet in an attempt to pull her trousers to her waist. As the fabric slipped over the wound in her leg, a muffled moan aired from her pursed lips. She tore off a strip of material from the bottom of her shirt to tie around her leg. She sucked in air, pressing her knee to her forehead as she tightened the piece of cloth.

"Yeah." Brenn tensed his jaw, dropping his eyes to the brown-eyed beauty. Half a day ago, he was prepared to never speak to her again, and now he felt the urge to whisk her away and keep her safe. While he did not have the confidence to protect her, the ire he felt toward her for deceiving him—seducing him and using the borra leaf to elicit the truth from him—had vanished. He hoped she would forgive him, too, considering he did not save her from Krel as promised. "I am sorry this happened to you, Taryn."

She turned her eyes away.

"I have returned the Nocnica to the Netherworld. I suspect Krel will be distraught by the number of hags roaming the frozen wasteland, hmm?" The dragon-man dusted off his hands as though the strain of summoning demons was all in a day's work. He bowed nonchalantly to Taryn as she looked up at him. "As always, I am at your service."

"Thank you," she said.

Brenn searched Rehor's face, seeing only a few wrinkles added, indicating the little amount of his own life he drained when casting the ancient magic. His eyes traced briefly to Krel again, and then he returned his gaze to the redheaded man.

"I have never seen anyone wield such power before in my life. If all Stuhia are this strong, it is a wonder the Anshedar have any influence in the north. You are a god among men." Brenn ran his hands through his hair, turning around in the glade. "I do not understand your magic. I watched you age yourself against the bauk and chort, and here you have summoned demons from the other side. I thought powerful spells would place a Stuhian in his grave."

"Some will. A simple summoning will only take a couple of years. Nothing I cannot readily acquire once more," Rehor said, folding his hands in front of him rather formally. "Are you asking me to explain the complexities of Koldovstvo to you while we stand here in the light of the rising sun? The most romantic way to spend our time together, it is not." Rehor puffed up one of his cheeks, twisting around to admire the patch of land amid the far-reaching forest. A breeze swept through the trees to the north, bringing the smell of morning with it. The sky seemed to lighten more as Rehor went on. "If I must educate you about the ancient magic, know that our bloodlines give us access to certain types of magic, whether that be profane, sacred, void, or primal. Profane magic is my gift, which among my own would classify me as an Eretik. A type of magic that is frowned upon, really. The very reason I have kept my feet from home all these years. Should I go on?"

"Are all Stuhia as strong as you?" Taryn asked.

"Many are, yes," Rehor replied. "I can assure you Eisliev Kluk would tear me to pieces in a fight."

Brenn shook his head, noticing Taryn stayed on her haunches at his feet. Blood colored the cloth around her thigh, but she ignored it. Instead, she wiped the blood from her face with her sleeve, careful not to touch her nose. The dried tears on her cheeks had splotched the stained crimson.

"That is why you gave him the ring," Brenn clarified with a nod. "Is he an enemy?"

"He is not my enemy," Rehor said. "Are there other questions about Koldovstvo I should answer? Do you need to know where our magic comes from? How it weaves through our blood to take shape in the physical world? Should I explain the very skeins of Aenar and how they are woven into Thrice Nine Lands to give us life? How about how we dragon-men once worked with the skin-switchers of Anaerfell to protect those monuments that gifted us with breath and promised us the hereafter?" Rehor stared strangely at Taryn. "Know more than most, I do. Though what use the information would be to you, I cannot say."

"I do not need a lecture," Brenn decided, rubbing his temples. He did not need to know the vast knowledge of the universe, information that had no business in the minds of mortals. He only wanted to know how his simple command to kill Krel led to such horror. "You surely could have been more benign in your execution."

"True." Rehor straightened his back, folding his arms across his chest. He grimaced, still looking at Taryn, who visibly gritted her teeth at Brenn's comment. Rehor said, "You spend a lot of time thinking about what *could've* or *should've* happened, hmm? Can you not accept that things simply go the way they were meant to go?"

Brenn slowly blinked at Rehor. "You mean Krel was meant to die?"

"Oh, he would have been dead before this adventure was complete, I guarantee you," Rehor replied.

Taryn groaned again, touching her nose with her fingertips. She rubbed either side, pushing gently and wheezing in response to the tenderness.

"What is that supposed to mean?" Brenn asked.

Shifting in his robes, the Stuhian studied him and then sighed heavily. He motioned for Brenn and Taryn to come closer, although he was the one who closed the distance between them. Once he was near enough for Brenn to count the red bristles on his upper lip, the dragon-man cast his round eyes back and forth between them. He let out another long breath, causing mist to dance across the air.

He whispered, "Time for me to come clean, I think it is, hmm? We have played this charade long enough, and while the two of you have performed beautifully, I understand neither of you knew the pretense?"

Brenn angled his brow in confusion. "What in the Nine Lands are you talking about?"

Rehor combed his hair back, then shook a finger at Brenn. "I like your spirit, so I am going to say this to you." He looked over his shoulder again to scan the clearing before leaning forward. "But if you do anything untoward or troublesome, I am going to have to return to my prescribed script, hmm? I really do not want to do that."

The pop of Taryn's nose being realigned followed her keened squeal, drawing Brenn's attention. He was almost thankful for the distraction, pulling him away from Rehor's insane rambling.

The young woman shook her hands, murmuring under her breath to distract from the sudden pain that was likely trailing up to her eyeballs. "Bad idea," she wailed with tears flooding down her cheeks again. She folded herself over again, grabbing handfuls of her jumbled hair. "Bad idea. Bad idea. Oh, gods. That hurts."

With a slow breath, Brenn faced Rehor again. The dragon-man's blue eyes were unblinking, ever-watching him, with his cheeks bulging and red. He might have been holding his breath since speaking his last words. "I do not think there is anything you could say, Rehor, that would—"

"I'm a legionnaire," Rehor blurted, smacking his lips closed again as quickly as they had opened. Brenn's breath caught in his throat, a knot the size of a fist swelling up from the base. He could not even mouth a question before Rehor spoke again. "That is to say, I have been a part of the Dusk Legion since before you picked me up in Egis with the two sisters. I was waiting for you since you left Lonmere. Sent me to retire you and Krel, the Dusk Legion did, hmm?"

Taryn turned her eyes upward, taken by Rehor's admission. "You are part of the Dusk Legion? All this time? Then what was all that talk about wanting to be a legionnaire?"

"A diversion," Rehor answered.

"Wait," Brenn backed away from Rehor, his fists clenching defensively. *He was sent to kill them?* He nearly tripped over Taryn in his hurry to put some distance between himself and the Stuhian.

"No, no, no, no," Rehor hurried his speech, raising his hands to Brenn to slow his movements. "I am not going to kill you. Not today, anyway. The senate wanted everyone exterminated after the mission was complete to keep it concealed."

"I have served the Dusk Legion for almost ten years; I do not know you," Brenn said, looking back to Krel lying dead in the dirt. He was not going to end up like his partner. "You are lying."

"Lying, I am not. Very few know me," Rehor insisted. "I would be terrible at retiring assassins if my identity was shared throughout the guild, hmm? Here, look." Rehor turned around and lifted the hair off the back of his neck. An orange orb of light sprang into existence, revealing the upside-down triangle engraved on his skin.

Brenn gasped. He, indeed, bore the mark of the Dusk Legion.

"Cock and pie," Brenn cursed. "All this time."

"Ah, yes. Doing this since before you were born, I have been," Rehor said, turning around. He gestured to the ground before sitting cross-legged across from Taryn, seemingly unconcerned by the corpse sprawled out a few feet away. The glow of his magical sphere illuminated the side of his face. "If we are being honest, you are not the only one I have let go free, hmm? Interesting, it is, to see how some live their lives," he paused, "when given another chance at life."

"You really are not going to kill us?" Taryn asked.

Rehor lifted his eyebrows. "Have you not been listening? I like you two lovebirds." He pointed to Krel, scrunching up his face with disgust. "Him, on the other hand—well, he was an ass, hmm?"

Brenn picked at his lip with his fingers, trying to wrap his mind around Rehor's confession. He and Krel thought they were in control, selecting the hired hands to join them on this mission; yet Rehor somehow put himself in the right place at the right time. Brenn's mind buzzed, trying to determine what was real and what was contrived. "What about Princess Nitalia? And the Crimson Sun? And the Uvil?"

"Oh," Rehor said, picking at his nose before answering, "I am afraid we are not quite done with all that, hmm? Princess Nitalia has been ordered to be killed, though I think the Crimson Sun is correct in assuming the entire plot is being arranged by the Uvil."

"After all of this," Taryn strained her voice, "we are going to attempt to kill the princess? I am not sure I can even walk."

"We have no reason to kill the princess," Brenn argued, "particularly if Taryn and I are planning to avoid the Dusk Legion anyhow."

"Yet running from the Legion, I will not be," Rehor said, "and I am meant to report that you were slaughtered after the mission was accomplished. Considering you cannot be *dead* until she is dead, we must see her to an early grave, hmm?"

"Blood and spit," Taryn said. "Do you still plan on making it look like the Crimson Sun killed her?"

"I think that is rather improbable, hmm?" Rehor shook his head, his curls bouncing wildly. "The Crimson Sun knows each of our faces. They must be dealt with fully for us to clear all accountability from ourselves and the Dusk Legion."

Brenn dropped next to Taryn. "How are we supposed to defeat the Crimson Sun?"

Rehor shrugged his shoulders. "She must die." He scrambled to his feet again and approached Krel's body, pulling the bag of

Gaetanean coins from his belt. He then turned around and tossed them at Taryn's feet. "You two will have a bag full of Gaetanean silver to start your lives with if we can figure it out."

Taryn grabbed the bag and peered inside its dark folds. Brenn watched her count for a bit before she interrupted her count. "I have never seen so much silver. Krel was carrying this on him the whole time?"

Brenn did not answer her, not wanting to point out the silver was originally meant to be used to frame her for the princess's death.

"Can we delay her death for a bit?" he asked.

"Possibly," Rehor replied.

"Can you really see without light?" Brenn asked.

"As though it were day," Taryn said.

Brenn clicked his tongue. "I might have a plan."

Chapter XXI

TYR, *The Crimson Sun*

ife was chaos.

The thought pervaded his mind as his axe slammed into the thick hide of the boarish creature. Its clawed fists raked against the ground, its horned head falling limp. Tyr jerked the two-handed axe from its split spine and quickened his steps to catch a second one on the end of his blade. Dark blood sprayed as his axe cut into the jowl of the monster.

Its roar was silenced.

"What are these?" Tyr barked, spinning to face the trees around them, ready for another to materialize from the wide trunks. The four-legged monsters were ethereal one moment and a physical threat the next. Even the Witiko, as large as any Ispolini, that he slaughtered in the Deep did not seem as perilous. Yet the dozen dead at his feet indicated his ease in trouncing them. The monsters were no match for his sheer size and strength, but if caught off guard, he guessed any one of them might get the upper hand.

"How should I know?" Eisliev lifted an eyebrow, standing calmly among the trees behind him. The Stuhian had not lifted a finger against the creatures, letting Tyr cut them down one by one. "They do not need a name for you to split their skulls."

Tyr scowled at the dragon-man.

"Glare all you want with that ugly mug. You wanted to abandon the princess, venture off to spill blood and clear your head, so…" Eisliev waved his hand dismissively at the carcasses, "…have at it."

Another beast burst from a poplar tree, the curled horns curving on each side of its elongated face. It roared, flashing its yellow fangs, and rushed him. Tyr gripped the long handle of his axe and swung, hitting the beast in the left foreleg. The creature lifted off the ground with the momentum, the blade almost cleaving off the limb before flinging the monster into another tree. In three strides, Tyr reached the spot where it landed and hacked his axe into its side like he was chopping wood.

With its fading breath, another horned beast burst from the bark in front of Tyr's face, snapping its jaws inches from his face. Pulling back, he released his weapon and caught the beast by either horn. With a snarl, he pulled the beast to him so that it fully materialized. The creature kicked its faun legs in an attempt to gain footing, wildly gnashing at him. Tyr jerked the beast off the ground and smashed his head into its center eye, dazing it, and then swung it by the horns into the side of the tree. Its insides cracked under the force.

Tyr roared, reaching for his axe and splitting the monster in two as it meekly attempted to drag itself away from him.

Suddenly, something else skittered above Tyr in a black poplar tree. He snapped his head toward the sound to see a different creature, hunched with clawed feet, leap from branch to branch, oak to planer, and dart deeper into the woods. He watched the fiend until it was gone from sight, swallowed by the darkness of the Dyndaer.

Beyond the thinning branches of the trees, the coming morning lit the heavens, the pitch of night fading to a soft blue.

He shifted his gaze to the three-eyed corpse at his feet. "I think we are done."

"I personally thought we were done once we crossed the river. The persistence of these mindless brutes is becoming a nuisance," Eisliev said, shuffling his red robes around his shoulders. He loomed closer, scraping the edge of his nose with his knuckle and glancing at the gore at his feet. "I suppose as long as we do not bump into a vila, we should reach Teodor in time to leave this cursed forest."

"Vila? You mean the maidens of Marheena?" Tyr breathed heavily through his nose, his chest rising and falling rapidly with each word. He cleaned the edge of his axe on the fur of the monster at his feet, still hearing his heartbeat thumping in his ears. He had not heard of the dryads since he was a child, fabled in stories told by the Elders. They were said to be creations of the Frozen Witch who did her will and channeled the magic of dragon-men without cost. "They are from the old world, remnants of a time when only dragons, rusalki, and the gods know what else roamed Aenar. I did not know any remained on Aenar."

"They are no deader than the dragons," Eisliev told him. "Is your brain so small you think all that exists is what you can see?"

Tyr scowled, noticing he had ripped open the wound on his arm again from the battle with the simargl. He frowned as he touched the blood, smearing it down his bicep. "Bah! I have enough to worry over as it is. The gods did not create mortals to be all-knowing for a reason."

Eisliev scoffed. "Speak for yourself. Not all of us are threatened by knowledge."

Not having the energy to bicker with Eisliev again, Tyr strapped the axe to his back and started off through the trees in hopes of finding Teodor and the others.

Eisliev trailed close behind.

Tyr was not sure how far they traveled in silence, having little to say to one another. He fought back thoughts of home and family, but the harder he resisted the quicker they came.

The seasons of the east were different than those on Tundris Mor, where the shorter summers were like autumn and the long winters were akin to death. His bare feet kicked through the withering leaves that nested on the ground, sending debris of red, yellow, and orange foliage out in front of him. Never had he seen so many trees in one place. Even standing in the Dyndaer, he was dumbfounded how piles of leaves sat at his feet while a dense canopy still existed above his head to withhold the light of day.

Tundris Mor was better known for its barren lands laden with ice and rock than its forests. In his heart, he had an eagerness to return to the lands from which he was banished, but the truth was that nothing was left for him back home. His father was in Lairhein. His mother and sister were dead. And before Eisliev, the concept of "friend" never existed; even in the Stuhian's company, he was not sure he could call the should-be-king a friend. He had reservations about even calling him an ally.

With a frown, he kicked at the leaves again. He spent most of his time in thought, and he recognized that he was rarely bound to rationality. To think he was ready to embrace death upon being banished from home a year ago gave him pause. For now, he traipsed outside death's reach, with the hope of restoring some sense of the afterlife before being sent to it. While he knew Eisliev was more motivated by revenge against his enemy, Dagmar Kaligula, than sending demons back to the Netherworld, Tyr had to hope the Stuhian would follow through with the promises he made. He needed to find the Blood Cascade.

Though even if his sister and mother were restored, Tyr was skeptical that he would ever stop fighting. He did not know anything but the thrill of battle and bloodlust.

"Stand steadfast," Eisliev said, pointing at a clearing to their right. "Someone has been here recently."

Tyr rubbed his eyes and shook his mane of red hair. For Eisliev to notice anything before he did was nearly insulting. The dragon-man was not a natural tracker like he was, often drifting into the shadow world of Klukas to scout ahead; his attentiveness usually lacked in comparison. Tyr needed to keep his mind from wandering so aimlessly.

Scanning the brush at the edge of the clearing, Tyr grumbled under his breath before attempting to speak in a deep, calm tone. "I see that, Eisliev. Though I do not see any sign of Teodor, Seigfeld, or the princess."

Eisliev curled his lip at the comment and shook his head. "Someone passed through the glade." He turned away from Tyr and stepped beyond the tree line into the open space. The already ruined grass, half-dead from the onslaught of cold weather, was further crushed underneath his boots as he stepped beneath the yellow glow hanging in the sky. Eisliev did not even acknowledge the Lightbringer above him, his eyes already fixated on something lying in the grass ahead.

Tyr, on the other hand, welcomed the warm light on his face. The chill of the Dyndaer did not impact him like it might the Anshedar that inhabited Maharia, but he would not shy away from the added warmth brought to him by the sun.

"We have a body over here," Eisliev said, hurrying his pace so that his robes made a swooshing sound against the grass as he moved. His footsteps were heavy, adding to the markings spread throughout the area.

"What happened?" he asked.

"I don't know, Tyr," Eisliev said. "I have been with you, remember?"

Tyr bit his tongue at the sarcastic tone and followed the Stuhian, seeing the twisted corpse in the middle of the meadow. The thick black beard and muddled hair were not unfamiliar to Tyr. Despite the skin being a shade paler than usual, he recognized the face as belonging to one of the assassins.

"Bah! How did he get around us? We should have been half a day ahead of the Dusk Legion at least," Tyr said.

Eisliev eyed him with dismay. "You find a corpse with the body twisted and broken, the face carved with fright, and you want to know why he was less lost than us?" Eisliev pointed off into the distance. "We spent half a day heading north up the river before we doubled back to find the bridge. Be glad he came by this clearing before we did." Eisliev looked over his shoulder. "I saw more blood back that way."

"I will have a look." Tyr gritted his teeth and turned away. He did not want to look at the mangled body at his feet anyway. Sure enough, after skimming the area, he caught sight of dried blood on several blades of grass. He continued to work his way around the glade, finding more splatters of blood, discovering a bolt lodged in the soil some distance away, and lastly, he came by a few teeth scattered in the grass.

"Is he missing teeth?" Tyr asked, lifting his eyes to Eisliev.

"If you want to put your fingers in his mouth and check, I will not stop you," Eisliev replied, kneeling by the corpse.

With a sigh, Tyr made his way back to Eisliev, coming closer to the corpse than he wanted. "Well, I found teeth. And there are also signs of a struggle and footprints heading back the way we came. Might have been the other assassins retreating from whatever did this."

"If they were with him at all." Eisliev crossed his arms, shaking his head.

Tyr followed Eisliev's line of sight. "Wait! Why are his pants around his ankles?"

Eisliev raised an eyebrow. "I do not know, Tyr, and I am not sure I want to. Though I think it is safe to assume whatever happened here would probably make a great story. Regardless, he is dead, and we are wasting time."

Tyr sucked in a breath, seeing a red-tailed hawk cry out overhead, gliding over the glade to the south. The wind etched through the top of the trees as Eisliev made his way westward to exit the glade. "Do you think he was trying to take a piss and a beast attacked him and knocked out his teeth? He must have gotten one shot off, right?"

He kept walking.

"Eisliev? Do you think it was a rusalki? Did one of those water nymphs try to have their way with him?" Tyr boomed.

No response.

"Eisliev! The tracks head back south," Tyr said, trailing behind the dragon-man.

"Yes, but Teodor would not be heading south. He wanted to go to Gaetana," Eisliev replied. "And that is northwest along with the end of the forest. I would prefer to return to Tamarri and get an assignment that will bring us closer to the Kadari and Dagmar. We are wasting valuable time." He grumbled. "With any luck, they were able to ride ahead on their horses and are already done with this wasted journey."

Tyr ran his hand along the scar on his arm, taking one more look at the corpse behind them. He did not have any interest in sticking around in the forest either, but he was not sure their adventure against the Kadari would be any less dangerous.

Chapter XXII

TEODOR, *The Crimson Sun*

Teodor was awoken by Seigfeld, feeling more tired than the day before. They had traveled late into the night as though the assassins were clawing at their backs, even though the Dusk Legion had not been seen since crossing the river. Nevertheless, Teodor knew he would feel better when they exited the forest. The Dyndaer would end soon, and if they could make it past the border, the threat of the cutthroats would considerably diminish.

With the sun barely giving light to the sky, they sat in a circle eating bread and dry meat, and then set off on their horses, trotting between the trees with little conversation and even less enthusiasm. The journey was more tedious than Teodor thought it would be when they first set out from Tamarri. He knew the journey to Cavell and then to Gaetana would be exhausting, but the twisted vines, moss-covered ground, burping mires, and the smell of rot were wearing on the mind. In reflection, he realized that weaving through the trees from north to south and then east to west was more than anyone should experience in a lifetime, let alone a fortnight.

If ever a place existed that would threaten the sanity of men, it would be the Dyndaer.

Looking forward to their return to civilization—or even a different landscape—Teodor rode alone on the brown mare while Seigfeld led Jab with Nitalia in the saddle ahead of him. He spun the signet ring on his hand, a token of his family and heritage in Eldhaft. Part of him was surprised his father let him keep the ring, seeing how the conversation they had before he left for the Crimson Sun was an exchange of insults.

He did not have his father's standards, or the lack thereof, which set him apart from most who hailed from Eldhaft. The overbearing thieves guild had their hands in every nook of the city, from the merchant shops to Harrowhal to Old Town to Count Vlassi's palace. At times, Teodor wished he carried a different surname, avoiding the onus of carrying the name Bacheva, but in the end, he was bound by his blood. His duty in protecting his family's interests, even while in the service of the Crimson Sun, never would escape him. To bring dishonor to their name would also shame him. In everything he did, he must consider the impact to the Bacheva family, even though the inheritance would be passed to his younger brother, and his father would forever refuse him readmittance to their estate.

As if fate wanted to compound his worries, Seigfeld turned his angular chin over his shoulder to gaze at Teodor. The sound of the horses' hooves clopping echoed for several steps before the principled man opened his mouth.

"Are you truly unconcerned about the repercussions in disobeying Count Frantisek? Despite your reason, I cannot see the king welcoming your insolence, even when delivering his niece to him safely." From his crisp tone, Teodor sensed Seigfeld had been wanting to speak to him on the topic for a while. Though Seigfeld's own family was not noble, but Teodor knew he'd spent enough time in the company of great men to understand their minds. Seigfeld continued, "King Frantisek is not known for walking outside of the law. The Gaetanean Kingdom was passed down to him by his father—well fought for and protected by his father, I might add—and since his induction, he has been known to do little more than follow what has already been written. I am not sure he will respect your deviation from what is considered proper."

Teodor bit his inner cheek, hearing Seigfeld seeming to say the same thing repeatedly in a single speech, much like a noble. Apparently, he did not only know their minds, but he spoke their tongue as well.

"You are still questioning the decision to take the princess to Gaetana? We discussed this already. Count Frantisek originally agreed to this plan. His wife can attest to it." Teodor said, looking to Nitalia on the warhorse. "If you recall, she made the choice to stick to what was agreed, not I. In fact, you suggested that her command could hold sway over her father's."

"I did." Seigfeld tightened his jaw, nodding at the princess with a hint of respect before redirecting his attention back to Teodor. No matter what Teodor might think of the man, Seigfeld was not a fool, he was a veteran member of the Crimson Sun and a man who would clearly see how Teodor had manipulated the situation to his benefit. "Princess Nitalia should know I hold no disrespect for her choice, but in the end, you will be the one whom the king will hold liable," Seigfeld said. "We both know this. You are a delegate of the Crimson Sun and the son of one of the most powerful men in Eldhaft. He will expect you to follow the law of the kingdom."

"But not his noble niece?" Teodor challenged, even though he knew Seigfeld spoke the truth.

"She is a child," Seigfeld said.

Teodor saw Nitalia tense at the comment, but she did not argue against the truth of the statement. She might hold rank over them, holding the capacity to tell them how to defend her and where to take her, but she knew the truth when it was heard too. The king would not punish his kin and damage the Frantisek name when he could run another noble's name into the ground.

"She will be safe, Seigfeld," Teodor replied.

"Yet Tomas is dead. Eisliev and Tyr are lost. The assassins live," Seigfeld said. "Our situation has changed since agreeing to advance to Gaetana."

Teodor winced, hearing the series of accusations fired at him without pause. "You think I am responsible for all this? I did not ask for Tomas to come along. Tyr and Eisliev left of their own accord. And those cutthroats were—"

Seigfeld interrupted him. "We were ordered by the count to return to Cavell with his daughter. The moment we stepped off the path instructed, the outcome of the mission fell on your shoulders. Such is the burden of taking charge."

Teodor grimaced. He could not outwit Seigfeld any more than he could the king if accused of the same failure in judgment. "You are right, Seigfeld."

"I expect you will not ignore the details when reporting to the king nor when speaking with Ivarr upon returning to Tamarri." Seigfeld frowned, facing forward once more.

"You should know me better than that, Seigfeld," he replied.

Seigfeld stopped himself, shaking his head. "I am sorry if I sound harsh, but I worry what will happen to you, Teodor. If the princess is safe, you may not receive more than a stern lecture or a minor punishment. But I have also been thinking that you run the chance of the king reporting to your father in Eldhaft. His wrath will likely not be so easily brushed aside."

Teodor gritted his teeth. "No, it will not." The ring on his finger suddenly held more weight.

They went on in silence. Teodor was left with Seigfeld's estimate of what dire response may be awaiting him in Gaetana and Tamarri. The trees thinned and became sparser as they ambled along. The swamps had disappeared, leaving little more to look at than white and brown spotted trees spread over the yellow and green landscape. Fewer leaves remained on the branches of the adjacent trees, unlike those in the deeper woods, allowing a fuller view of the looming yellow light of the sun behind a thin layer of grey clouds.

After stopping at midday, Seigfeld took his turn on Jab, and Nitalia rode the brown mare. Teodor lumbered ahead of them, pushing off each tree as he passed by as though it would push him closer to the forest's end.

It was nearing eventide when Nitalia pointed behind them, nearly shouting. "Look! It is Tyr and Eisliev!"

Not knowing how tense he had been, Teodor's shoulders relaxed at the sight of the two trailing behind them, hoping that their fortitude might lessen the grimness of the tale he would have to tell.

Shouting out to them across the expanse drew their attention and evoked a wave in return; the Ispolini and Stuhian then started to trudge in their direction. Realizing they would not make it much farther before morning, Teodor gave the order to break for camp while they approached. By the time the two finally reached them, the horses had been tended and the fire started. Nitalia sat cross-legged next to Teodor, who was changing a bandage on her back while Seigfeld prepared their supper.

"We figured you for dead," Seigfeld said as Eisliev and Tyr entered their small camp. The Stuhian wrapped himself up in his red robes, sitting on the opposite side of the princess. He scooted closer to the fire to warm himself. Tyr fell to his side on the opposite end of the fire.

Eisliev pulled his hands from his robes and hovered them over the flames. "Enough unmarked graves in the Dyndaer without us needing to add our own."

Teodor scratched at his beard and attempted to read the impassive expression of the dragon-man. When they last spoke, he learned Eisliev held position and sway over the Stuhian kingdom. While he planned to inform Ivarr, he knew building a relationship with Eisliev would be important if they intended to use his connections for their benefit.

"I am glad to see you both alive and well," Teodor said. "We had grown worried."

"Bah! Eisliev and I have been through worse than the Dyndaer," Tyr said, looking over a gash on his arm before returning his gaze to Teodor. The flames flashed in his blue eyes. "We thought you had buggered off to Gaetana already. We were about to return to Tamarri."

"Did you find the Dusk Legion again?" Nitalia asked.

Tyr bowed his head, leaning up on his elbow. "We caught up to them fairly quick after doubling back. We hurt them, too—badly but we were attacked by simargl during the fight. They took the opportunity to escape farther into the forest while we fended off the beasts, but…" The giant eyed Eisliev as if he was expecting the red mage to cut in and finish his story.

"But what?" Teodor asked.

Eisliev furrowed his brow, catching Tyr's expression, and then looked over to Teodor. "We found one of them dead earlier this morning on this side of the river. Not sure what killed him, but he was left in a bad way."

Teodor leaned closer. "What do you mean?"

Eisliev shook his head. "You would not believe me if I told you."

Tyr cleared his throat. "He wasn't wearing his pants."

Teodor widened his eyes. "What?"

The princess visibly gulped, folding her hands in her lap. "Might be best not to tell gruesome stories before bedtime. Did you see any sign of the others? On this side of the Drayrich?"

Tyr did not seem capable of doing anything more than shaking his head, his red curls bobbing over his ears.

Seigfeld's mouth was agape, eyes bouncing back and forth between them. He said, "We know one of them was more intent on getting ahold of Nitalia. Maybe he followed us across the river and the rest went back. It does not explain the pants situation… You think they had a spat among themselves?"

"Maybe," Teodor said.

Eisliev butted in. "Is that how the Anshedar solve feuds. Depantsing? I mean, what in the Nine Lands are you talking about?"

"No. Forget the pants." Teodor watched the flames spark in the fire, shaking his head at Eisliev. "We crossed the assassins again while you and Tyr were wandering through the Dyndaer. Luckily, we did not fight them. We spoke with them."

"Briefly," Seigfeld added. "Very briefly."

"Spoke with them?" Eisliev perked up next to the princess, darting his eyes around the fire. "How did you manage that? What did they say?"

"Not much," Teodor said.

Eisliev squinted in confusion while Nitalia piped up. "We came across two mercenaries going to fight in the war against the Uvil—I do not remember their names—but they told us the Uvil had been turning factions against each other."

"The mercenaries said the Dusk Legion was set up by the Uvil, who may have also been the ones to warn us of the attack on the princess," Teodor said. "We thought we could steer the assassins off by revealing the truth." Teodor eyed Eisliev. The man tapped his fingers against his knee with every word, his face frozen in the light of the fire. "We cannot be sure, of course, but a few of the assassins took the time to listen. One was disinterested in hearing us and moved to attack the princess, but the other three held him back while we escaped."

Eisliev shook his head in disbelief. "Did the Stuhian say anything?"

Teodor shook his head.

"You risked a lot facing them," Tyr said. "You would have been helpless to defend against them."

Teodor sighed. "To our benefit, knowledge swayed them, or at least most of them. If the body you found was the agitator among them, I do not think we will be seeing the likes of them again."

"The Lonmerean senate and the Dusk Legion will always be a threat to Maharia, but I agree we will not see these cutthroats again on this journey," Seigfeld clarified as the horses whinnied behind them where they were tied to a tree. He moved toward them to feed them apple crisps. "The faster we can get to Gaetana and deliver the princess, the better."

Nitalia pulled her shoulders back and tucked her legs closer in a crisscrossed fashion. "If the Dusk Legion is no longer a threat, then I should head back to Cavell. I do not see a reason to continue to Gaetana. My mother will be worried over me."

Teodor cleared his throat. He had no interest in traveling back through the Dyndaer to return the princess home. The threat of beasts alone was enough to make him wary. "I think seeing you through to Gaetana is the best choice, Princess, but maybe we can hurry the process."

"What do you mean?" she asked.

"Seigfeld, Eisliev, and Tyr can return home to Tamarri. They can report to Ivarr," Teodor explained, "while I escort you to Gaetana. We have the two horses to carry us, so we could arrive in a couple of days at most. That is, if it is okay with Seigfeld for me to take Jab the remainder of the way."

"As long as you return him safely to me," Seigfeld said, returning to the circle and taking his seat. "I will hold you to your promise."

"I will return your horse," Teodor replied, a half-grin splitting his lips. The expression felt odd after the stress of the past couple weeks.

Eisliev scratched his head. "Do you really think it is wise for us to split up? Do not get me wrong, I would rather head back to Tamarri, but we cannot know whether the assassins have gone."

"I could stay with you, if needed," Tyr said. "I can keep up with the horses well enough."

Teodor scrunched up his face at the Ispolini's swollen eye. "Best go and get your injuries taken care of, Tyr. Though I appreciate the offer."

"I think it is a safe assumption that the assassins have moved on; I would like to be a fly on the wall when they return to the senate in Lonmere," Seigfeld said. "No matter what is decided, Teodor, you will be answerable for the outcome. Be sure you are comfortable with the possible consequences."

The smile vanished as quickly as it had surfaced as he did his best not to glare at Seigfeld. "I heard you earlier, my friend. From what we know, I think this is our best course."

"If you refuse to let me return home and think I need to go Gaetana," Nitalia said, "I am perfectly capable of going on my own. You have escorted me through the brunt of the Dyndaer. The road north is not far, and few are going to deny me aid once they know my name."

"I think it a bit too dangerous to have you travel completely alone," Teodor said. "We have had a difficult enough time fending against the beasts in the region. We have been lucky to survive the journey."

Nitalia leaned away, blinking at him as though his words were insulting to her. "I don't carry these billhooks to look scary. I am not helpless. In fact, if I recall, I protected you the last time we fought side by side."

Teodor tilted his head. "I did not mean any disrespect, Princess. It would not be suitable for me to have you arrive at Gaetana without an escort. It would be a stain on my honor. You are injured and my position with the Crimson Sun demands I report to the king."

Nitalia relaxed her face, turning her eyes back to the flames. "Very well, Master Bacheva."

Teodor took a breath. "It is settled, then. We will part ways in the morning."

Chapter XXIII

BRENN, *The Dusk Legion*

"Morning will be here soon," Taryn said, leading them to the fringes of the Dyndaer. She brushed the dark hair from her cheeks, favoring her right leg as they bolted westward.

The trees were nearly nonexistent, scattered across the flatlands south of Gaetana. Brenn was surprised they had not reached the river that separated them from the civilized world. He only hoped they were far enough north to avoid the war against the Uvil altogether.

As they advanced across the terrain, he noted that the wild grasses sprouting around their feet would be tall enough to hide them from the Crimson Sun if they were to lie down, but even so, the slightest movement might give away their position if they were not careful. First, however, they needed to set the ambush.

Brenn swallowed the little handful of milroot powder that Rehor had given him and slowed down behind Taryn. Even though he barely saw past the nearest tree, he looked over his shoulder for the mercenaries. More specifically, he searched for Princess Nitalia and Teodor Bacheva. He suspected they had not broken camp yet, but the Crimson Sun would be shadowing behind them by first light. He was anxious to see how events would unfold, hoping his plan went as flawlessly as he anticipated. Taking the princess from Teodor and returning her to Cavell without him noticing would be easier said than done.

"Are you sure he is sending the other three back to Tamarri?" Brenn asked Rehor, who shuffled to a slow walk at his side.

The dragon-man breathed heavier than Brenn or Taryn. Brenn suspected Rehor had taken a smaller dosage of the milroot, giving Taryn more to combat her injury. Rehor nodded. "That is what they said. He plans to travel solo with the princess the rest of the way to Gaetana. I stayed with the horses until they spooked, and I had to abandon my position. If the Crimson Sun sticks to what they said, I cannot imagine a better scenario."

"It would be nice if they did not have their horses or if we had their horses," Brenn suggested, his mind reeling. "Or if you would let us kill Teodor. I can easily think of several better scenarios. Do not forget, we must make our way to Cavell again without Teodor chasing us down. I cannot imagine the path back through the Dyndaer will be any easier going east."

"Do not worry about Teodor," Taryn said. "I will make sure he does not follow you."

"How can you be sure?" Brenn asked. "He might kill you if he catches you."

"I will be fine," she said.

"Worry about her, you should not," Rehor agreed with a grin. "She has skin-switcher blood in her veins."

Taryn looked to Brenn, momentarily slack-jawed, and then questioned Rehor. "I have *what?*"

"Skin-switcher blood," Rehor repeated. "As far as I can tell, your unknown woman-plundering father was not a god, but a Vucari from the northern lands of Rhian, hmm? Thought they were all dead, I did. Yet living proof of their existence, you are."

"What are you talking about?" Brenn asked. "How do you know who her father is?"

"I do not know *who* he is," Rehor replied, "but I can tell you what he is. The Stuhia waged war against the skin-switchers for hundreds of years. Familiar with their kind, I am. Enhanced hearing and vision, insusceptibility to the elements, and resistance to pain are only some of their qualities."

Taryn pressed her hand to her chest. "Why do you call them skin-switchers?"

"Because they can twist their bodies to take the form of animals and beasts at will," Rehor said. "A nasty sight, really." He leaned over as they walked. "Do not worry yourself. An enemy to the Vucari, I no longer am."

"Blood and spit." Taryn gulped.

"How long have you known?" Brenn asked.

Rehor scrunched his face. "Slowly putting the pieces together, I have been. Unless she can twist herself into a sparrow or a wolf, it appears she has but a fraction of her father in her, hmm?"

"I-I cannot—" Taryn said, seemingly trying to digest the information.

"Anyway, I will keep us safe in returning to Cavell," Rehor said over her. "But back to the matter at hand, I will point out that you wanted to keep the princess alive. Kill her and be done with this adventure, I say." Rehor wagged his finger at Brenn. "All you must do is turn the other way for a bit, hmm? I will take care of the rest. We could bury her in this very field."

"No. The entire mission was a farce." Brenn grimaced, scratching at his beard. He was still trying to wrap his mind around *skin-switchers*. "We will stick to the plan and wrap this up as peacefully as possible."

"As you wish," Rehor said, smirking, "but the Dusk Legion will send me back to finish the job, even when hearing the Uvil betrayed us. You are only delaying the inevitable, hmm?"

"I understand." Brenn sighed. Rehor had argued the senate would stall the princess's death a year or two to see how the Uvil reacted, giving hint to their true motivations, but Lonmere had already fallen in love with the idea of murdering the Frantiseks. No matter what happened, Rehor believed they would want her dead. "Time might sway their interests."

"Doubtful," Rehor said.

"Can we focus our attention on something else please?" Brenn replied. "We need to think about how to keep them from pushing past us."

Rehor smiled. "I will be summoning a *Poludnica*."

"A what?" Taryn stumbled next to Brenn and grabbed his arm to keep herself from falling. He kept her steady, and she chose to hold on to his arm for a bit longer while Rehor explained.

"A noonwraith," he said. "We will not be able to dawdle long once it crosses over the threshold. It is not like the Nocnica from the Netherworld. Poludnicas are brought from another place in Thrice Nine Lands, hmm? Summoning one requires a constant connection, meaning my life will drain as though I were in constant battle with Koldovstvo."

"And what does a noonwraith do?" Brenn asked.

"Oh," Rehor rubbed his head if he were trying to remember. "Paralyze those captured by their gaze and lead them through dreams, nightmares, or alternate experiences, they do. Sometimes a Poludnica will tell you riddles or stories, or they might have you live through multiple paths of your life; that is, if you were to make different choices. I do not really know the full of it, hmm?

Only what I have heard, but you will have to remain out of her gaze. She must captivate Teodor so you two can get the princess."

"Wh—" Taryn looked at Rehor with wide eyes. "If you had the power to bring forth one of these Poludnicas, why have you waited this long? We have come across the Crimson Sun multiple times when one of those creatures could have been helpful."

"Helpful for whom?" Rehor furrowed his brow, rocking his head back in surprise. "Hear me, you did not. The Poludnica affects one person," he lifted his finger up to make his point, "and does not do any real harm, except to me while I maintain an open channel to Koldovstvo and hold it in this reality, hmm? I fail to see how dropping them amid a battle would have helped." He shook his head at Taryn, who regained her footing to keep stride with Brenn. Rehor huffed. "I want to like you, but you are awfully insistent I kill myself for your benefit."

Taryn tightened her lips. "If I had magic, I would be using it a lot more often."

"Then thankful you do not, I am," Rehor scoffed.

The scent of winter clung to the evening breeze, catching in Brenn's nose as they pushed forward. He could not remember the last time they had a full night's rest, but he guessed it was before leaving Cavell. Without complaint, the three of them marched on through the grasslands, only stopping briefly for Taryn to rest her leg and then moving westward again.

Brenn was surprised the milled magic allowed her to keep up with them. With a fresh bandage wrapped around her upper thigh, the bleeding nearly stopped, but the hole in her leg looked agonizing. To her benefit, the quarrel missed the bone and only passed through the meat, but he suspected it hurt to walk, let alone run across the uneven terrain. Even when taking twice the milroot that was meant to give her newfound vigor while numbing her pain, Brenn never imagined she could keep up.

He wondered if anything could stop her. A broken nose, injured leg, dead sister, and crushed spirit, yet she continued as though she were anything but a mere woman. The story of her father being a god played in his mind as they headed westward. Whatever she was, Taryn was not human.

No, she was something more.

His thoughts were on her origins when morning finally came, a grey sky coming with it, which would continue into the afternoon. He was glad to see rain did not follow as they traipsed over the clumps of dirt and grass, ambling through the diminishing trees. He could feel a sense of calm washing over them as they walked through the widening fields, a pleasant change after the crushing experiences that would likely haunt them into old age.

"Where will you go after we are done here?" Taryn matched him stride for stride. Her brown eyes met his, holding his attention.

"I don't know," he said truthfully. "I cannot rightly return to Lonmere if I am meant to be dead. My mother and father will be heartbroken, my brother too, but it will be for the best if I simply disappear."

"A choice, you will not have," Rehor agreed, eavesdropping on their conversation from the front.

Brenn ran a hand through his hair. "How about you?"

"I will return to my mother in Mecka," she said. "It is not far from here. North of the Gnyn Waters on the outskirts of Gaetana." She touched her nose tenderly and winced. "You could come stay with me, if you'd like?"

Brenn nodded. "I would like that."

Rehor chuckled to himself. "Oh, are you two not the sweetest?"

The sound of approaching horses' hooves beating against the ground behind them caught Brenn's attention.

He motioned for them to take cover. "Here they come. Hide."

Chapter XXIV

TEODOR, *The Crimson Sun*

A strange restlessness swept over Teodor as he neared the open prairie. Anything could be lurking in the weeds and scattered scrubs. Although he could not see anything uncommon, the back of his neck itched and his skin prickled, causing him to bring Jab to a halt. He heard Nitalia coax the mare next to him as it, too, slowed to a stop.

As he searched the landscape, Seigfeld's warning rang in his ears. The words had stuck with him through the night and into the morning, even when he watched his three companions set off north for Tamarri, and so he was not shocked when they returned once more. He knew whatever happened on the final trek to Gaetana was his concern and his alone. If he failed to deliver the princess now—if any ill-bearing crossed their path—his name would carry dishonor that he could not see undone.

The omen is what kept him from proceeding into the prairie. Yet Teodor noticed Nitalia scanning the grasses with equal measure as if expecting beasts to sprout from the wilted blades, and she had been given no warning.

"Do you see the grasses moving?" Teodor narrowed his eyes. "Besides the wind, I mean. Did you see anything stir?"

He gripped Jab's reins, drawing his sword while fighting the urge to drop to the ground.

"It is hard to tell in this light. Should we wait until the sky clears before continuing? The clouds will not be with us all day," Nitalia said.

Her words brought his attention to the shadow cast by the clouds. The day was only half over, and the color above suggested twilight was nearing fast. He hoped the rain withheld until they reached Gaetana.

He shook his head. "No matter what is out there—a polevik or some other beast—we should not tarry. The river cannot be much farther."

Teodor heard the faint sound of weeds crunching and then a small breeze fluttered against him. He strained his eyes until they burned like hot pokers in a fire but still could not see anything. He led Jab forward a step when the breeze escalated to a gust.

Nitalia cried out next to him and then a silvery light glinted in front of his eyes. The unearthly wail that erupted from the flash drew Teodor's attention, keeping him from turning toward the princess. His legs tightened on either side of Jab to keep him from bolting, but the warhorse seemed unbothered by the sudden disruption.

The hollow howl was breathy like the wind, cold and lasting. Deafening. Intimidating. A feminine figure formed from the light, her golden hair like strands of harvested wheat; her legs and hands were stained black like tar. She floated from nothingness, suspended in the air like a ghost. A wraith-like white gown, worn to the point it covered practically nothing, hung from her thin frame, her face wanner than the light of a distant moon.

A pristine, primeval voice filled his mind. *'Fallen from the world; fallen from memory; fallen from grace. Tread down this untamed path of darkness."*

The rainclouds overhead churned, speeding by as though time raced along, churning day to night and winter to spring.

"They are coming!" Eisliev Kluk's voice rang from behind Teodor. Before he could turn to question the Stuhian's sudden presence, howls and screeches arose from the fields in front of him.

The ghastly woman had vanished.

Tyr stepped forth to Teodor's right, his blue eyes looking black in the veil of darkness swirling around them, agitating from a mist boiling beneath Teodor. He twisted on Jab to look for its origin, finding nothing except a sea of black-filled waves of fog.

Tyr pulled the familiar battle axe from his back. "We will have to cut these curs down."

Teodor's mind spun, wondering from where the two mercenaries had come. He noticed that Tyr was absent of his injuries.

This was not real. It could not be real.

"Hm." A grey horse stomped against the soil next to Jab. Teodor turned to see Ivarr Gauthus, the leader of the Crimson Sun, sitting on the mount. The silver in his goatee patterned against the brown strands of hair matched the trimmed bangs hanging from his leather helm, looking all-too familiar. He was trying to figure out why Ivarr was with him when the man tossed his red cloak to the side, revealing a quiver of arrows and a longbow. The weapon looked as though it had been carved of a strong wood. The outer surface was smooth, save the small notches on the top and bottom of the strip of timber where a string of horsehair bent the wood into a simple curve. He recognized the weapon as one that once hung on the wall in his father's study back in Eldhaft. A faint memory of Gaspar gifting the bow to Ivarr when Teodor joined the Crimson Sun surfaced.

"I see them," Ivarr said. "They are many."

Strength fled from Teodor, turning to examine the grasses again. He could see nothing even though the howling sounds grew louder in his ear. The harder he looked for whatever came, the higher the grasses grew, soon rising over Jab's head. The ground shook as though pure evil walked upon it.

He was going to die here.

"Where is the princess?" Teodor asked, turning to his three companions. He could not see the brown mare or Nitalia anywhere.

The sun lifted and fell in the distance, giving and taking the light so quickly, it might as well have been a flash of lightning.

"What princess?" Ivarr asked.

"Bah! There is no princess," Tyr said.

Teodor's heart pounded inside his chest. His breath was a heavy wind blowing through a hollow oak.

Was there no princess?

A shadowy figure thundered through the weeds toward him. He could not make out its form in the weak light, only hearing the grunts as it rushed forward, holding a weapon that seemed to slash away the blades of grass. It moved quickly; it was too swift to outrun. When it finally leaped in front of Jab, Teodor thought his heart would bound into his chest from fear.

The large hoofed feet slammed into the ground, sending up a small vapor of dirt into the air, eddying the dismal fog. The legs leading up to the body were somewhat thick and strong, covered with a wild mane of black hair, disheveled and shaggy. The upper body and arms were that of a man but with the potency of a beast, with enough muscle to snap Jab's neck.

He promised to return Jab to Seigfeld.

Staring into the repugnant face shaped like a bull and covered in the same unkempt hair as the legs, Teodor saw two beady brown eyes under the unshorn bangs. In addition, the creature had two triangular ears hidden under leagues of hair, protected by curled, razor-sharp horns that jutted past the forehead like a ram. The face was elongated and had thin black lips.

Remembering the beast held a weapon, Teodor guided Jab backwards. The curved blade of the falchion shimmered in the beast's hands as it raised it above its head.

An arrow flashed by Teodor, breaching the monster's chest. Red blood spurted across its skin, coloring the dark fur with red spots. A second arrow followed, nearly striking the same wound again, causing the beast to raise its chin to the sky and roar with the vitality of a thousand men on the battlefield.

Teodor jerked his eyes to Ivarr, who placed another arrow on the string of his weapon.

"Again!" Teodor cried. The bladed shaft tore through the monster's neck. Blood sprayed like droplets of rain across the ground, Jab, and Teodor. The warmth of the gelatinous liquid on Teodor's face sent a chill across his body. He pulled his sword from its scabbard, raising his eyes from the dying creature, its roar becoming nothing more than a mere whimper.

The red mage came into view on the far end of their line, riding his own painted gelding. "We must fight our way through," he said. "Be sure to protect me. I am an Arkhon, after all."

Tyr rumbled next to him.

"What? You said you were no longer the king of your people." Teodor raised an eyebrow, balancing the weight of his blade in his hand. Ivarr made no reaction to Eisliev's claim. "Did these beasts come for you? What are they?"

The dragon-man did not answer, almost frozen in time, gazing over the fields. Tyr, too, was motionless.

Teodor twisted back to Ivarr. "We will make a run for the river," the leader of the Crimson Sun directed, adjusting his helm. "Tyr, you stay close. I have heard Ispolini can run as tirelessly as a horse. Hm?"

The Ispolini grunted again next to Teodor.

As though the warning spawned another beast in the grasses, a howl bellowed immediately in front of them and a second creature crashed into their space. Tyr twisted in time to catch the flailing falchion with the blade of his battle axe. They stood face to face for a moment, staring directly into each other's eyes. The creature was as lofty as the barbarian. With a growl of his own, Tyr pushed the monster backwards. Then, with unbelievable speed, he swung the battle axe underhanded and sliced the monster across its belly. The fiend dropped its own weapon and slumped backwards, sliding off the deliverer of its death.

Where was Princess...Frantisek?

A horned brute emerged to Teodor's right where Tyr had stood moments ago. His thoughts fled his mind. He slashed his sword at a downward angle, striking it across its muzzle. The beast roared, reaching for him, despite the blood oozing from the fresh wound. He swung again and cut through its arm before it could grasp him.

The beast fell away with the sound of Ivarr's booming voice. "When is the last time you spoke with your father?"

"This is hardly the time to discuss my father." He twisted to face Ivarr. "My father doesn't want to see me."

Ivarr paused for a second to give Teodor a scowling glance, then nodded. His mouth moved but the sound in Teodor's head sounded nothing like the man's voice.

He heard the familiar tone of a female instead.

"If you listen, every story is full of life lessons with no exceptions, except for this one."

Chapter XXV

BRENN, *The Crimson Sun*

Exhaustion weighed heavily on his bones, the milroot all but depleted from his body. He had to rely on his natural adrenaline to push him through. He could already feel his side beginning to ache again.

The moment Rehor's gust threw Nitalia out of her saddle, Brenn pushed off the soil, springing from his hiding place to rush her. He saw her hit the ground with a solid thud, tumbling head over feet into an awkward lump. With his cestuses already fastened over his hands, he hoped to knock her senseless long before Rehor risked draining his life, though he knew he could not reach her before she stood.

"Hurry, Brenn!" Taryn's voice carried behind him. She was without her daggers—having lost one when striking the princess and the other in the glade when fending off Krel—and with the sapped milroot, she was helpless in any fight. If her broken nose was not enough, the injured leg would make her more of a liability than a threat.

He did not need her next to him in combat. He only needed her to collect the mare before it fled across the field.

To his right, the Poludnica had already erupted from a silvery light, beckoning him to look at the wonder, but he fought the impulse, heeding Rehor's advice not to look at the otherworldly creature. The screech of the feminine spectre, however, rang in his ears, stinging at his heart as much as his mind, and still he pushed forward. He would not allow his curiosity to ruin them. The most he saw was the Poludnica's wispy gown and flowing golden hair from the corner of his eye as he bolted by her. Based on the sounds she emitted, he conjectured her face would bear a resemblance to death.

He had seen enough death to last him a lifetime.

Teodor Bacheva, on the other hand, he did see entirely, sitting on his horse with a lifeless expression as he gaped at the noonwraith. The horse under him nickered, tossing its head without a care. Yet the swordsman was compelled to keep his gaze on the Poludnica, ever-mesmerized by the hollow howl.

"No!" Princess Nitalia forced the word from her mouth as she rolled to her knees and caught sight of him approaching. She stumbled to her feet in a rush, causing the brown mare to bolt in a short circle before stopping and stomping its feet. The animal certainly had less training than the mount beneath Teodor, but it had not fled far.

Stumbling to the side, Nitalia jerked her billhooks from their sheaths, holding them shakily at Brenn as he approached. The wind whistled between them, rustling the grass and the few trees scattered over the terrain.

Brenn glanced across the lowlands. Nothing stirred out here except them.

She wheezed, showing favor to her left side. He could not tell if she hurt herself when falling or if it was in response to an injury from a previous fight. She gritted her teeth. "You will not… find me to…to be an easy opponent, assassin."

Lifting his hands to protect his face, Brenn did not give her a response. Instead, he strode closer, rocking his shoulders back and forth as though he were ready to brawl against the Ispolini.

"Master Bacheva!" she screamed, stumbling back a step. Her hooded purplish cloak swirling near her boots as she readjusted her feet for a better stance.

Her juvenile movements told him all he needed to know.

She swung the first billhook wildly at his head. He ducked underneath it, then jumped back to dodge the second that aimed for his midsection. She must have taken his movement as a retreat because she advanced, twirling the one in her left hand harmlessly while slicing the air again with the blade in her right.

She admittedly had enough force behind a blow to cut him open if he were stupid enough to dive in front of her attack. Unfortunately for Nitalia, he had fought more experienced fighters, many of whom held more skill when half-drunk and unarmed.

With a snort, he jabbed at her twice. She stumbled beyond his reach and steadied her footing. Curling her lip, a sudden ferociousness came over the young princess that Brenn did not expect. With a guttural scream, she assailed him, spinning her curved blades in deadly proximity. The iron flashed like beams of moonlight, blurring in front of him. He spun to and fro, scarcely missing each pinpointed attack. The sharp end zipped on either side of his flesh, her final thrust nearly shaving the hairs off his chin.

He kicked at Nitalia to knock her back, only to have her duck under his leg and sweep his other leg with her billhook. With a surprised grunt, Brenn flew into the air and slammed against the ground on his ribs.

He roared, certain he could hear the bones splinter further. Gritting his teeth, he rolled back as she advanced, a sudden sweat roiling off his brow and threatening to blind him.

"You will not have me!" Nitalia screamed, slamming her weapon down at him.

Dumb luck saved him as he rolled to the side and skittered to his feet. Her head snapped to him, twirling her blade and preparing to come at him once more. Heaving for breath, he retreated with wide-braced legs and lifted his hands in defense. He needed to end this fight quickly, or Rehor would rot away to nothingness.

He stepped left and then right, ready for her next attack. She hacked her left billhook downward. Turning sideways, Brenn smacked the flat edge of her blade with the iron plating on the palm of his glove, throwing off her balance and momentum. He then grabbed her right wrist, halting her second attack completely. She twisted in close to him in an attempt to stop herself from falling over. The shocked expression on her face was brief as he pulled her into even closer proximity and punched her in the chin with a right jab.

He did not even see her eyes close as her head rocked back. Both weapons slipped from her hands. He let her go and watched her smash to the ground in a heap.

"Gods." Taryn limped, reaching out for the reins of the mare behind him. The horse did not even attempt to flee from her. "You took her down fast."

Brenn ruffled his brow, sucking air through his nostrils hungrily. "What did you expect? She is a child with farming tools for weapons."

"Rehor," Taryn yelled. "Be ready!"

Brenn looked to the dragon-man standing in the field, his arms shaking in front of him as Koldovstvo channeled through him. Even at a distance, he could see the man aging with wrinkles forming under his eyes and on his cheeks. He was glad to see Rehor's hair had not yet started to turn grey.

Kneeling next to Nitalia, Brenn unfastened the purple cloak from her neck and pulled it from around her body. He touched his ribs as he stood back up. He forgot how much damage the Ispolini had done to him; the strain of moving in battle, even against the young princess, was enough to make him ache.

"Here." He offered the cloak to Taryn, and then extended his hand to help her onto the horse. "Put this on and get moving. Whatever you do, do not let him catch you."

Chapter XXVI

TEODOR, *The Crimson Sun*

The silver light burned his eyes, leaving spots on the edge of his vision. And then, the illusion was gone.

As though he were waking from a dream, the fields in front of him blurred. The wind stung his face; the horse's hooves pounding the ground under him sounded like thunder in his ears as his mind tried to adjust to the world around him. He could not make sense of how he had come to be in the field, blinking against the haze of the roiling clouds and the greyness of winter.

He fought to remember where he was and how he came to be there. Nowhere did he see Eisliev Kluk, Tyr Og, or Ivarr Gauthus. The field ahead was empty. The grasses were dying.

What happened?

Reality formed around him, making him question whether he had fallen asleep on the horse while riding westward. The faint memory of some spectre materializing in front of him with hollowed eyes and hair like a field crop haunted him. Yet tracing over the lowlands ahead revealed nothing but—

Nitalia! The princess!

The mission of delivering Nitalia to Gaetana rushed back to him tenfold, ridding his mind of the temporary madness. He was not battling beasts in the prairie or traveling with Ivarr on distant adventures. Nitalia Frantisek was his charge.

The young woman sped across the terrain atop her brown mare, the purplish cloak flapping behind her, barely visible at the great distance with the hood pulled over her. She was almost crouched into a ball, save her legs dangling on either side with her feet securely held in the stirrups.

She must have been frightened by whatever had captivated him.

"Princess!" he screamed after her. "Sard! Gero's yard! Princess Nitalia! Stop!"

She did not slow in the slightest, not even turning her head in his direction.

Fearing his desperate cries were being stolen by the wind, Teodor kicked the warhorse in the ribs to give chase.

Jab lurched forward into a full gallop, its forelegs and hindlegs alternating over the uneven ground in a desperate attempt to catch the young noble ahead of them. Teodor was responsible for her safety. He could not let harm come to her for fear that he would lose position among the Crimson Sun and tarnish the Bacheva name.

"Nitalia!" he roared over the wind whipping against his ears.

No response.

The scattered trees and shrubs blurred by him. He had no clue how to close the distance between himself and the fleeing princess. He could only hope that Jab held more stamina than the mare.

The time he spent chasing her surprised him, lasting nearly a league before he saw the other animal slowing to a trot on the horizon. The shimmering waters of the Deep Run, flowing north from the Gnyn Waters all the way south to the ocean, could be seen on the opposite side of her. She could not flee any farther without traveling north to a ferry or south to find a bridge. She would not dare try to cross the frigid waters on horseback.

What little light in the sky remained nearly faded by the time he closed the distance between them.

Encouraging Jab to continue, he peered through the dimming light at the hooded figure. She paused, turning her head ever so slightly to look back in his direction from the shadows of her hood. His breath quickened, realizing she took notice of him and continued trotting north along the water's edge.

"Nitalia!" Teodor cried out again. He remembered her claiming she would go to Gaetana without him, but her behavior was beyond understanding. He growled between his teeth at the horse, trying to make sense of what she was doing. "Come on, Jab."

He smacked the reins against the horse, guiding the mount to follow her. Squinting at the colored cloak, he realized he could not see her billhooks over her shoulders.

Nitalia?

"Stop!" he shouted with only a few hundred feet between them. "By the gods, you will stop right now, or I will run you through myself!"

To his surprise, the rider pulled on the reins to halt the mare, turning the animal slightly so Teodor was forced to come closer to see her.

"Take off your hood," he said, his hand falling to the blade at his side. The hooded cloak definitely belonged to Princess Nitalia, and the mare belonged to the Count of Cavell, but this rider could not be the young noble.

Thin fingers reached for the hood as she twisted her horse around to face Teodor.

"Good evening, Master Bacheva," the pale-skinned assassin said, pulling the fabric from her dark strands of hair. Her light skin was blotched by her swollen nose and the dark circles under her eyes.

"You!" Teodor recognized the brown-eyed girl as being with the Dusk Legion. He twisted his horse in a circle to check his flank and the riverbank, expecting the other cutthroats to come charging out from all directions. He pulled the blade halfway from its sheath before realizing he was not being ambushed. "Where are your friends? Where is Princess Nitalia?"

"They are not here," the woman said softly, folding her hands in her lap. "It is only you and I who have come this far west. You can cut me down if you wish it."

Teodor flared his nostrils, looking for some sign the woman was lying before raking his eyes along the river's edge again. He could not make sense of what had happened.

How did he lose the princess?

"You attacked me outside the Dyndaer, in the field, with some spell," he concluded, eyeing the darkness settling over the land behind him. "You somehow swapped places with Nitalia while enchanting me with magic." He turned his horse, unsure of whether he should race back the way he had come or if it were even worthwhile. He could feel his face twisting with anger; he had lost. "Sard! You killed her, didn't you? I should take your head here and now."

"You may," she replied, lifting her hands in the air innocently. "I have no weapon. I cannot stop you."

"How could you take an innocent girl's life? And for what?" He sneered, pulling his sword fully from his belt and pointing it at the assassin. "The Uvil will not gift you with anything but the death they offer the rest of Maharia!"

The woman shook her head gently, her brown eyes soft. "I do not know anything about any of that. I do know the Svet under your command killed my sister."

Teodor gulped, unsure if he was meant to feel remorse for the death of this stranger's family. "Your sister died attempting to assassinate a noble," he said. "I am sorry for your loss, but I cannot say it was undeserved."

The girl tensed her jaw, turning her eyes from him as though she might be hiding tears. He wondered what response she expected from him.

Her next words came out in a choke. Perhaps his simple truth weakened her taste for vengeance. "The others have not killed the princess."

"What?" Teodor gaped.

"They have taken her back home to her father."

Teodor choked. "What? Why? Gero's yard! Why would we go through all of this for them to return her home safe?"

She shrugged, hiding a sniffle in the failing light. She was clearly fighting back any emotional display, probably brought on by the thought of her sister. She said, "To keep peace in the north as you claimed should be done. Seems your tongue wagging convinced them to do better."

A cold chill ran over Teodor's body that came from something more than winter's rawness drifting over the Deep Run. He steadied Jab. "It cannot be that easy. At what cost?"

"It does not matter. You can no longer do anything about it," she said.

"What cost?" he snapped.

The assassin sighed. "The Crimson Sun will take the blame for snatching her without cause. There is nothing you can do about it," she reiterated. "Your horse is too tired to chase them back to Cavell, and even if it were not, you could not possibly traverse the Dyndaer on your own. Your company is gone. You are alone."

Teodor gripped his sword until his knuckles were white. He could feel his blood pulsating through the veins in his arm. Her words rang true to him, knowing the count was too confused to know fully why the princess was taken to Gaetana to begin with, and they had gone against their word to return her back safely.

"Princess Nitalia will never agree to its veracity," he said.

A weak smile touched the corner of the assassin's mouth. "She is young and malleable."

"We will send an emissary to Count Frantisek when I return to Tamarri. The Dusk Legion will be held accountable!" Teodor could not stop his hand from shaking. Even as the threat escaped his lips, he knew the idea was worthless. No evidence of the Dusk Legion would be found in Cavell, and any attempt to rid the Crimson Sun of accountability would come across as being an act of artificial diplomacy and panic. If they frightened Nitalia into lying for them, the Crimson Sun would lose what little credibility they had with Count Frantisek.

"Do what you think is right. Though one way or another, I imagine you will not survive another trip to Cavell," she said. "If I may suggest, twist the truth for your own benefit. The princess is safe with her father again, which I believe was your overall intention. What could you do with that truth, Master Bacheva?"

Teodor grimaced, trying to wrap his mind around her line of reasoning. He did not have to contend with King Frantisek and therefore did not have to worry about word of any type of failure reaching his father. Outside of convincing Ivarr that the mission was a success, he could possibly skirt any consequences. The chances of anyone from the Crimson Sun coming to Cavell in the following months and learning anything different was nearly impossible. Mercenaries would be distracted by the war for years to come, not the inner politics of the kingdoms of men.

The assassin dipped her head, readjusting her hands so that

they clutched the reins once more. "The four kingdoms are at peace, Master Bacheva. Your position is secure. The Crimson Sun can continue on as they always have, and the Dusk Legion will return to their feud with your father in Eldhaft." She licked her lips, swallowing harder than she probably intended, her eyes settling on the longsword in his hand. "So, if you are not going to put me out of my misery—if we understand one another—I will be on my way."

He twisted the blade in his hand, admiring the iron.

"We let you live back there. We could have killed you and did not," she said, the sweetness of her voice swirling in the evening air. "I will not stop you, however, if it is your wish to take my life."

He met her brown eyes, laced with grief. "You have lost enough."

He tossed his blade to the dirt.

Chapter XXVII

BRENN, *The Dusk Legion*

He lightly smacked the princess across the cheek to wake her for what felt like the dozenth time. She moaned, turning her head, but did not open her eyes.

"How much did you give her, Rehor?" Brenn ran a hand nervously through his hair and then lifted it to smack her in the face again. "I am running the risk of leaving red marks across her face."

"She has a knife wound in her back. I think a few handprints will be overlooked, hmm?" Rehor replied, sitting near the princess's head.

He pushed the grey-red hair from his blue eyes, reminding Brenn of the years he had spent to keep them safe on the journey back to Cavell. Brenn did not want to think of the number of monsters he had slaughtered in his wake. At first, he was concerned the dragon-man would waste his life away, but Rehor assured him that he would siphon the essence out of someone soon enough to restore his youth.

"You have to be tired of dragging her along on that *thing*," Rehor said. "Besides, I do not think our story will hold up if you are tugging her along behind you when we pass through the gates. Think she came with us of her own free will, the guards and her father must."

Brenn eyed the stretcher made from long branches and torn fabric on which he had dragged the princess for the length of the Dyndaer while Rehor kept her drugged with whatever plant mixture he concocted.

"I hope this works," Brenn said.

"It was your plan," Rehor said. "I prefer we drown her in the swamp and be done with it."

"We are not going to kill her," Brenn replied. "If we deliver her safely back home, we can blame the Crimson Sun and prevent Lonmere from being targeted."

"Yes," Rehor agreed, "but I must return to Lonmere and convince the senate and the Dusk Legion that the lot of you are dead, and they have to be okay with the mission being incomplete. I do not believe they will respond positively."

Brenn gritted his teeth. They had gone over the plan time and time again for the past several days. He did not know why they were still talking about it. "You will think of something. We do not need to embolden the Uvil or leave Lonmere on the chopping block. We return the princess, cause some dissonance with the Crimson Sun, and move on with our lives."

Rehor lifted his shoulders to his ears and sighed dramatically. "I was looking forward to killing her. Are you going to hit her again or not?"

Popping her in the cheek again, Nitalia's eyes fluttered open. Upon seeing him hanging over her, she shot up with her arm flailing, attempting to scream. He shoved a hand over her mouth and put his weight down on her.

"You are alright, Princess." Brenn leaned down to whisper in her ear, hoping he would be louder than her muffled whimpering. "You are alright. We are not going to hurt you. You are home."

Her thrashing lessened, and he slowly lifted himself from her.

"I am going to take my hand off your mouth. Don't shout. Please," he said.

She responded with a subtle nod, her blue eyes darting between him and Rehor, who hovered over his shoulder. Her golden hair was wild and frayed, stuck to her pale cheeks. As he let her loose, she remained frozen in place.

"What have you done?" she asked hoarsely.

"We have brought you home," Brenn said, reaching behind him for the waterskin he had prepared. "Do not move too quickly or you might faint. You have not eaten in several days."

She eyed him warily but reached for the waterskin, eagerly gulping the day-old water.

Brenn moved the long strands of hair from his face and leaned out of Nitalia's space. Even after dragging the young woman through the Dyndaer, it was a different experience having her looking back at him. In the past, killing people rarely involved him speaking to them directly, and even then, they were disgusting overweight men who probably had done something in their life deserving of death. The young princess looked to be as innocent and gentle as a newborn child.

He did his best to sound menacing, foreboding, crossing his arms over his chest. "I need you to listen to me, Princess. If you agree to cooperate with us, we will take you through the gates of Cavell and back to your parents. If not, we will put you back to sleep and slip you into one of these marshes to drown, never to be seen again."

"Oh, no, no, no," Rehor said. "I would not drown her. I would bury her near the swamp and let her wake up several feet underground. She will have no way of knowing which way is up, hmm? Let her dig until she suffocates or starves to death or digs her way into the mire, clawing helplessly at her prison."

Nitalia swallowed a mouthful of water, gagging slightly while trying to maintain her composure. Brenn knew fear. It was evident in Nitalia's eyes no matter how hard she tried to hide it.

"You are only alive because he insisted," Rehor went on, eyes large and jaw clenched. "If it were up to me, I would rip every Frantisek to pieces, leisurely peeling meat from bone, starting with their fingers and toes and working my way to the middle, so every sliver of pain could be experienced before the blood loss put them to sleep. I pray you give me reason to come back here and flay your parents in front of you, hmm? The gods know I could strip the fat off your father, layer by layer, for days."

Brenn leveled his gaze at the princess, clamping his teeth together. Nitalia handed the waterskin back to Brenn. He was not sure whose hands were shaking more, hers or his.

"You aim to frighten me," she said, defiantly meeting Rehor's blue eyes.

The dragon-man leered, and in the beat of an eyelash, snatched her wrist between his fingers. Her wail was immediate as she tried to pull back, her skin sizzling under his touch, the flesh blackening.

Rehor snarled. "I can rob you of your life and have you wither away like a corpse here and now, or infect you with a rot to keep you from ever bearing children, or perhaps I can fill your belly with my own seed if you so wish it, hmm?" Nitalia fought against his grip, her flesh bubbling against his touch. "I tell you, if ever there was a thing for you to be frightened of in this world, child, it is me."

He released her. She pulled her arm to her chest, examining the scorched flesh, seeing a ring of discoloration as though a circle of hot iron had burnt her.

Brenn was surprised at how forceful his own voice sounded in addition to Rehor's threats. "You will do as we say."

"What do you want?" Nitalia stammered.

Brenn popped his knuckles. "You will tell your father the Crimson Sun took you against your will and that I rescued you."

"What about him?" Nitalia asked. "Did he rescue me too?"

"He will not be with us," Brenn said, lying with a straight face. "He will be watching from the shadows, ready to respond if you choose to speak against us."

"I will not," Nitalia said, examining the skin on her wrist. Inevitably, the mark would scar. "My father has no love for the Crimson Sun anyhow. If you leave me home and let us alone, what do I care who carries the blame?"

"Good," Brenn said. "Let's go."

Nitalia struggled to her feet, her legs wobbling from lack of use. She looked up at him. "What should I say the name of my savior is?"

"Krel," Brenn replied. "Krel Traelador."

The Cavell gates were no more impressive this go around as they were the first time Brenn had approached them. Stone upon stone was well crafted over the archway and designed in a way that would last ages, but it was nothing compared to the fortress of Lonmere, built in the side of the northern mountains.

As they approached the open gate, Brenn glanced at Castle Frantisek on the ridge behind the town. He could see light burning in the open windows of the small fortress.

He could hear the low murmur of life beyond the gates. The inhabitants of the hamlet were moving along in their accustomed manner, busily going about their business as if it were any day. Brenn stretched his neck to peer at the people beyond the stone-faced guard who stood at the ready.

A man with a full dark beard and mustache, wearing black armor like the other sentries of Cavell, stepped forward with his polearm at his side.

"Czern's blessing. What is your purpose…" he started saying before stopping himself. "Princess Nitalia, you have returned."

He folded his body in half in a typical fashion, while Brenn stood silently at her side.

"Master Tam," Nitalia bobbed her head. "If you would be kind enough to escort us to my father, I must speak with him."

"Of course, my lady," he replied.

Tam signaled to another guard inside the gate to take his watch, and then he led them through the dusty streets and up the spiraled path to Castle Frantisek. Those along the way who recognized Nitalia's golden hair called out or waved to her. The mixed expressions of the people they passed gave Brenn some impression of who knew of the recent attack on the castle and the princess's departure, and those who were completely unaware or, at least, intelligent enough to hide their knowing.

The guard, Tam, was calm but attentive, not bothering to pay too much attention to Brenn while giving Nitalia a few side looks. As they traversed closer to the doors leading to the castle, putting distance between themselves and the hamlet at their backs, the wind picked up, hinting at an early winter storm billowing in the north.

It was then that Tam broke the silence. "I hate to ask, my lady, but did Master Ethelred not escort you from home? Where is he?"

Nitalia turned to Tam with sadness in her eyes. "I fear he is dead. I will speak to my father about giving recompense to his family for his service."

Tam swallowed hard, his eyes lingering on Brenn for the first time. "How did he die? His family will want to know."

"Protecting me. He should be remembered well."

Brenn clenched his fist, the same fist that had taken the life from the guard. "We should leave the bulk of the details for Count Frantisek," he said. "Come along, Princess."

Leaving Tam outside, Nitalia and Brenn made their way through the hallway and to the chamber. The large tapestries hanging on either side of the hallways were black and purple, denoting the great battles of the Frantiseks and their family lineage. While Brenn was prompted to remind Nitalia of their agreement before entering the chamber, he suspected the woven artwork was reminder enough.

In unison, he and Nitalia stepped through the familiar doors to find Count Vlaskhorn Frantisek and Countess Maja Frantisek situated on their thrones on the opposite side of the centered hearthfires. The room had been cleaned, the long tables and chairs replaced, several tapestries removed, and the rug cleansed of blood.

"Czern's breath!" Count Frantisek cried, standing up from his chair. A stone crown Brenn did not remember from before sat on his head, elegantly shaped to fit him. The crown looked drab in the firelight, enough to make Brenn think the count could have been the God of Darkness himself, an idol of madness and destruction and gloom. "Nitalia, you have finally returned. I expected you home days ago!"

The count's cloak was heavy and thick, purple with black embroidery, dragging behind him as he made his way to his daughter. His stomach bounced over his belt line as he walked. Brenn did not intercept, taking his time to absorb the details. The soft, padded jacket, decorated with the finest thread, matched the pale gown of Maja as she, too, lurched from her seat.

"Oh, my daughter," she said, her eyes already brimming with salted tears, "I feared you were dead. The madness wrought within these walls over the past days has left us all to wonder what the gods had in store. Bless Czern for returning you home safe."

Maja steadied the bun on her head, centered in her own silver crown, weighing down her mass of golden hair. She rushed from the dais toward Nitalia with little elegance.

At the first sign of her mother's tears, Nitalia began to cry, losing all composure. The sight gripped at Brenn's heart. Yet instead of compassion for the familial moment, he found himself fearing that Nitalia would not hold to their lie under the duress of the sudden emotional toll of the reunion.

The count wrapped his arms around Nitalia, soon to be joined by Maja's warm embrace, her lips pressing to her daughter's cheeks through the uncombed golden locks. The count's ring, more extravagant than anything Brenn had ever known, tapped against his daughter's back. Brenn eyed the jeweled band for its worth, overlooking its obvious beauty and knowing Count Frantisek's prosperity was given to him by his brother and no other. The nobles in Lonmere had no access to such luxury. The strength of the Gaetanean Kingdom was found in their flowing riches. Lesser men, poorer men, longed to gain the respect that the Frantiseks could simply purchase.

It struck Brenn that those in Lonmere could only gain power by inciting war. They did not have the coin, nor the words, nor the status for influence; only war.

War was for the weak.

As they let Nitalia go, she covered the injury on her back with her hand.

"Have you been hurt?" Maja gasped.

"I will be fine," Nitalia gulped, fighting to regain her composure. All serenity was gone from the young woman. Brenn could not blame her. He and Rehor had tainted her vision, tested her truth, and challenged her fate. He feared they had broken her from whatever path had once lay at her feet. Perhaps death would have been a better destiny than to have her ideals wrecked. He watched her push any sign of her misery behind a fake smile. She met Brenn's eyes as she spoke. "Thanks to Master Traelador, here, I will be absolutely fine."

He may have heard a hint of sincerity in her tone.

"And who are you, Master Traelador?" the count asked, lifting his hand almost protectively across his daughter as he stumbled around her.

"I am but a stranger who came upon your daughter, my lord," Brenn said.

"A stranger?" the count repeated, looking over his shoulder at Nitalia. "I thought you were with the men of the Crimson Sun. They were instructed to return you home. As well as Tomas Ethelred. Where is he? I will have his head if he has disobeyed me."

"Tomas is dead, Father," Nitalia said. "He tried to protect me against…" she sucked in a breath, her chest swelling inside her armor. "…against those who were meant to bring me home. The Crimson Sun betrayed you."

"Betrayed me?" the count huffed. "What did they mean to do with you?"

"I—I don't know," Nitalia said.

"Czern's breath!" Maja cursed, pulling Nitalia close to her again. "We cannot trust those who align themselves with the Lightbringer, the Kadari, or…" She looked to her husband.

"My brother," the count finished, his face reddening at the mention of the king.

"What will you do?" Maja asked.

Count Frantisek looked at the princess and then his wife, his left fist clenching at his side. "What can we do against them? Even a letter of inquiry might incite madness in the realms, meaning little when war threatens our southern borders. We do not even know what they were planning or if they only used the name of the Crimson Sun to worm their way into the castle." He lifted his eyes to Brenn. "What we can do is reward the hero who brought my daughter home safely. How does five hundred Gaetanean silver sound, Master Traelador?"

"My lord." Brenn stooped as a commoner would before royalty, catching Nitalia's shock before she turned her face into her mother's shoulder. "You are too kind."

His exodus from the castle and Cavell was quick, knowing Rehor would be waiting for him beyond the gate and Taryn farther north at Mecka. His stride was comparable to a man about to enter an endless war. With his charge satisfied and the Dusk Legion soon believing him to be gone, he could live his own life until death carried him away to Thrice Ten Kingdom.

Epilogue

REHOR, *The Dusk Legion*

White flakes swirled around Rehor's black boots as he guided the horse carrying Nitalia Frantisek between the trees beyond the gates of Cavell. Light snow scattered over the blackened earth hinted at the state of the world—divided by extremes without giving pause for what other truths might exist. With little thought, he marched on, erasing his footprints under the eddying snow with Koldovstvo, leaving only the tracks of the horse.

The princess wept nonstop since he gathered her in secret from the castle, coming and going the same way he had a couple years ago. A few draughts laced with felpoppies made their exit from the town rather uneventful. Unless some obscure bystander caught sight of him, he was confident he had come and gone without being noticed.

Nitalia struggled against the bindings on her wrists, fighting against the balled-up cloth in her mouth. Her sobs, along with the trees bending against the wind above, creaking and cracking, were akin to a dark melody. The burbling swamp nearby only added to the rare harmony. He listened for a bit before interrupting the overly dramatized sniffles.

"Granted a couple more years to live, you were, Princess," he said, patting the noosed rope at his belt. He turned the horse onto a darker path in the forest, his orange orb of light floating over him. They should be coming on the tree he had chosen for the occasion.

She moaned the louder, fighting to speak against the gag.

"I do hope you spent the time well, giving the count and countess memories to cherish," Rehor said. "Yet I cannot say the condition in which they find you will bring them much solace, nor will it prompt them to think over the *better times*, hmm?"

He did not bother looking at the golden-haired noble, the sounds of her crying increasing with his every word. The twisted juniper tree, growing from a mound of dirt, appeared ahead, reaching over a small clearing in the wake of several saplings and larger types familiar in the Dyndaer. The straight branch of the juniper, however, is what beckoned to him.

It was perfect.

"It will be over soon, dear princess. You will not feel…much."

Her mumbled row against his actions filtered through the fabric so he only heard the suggestion of words, most of which were less than pleasant. Against his better judgment he approached her and removed the binding over her mouth, rolling the fabric back in his hand and stuffing it in his pocket.

"Do not scream, hmm?" he said. "Not only would no one be able to hear you, but destroy the ambience, you would."

"Why are you doing this?" Salty drops rolled from her bright blue eyes. She was shaking in the saddle, her thighs trembling with fear as much as her narrow shoulders. He noticed she tried to express courage, elevating her chin enough to be noticed, but her admired spirit was as captive to the terror in her heart as she was to him. "I did not tell anyone anything. I did as you asked. Please!"

Rehor pulled her from the saddle. The brown animal, unaware of what would occur, roamed to the side and began to nuzzle against the ground in search of fresh grass.

"I know, Princess," Rehor replied, pulling the coiled rope from his belt. He positioned the noose around her neck, gently pulling her hair out from around the knot. He nudged her in the small of her back so she would walk toward the juniper tree. "You did remarkably well, and for that I am grateful, hmm? You gave me enough time to travel home and, *well*, that was a mistake. Did you know Eisliev Kluk is no longer the Arkhon of Lairhein, hmm?" He tilted his head to study her features. He puffed out his cheeks and waggled his head with enough force to give himself a headache. "Oh, no, no, no. He is not! He is nothing but a cockered, lying thief. He is going to rue the day when I find him again and reclaim what is mine."

Nitalia's face twisted in confusion as he tossed the rope over the branch of the tree and then erased his set of tracks from the snow again. "You do not have to kill me," she pleaded. "The Uvil have advanced farther into the Gaetanean Kingdom. They are winning the war, right? They did not even want me dead. It was all a scheme."

"All true. I told them about the Uvil's scheme and they allotted a couple years to see what truth would be revealed. When nothing surfaced, the politicians debated back and forth. In the end, they like the idea of you being dead. I said I'd see it done, hmm?" Rehor replied, tossing the rope over the branch again. "I cannot leave you alive this time…give reason for the Legion to question me, we cannot. Die, you must."

"Plea—"

Rehor yanked the end of the rope, cutting off her petition. Her feet kicked as her petite frame lifted into the air. Her face turned red and then bluish, eyes bulging at him in desperation. He held her steady for a moment, fascinated by the slow death before realizing that a strangling would not give the impression of suicide; she couldn't do that on her own. But a hanging...

With a sigh, he expended a bit more of his life. Using weaves of air to throw her body over the branch, coiling the rope a third time over itself, he lifted her body several feet into the air and released.

The rope caught seamlessly on itself, snapping her neck with enough force that it reverberated into her spine.

Satisfied, he positioned himself on the mound of earth to remove the bindings from her wrists, then marveled at his latest opus.

It was then, and only then, that Rehor noticed the borra tree in the background. Packing his cheeks with air to contain a shriek of excitement, he unfastened the herb pouch on his belt and set out to collect its leaves.

ABOUT THE AUTHOR

Joshua Robertson was born in Kingman, Kansas on May 23, 1984. A graduate of Norwich High School, Robertson attended Wichita State University where he received his master's in social work with minors in psychology and sociology. His bestselling novel, *Melkorka*, the first in The Kaelandur Series, was released in 2015. Known most for his Thrice Nine Legends Saga, Robertson enjoys an ever-expanding and extremely loyal following of readers. He counts R.A. Salvatore and J.R.R. Tolkien among his literary influences.